# GIN AND TOXIC

Rita H Rowe

This novel is a work of fiction. All names, characters, businesses, places, events and incidents in this book are either the product of the author's imagination or used in a fictitious manner. Any resemblance to actual persons, living or dead, or actual events is coincidental.

For my mother.

"As an alcoholic, you will violate your standards quicker than you can lower them."
Robin Williams.


"You never know how strong you are until being strong is your only choice."
Bob Marley.

# Foreword: Gin and Toxic
*By Julia Kalman*

*Gin and Toxic* grabbed me from the start with its unsettling yet exciting story.

This book isn't just words on pages; it's a wild journey that holds on tight and doesn't let go.

Rowe creates a world where personal struggles and social pressures crash together spinning a tale full of intense emotions, fights, and self-understanding.

The prologue left me thinking, "I wish I'd written this"— you know that feeling I'm talking about.

As I kept reading, I felt like I was hunting for something ineffable, with each chapter hiding a little secret. When I got it, it hit me like a bolt of lightning. The gin in the story packs a punch—rough, unforgiving, and too much to handle. I soaked up so much of it through the book that I might never want real gin again. It's a strong and heady mix, but as the plot moves along, that gin turns into something healing offering a release that's both cathartic and a bit unsettling.

Rowe's writing mixes the edge-of-your-seat feeling of a thriller with the deep thinking of serious literature.

She brings Elizabeth's world to life in a detailed, moving, touching, sometimes sensory, and even synesthetic way, creating a story that feels both personal and universal.

## About the Author: Rita H Rowe

Rowe is a prolific Australian author who often writes about the ups and downs of human relationships and social limits. It's interesting that no matter how tough the topic is, like in this book, she manages to lift up the reader, to teach them, without being too preachy. With her background in literature and teaching, Rowe brings a special view to her writing, mixing feelings, understanding of the mind, values, and artistry of writing.

Rowe deserves her reputation as a great storyteller. She knows how to write stories that touch your heart and make you think, which sets her apart from other writers.

## Contextualizing *Gin and Toxic*

*Gin and Toxic* shows us a changing India after colonial rule.

The book reveals a country stuck between old ways and new trends, showing how big changes affect the characters' lives. This setting does more than just set the scene - it pushes the story forward and shapes Elizabeth's choices and problems.

Rowe mixes old-school storytelling with innovations. This gives us a new look at love, freedom, and what society expects. By showing these ideas through Elizabeth's personal struggles, the book comments on the limits women face in a fast-changing world.

The novel showcases the creative freedom of fiction, offering a deeply captivating experience that stays with you long after the last page. Perhaps that's why reading it brings to mind the emotional reflection often found in memoirs.

## Themes: Unpacking the Essence of *Gin and Toxic*

In *Gin and Toxic*, the writer looks at personal, social, and global themes, including post-colonial expansion or emigration, with some recent history thrown in.

At its heart, the book looks at the fight between what people want and what society expects, which we see in Elizabeth's journey.

The book digs deep into love, freedom, and finding yourself. This depth makes readers think about their own lives and the rules of society.

## Character Sketch: Unveiling the Figures in *Gin and Toxic*

Elizabeth is the soul of this book, a protagonist whose journey is riddled with intense internal and external conflicts.

Everything seems to drive her toward a unique path, including her own parents.

What will tip the balance?

Will it be her talent, energy, beauty, rebellious nature, feminine intuition, or motherly instinct? Or perhaps the customs she was raised with? Maybe something—or someone—else? Continue reading to uncover the decisions and experiences that have shaped her life.

The novel places great emphasis on her struggle to balance desires with reality as it highlights a shift from careless youthfulness into troubled maturity.

While there are numerous male characters in the book, Elizabeth's choices very well mirror her inner tensions - they could be seen as projections of the self.

Therefore, despite a wide circle of admirers, a passionate and exciting life, and all the contradictions, harshness, departures, rebellions, denials, and separations, I would say that Elizabeth remains a woman devoted to just one man.

What can I say about the male characters?

I believe that the three dominant male characters are essentially variations of a single archetype: the societal ideal of stability and tradition. Their differences primarily lie in their individual personalities.

Elizabeth's children, Genny and Robert, play significant roles in the narrative, inspiring us to change our lives and pay closer attention to the younger ones among us—their emotions, thoughts, and words. We are disarmed by Genny's innocence and vulnerability, as well as by Robert's protective instincts.

Ultimately, the book is called *Gin and Toxic*, and the only solace for trauma is either forgetting or, perhaps... the reflective gaze of understanding—the gaze of someone who loves, of a woman who reinvents the past and herself.

### The Art of Style in *Gin and Toxic*

Comparing Rowe's style with that of other authors, you can see echoes of Virginia Woolf's stream-of-consciousness technique.

Like Woolf, the author delves deeply into Elizabeth's psyche, exploring her inner landscape with similar depth and sensitivity. Woolf's influence is evident in the fluidity of Elizabeth's thoughts and emotions.

In conclusion, the author's style is marked by a careful blend of introspection, vivid description, and natural dialogue, creating a narrative that is deeply engaging and emotionally resonant.

### Personal Reflections: Insights on *Gin and Toxic*

Reading *Gin and Toxic* was a profoundly moving experience, both touching and illuminating.

Rowe's masterful storytelling and the depth of her characters make this novel a captivating and thought-provoking read.

I invite you to immerse yourself in this world and reflect on social norms and broader themes in your own life—such as personal independence, the many forms of love, pleasure and vice, dreams, and purpose, finding the right path, and the quest for liberation and fulfillment.

Although this work is written by a female author and features a female protagonist, it should not be automatically categorized as "feminine literature." Approach it with an open heart and mind.

Let the story embrace you like the wonder it is and inspire a deeper understanding of the complexities of human experience.

With deep admiration,
Julia Kalman
Editor-in-Chief, New Literary Society
July 25, 2024

# Prologue

## 1982

She tiptoed through the side gate, not noticing the brambles that poked at her bare feet, scratching the tender skin on her ankles, drawing tiny streaks of blood. She paused at the window, her heart pulling at her to stop, to take just one last look, knowing what she saw would render her weak, but she relented and peered through the dusty glass, her eyes darting about trying to see through the shadows in the dim room within.

Her eyes adjusted and caught a movement. Genny, her youngest, just five, her little body raising itself in fear, faced the window, and she imagined the big brown eyes staring straight through the lace curtain, piercing into hers. Her daughter didn't rub her eyes; no she hadn't been asleep, none of them could have slept through the commotion, and her heart tore again. What was going on in their little heads?

She gripped the steel bar on the window tightly. It was wet. She knew Genny couldn't see her clearly, but her silhouette against the light of the moon reflected on the windowpane. Genny knew she was there. The tears she had been trying to keep at bay burst free, mingled with drops of rain that fell on her face and her head and her bare arms. She pictured the tears that would most certainly be on her daughter's face, tears that would brim her eyes, her face unmoving, except for her bottom lip which would quiver wildly.

She heard a sob, a guttural sound that she realised was coming from herself. She put one hand over her mouth, the other, white-knuckled, still gripping the bar, the piece of steel that held her there. She was unable to move away, her eyes fixated on the figure that still sat rigid, frozen. She wavered. She could go back. He still hadn't discovered her gone; if he had, the still that surrounded her would have been broken by now. He was still waiting for her outside the bathroom door. She could climb in the same way she had crawled out and he would never know she had escaped. It would be okay ... maybe.

The pain seared though her hip and her left leg gave way, the rod she was clinging to saving her from tumbling into the sludge that now immersed her feet. She was unable to grasp fully what had happened just minutes before. Her thoughts were jumbled. She hesitated. Could she do this? She knew she had to. She put her fingers to her cheekbone and flinched, feeling her resolve strengthen. She knew they would be okay. He loved them, he would never hurt them, not the way he hurt her.

Her mouth was dry and she ran her tongue over her teeth. She tasted rust but held tight to the fading taste of the gin they had shared not fifteen minutes earlier. She rested her head on the windowpane. It felt so heavy and she squeezed her eyes tight, still in two minds. She raised her head again and looked at the other dim figures still lying on the two beds. She knew they were awake too, but they didn't dare move. They had heard it all but they were powerless to stop it. At times, they tried to intervene, to pull her away from him or him from her. Robert had even pushed himself between them once, and had gotten his finger bitten for his trouble.

This time it wasn't as vicious, but she was broken, she needed time away from him. She knew she would eventually go back as she always did. But right now, she needed to go. There would be more if she turned back and her body ached from the clouts, her brain was battered from the words he flung at her. He had begged at the door, pounded and pleaded, making promises that they both knew would be broken, even that very night.

She let herself look through the glass once more. The figure still sat. It was pleading with her too, calling her back. She looked down at her cotton nightdress and bare feet, knowing it would be best to return for everyone's sake. How could she leave like this? She had nothing, no one else. She could hear the faint banging on the bathroom door now. Her heart ached and not only for the children. She loved him, had from the moment she laid eyes on him. It was not too late to go back, he still didn't know she was gone. She raised her eyes once more to the child and mouthed, "I'm sorry."

She turned towards the gate and ran.

# Part One: The Wonder Years

## 1947–1965

# Chapter 1 - Too Wild

*The photograph used to sit atop the mantel in her parents' home. An athletic teen, wild hair flowing around her shoulders, loosed from a ponytail that had drooped to the nape of her neck, her olive skin glinting from the tingles of perspiration still on her forehead. She holds two trophies and stands atop a makeshift dais, her mouth wide in a smile, not looking directly at the camera but a little off towards the left. Her knees are dirty and her joggers are scuffed but her shoulders are squared and her chin is high. She is proud of her achievements. You can tell that this isn't her first victory and probably won't be her last. She has that confidence about her, that winner's glow.*

She knew she should run the moment she met him. And as fast as she could, like the athlete she was, destined for bigger things, for a life that was waiting to be caught and held in her grasp. She had the spirit, the gall to challenge even the toughest heart, and the grace, the beauty to drop a man to his knees, and most women too. She had too much spirit for anyone her age, no matter what age she was. It had been a bone of contention between her parents from as far back as she could remember, her guilt when they discussed her, when she heard snippets of conversations that were not meant for her ears.

"She's too wild, Jimmy. Too passionate, impulsive." Her mother's words, low but urgent.

Elizabeth paused at the door, wanting to hear more. She already knew they were talking about her; she could hear it in her mother's voice, the distress, the frustration she felt for her middle child, the disorderly daughter. Her parents sat in the moonlight, her mother's hand rested on the arm of her chair, her father's placed lightly over hers.

"That's not a bad thing, Doris," said her father, tapping the hand. Very rarely did her father raise his voice and Elizabeth stuck out her chest in pride. He always backed her when her mother tried

14

to turn her into a prissy young lady. "Passion is good in a young woman these days."

"No, Jimmy." Her mother's tone was regretful. "She'll be a woman soon. What hope does she have to get a man, the right type of man?"

A low chuckle escaped her father's lips. "There's much time for that, my dear. Much time."

"Time will fly." Her mother's voice now took on a faraway note. "Tess and Audrey are already being courted."

Elizabeth screwed up her face. Tess and Audrey. Always Tess and Audrey. Both over sixteen, beautiful as anything, refined and worldly, they took every opportunity to rebuke Elizabeth for her youth and inexperience. She looked down at her clothes, tattered, a hole broken through her coveralls. She poked her finger into it and scratched at the scab on her knee. She frowned. Maybe her mother was right. A fifteen-year-old 'young lady' probably had no business scuffling with the boys in the neighbourhood. She couldn't help but smile. She had just brought Felix to his knees, quite literally, only letting him go when he squealed for mercy. Felix, two years older than her, who had pushed her little sister to the ground. She frowned again. Molly, whom she had just rescued, ran back to the house hollering that Elizabeth was fighting again. That was her reward.

"Hush, Doris, you worry too much."

"I think we should do something," said her mother.

"You forget the passion you felt when you were young?" He said it in a whisper but Elizabeth's sharp ears heard and she cocked her head.

Her mother tittered shyly. "Jimmy!"

She watched through the door as her father reached right over and planted a kiss on her mother's cheek. She blushed. "What is the worry, Doris?"

"Her future," Doris insisted. "In this country ..."

"For one, my dear, we may not be in this country for very long. And what's wrong with this country?"

"Oh, Jimmy, I love this country. India is my home. But ..."

"This country is advanced, on par with the world. I don't ever want to leave here."

"But for the children ..."

Elizabeth had heard this conversation too many times. They

would talk about migration to Canada or America. Soon they would start discussing politics and she rolled her eyes, tiptoeing back into the house, where she found Fred, her younger brother, lounging on the sofa, the guitar cradled in his arms, his long fingers strumming lightly on its strings.

Fred was the only sibling Elizabeth felt any camaraderie with. He was calm, a thinker, and he couldn't deal with the girliness of her other sisters as much as she couldn't. Besides, although he was younger, Elizabeth felt she learned a lot from Fred. He said things in such a way that they seemed matter-of-fact, not like advice, which she eventually took as advice anyway.

"Hey, Fred?" Elizabeth sat on the edge of the sofa so as not to disturb the position he was in.

"Hmm?" Fred replied without looking up from his instrument.

"Am I too wild?" Fred snickered and Elizabeth narrowed her eyes. "Is that a yes?"

Fred's fingers stopped twiddling the strings and he gave the guitar a little thump and put it beside him on the sofa. He loved that thing so much, it wouldn't be put on the floor. "No, I don't think you're wild."

"That's it?" Elizabeth was disappointed. She wanted Fred to elaborate, tell her that it was okay to be a little wild.

"Better than being a girl who spends too much time doing her makeup in the bathroom and coming out looking like a cake shop." He giggled.

Elizabeth touched her face. She didn't like the stuff but she would have to get used to it. Her mother was already subtly leaving a tub of face cream on her side table every other day. How she could afford it, Elizabeth never knew, but Doris had many people who loved her in the neighbourhood, who always brought something or the other over to make her happy.

"Hey, Fred?" Elizabeth said when she saw her brother reach over to pick up the guitar again, assuming their talk was done. His hand stopped mid-air and he placed them both in his lap.

"Nothing." Elizabeth knew her brother didn't have the answers. He told her to be herself, just like her father did, but her sisters and her mother, no, they thought she should behave more like them, reserved, ladylike.

She wandered to the terrace and sat on the ledge where the wall had fallen away, hanging her legs off the edge. Her mother would have a fit if she saw her here, but this was where Elizabeth came to think—her favourite place, where she could observe the world without being seen, take in almost the whole of Derrum, a hub of activity, from children playing in the street, to servants washing clothes over the hill. She could watch her friend Carolyn, a little speck some two blocks away, as she sat on her own porch, trying to get away from her mother for a few minutes, or Jayna, her classmate, who walked along the footpath, her head down, trying to prepare for some test or exam.

She marvelled at the streets of Derrum, tiny alleys going nowhere, washing lines at the back of houses, most with no fences, some roads unpaved and dusty, cats and dogs skulking in open garbage bins, and not even a few metres away, the streets widened and became clean, almost shiny, lined with restaurants and dance halls. How she loved to come up here on a Saturday night and watch the people go in and out of those places, arm in arm, almost dancing as they went in. Her feet would tap and her body would move even if it was just to the music on her mother's old radio that wafted from the kitchen below. She wanted to be out there already, dancing on that shiny floor, watching the faces and feet of the people whom she grew up with, transformed into frenzied strangers, the dark mixing with the white, like there was no place for discrimination; no, not on that dance floor.

Elizabeth looked at the skin on the top of her hand, darker than the white people, like her very English father, and a lighter shade than that of her mother. She was stuck somewhere in between. She didn't know which she preferred as it had never been an issue for Elizabeth, but she knew the way the townsfolk talked. For them, typical Anglo-Indians, half white, half dark and half something else, they were in-betweeners, stuck in a no-man's land, shunned by white folk and dark ones alike. Oh, they belonged to Derrum all right; her mother's family had been a part of this community for as long as they could remember, and it seemed that Derrum was a cluster for Anglo-Indians, so they rightly fit in. But she heard conversations, between her aunts and uncles, even some of her older cousins, the way they felt about Indians, the pure Indians, whom they looked down upon for the colour of their skin. Elizabeth would look at her own skin and found that it was as dark as it was white—she knew she really didn't belong to anyone, dark, white or otherwise, and refused to be judged because of where her parents were born. And now it seemed that her parents wanted to get out of Derrum, out of India completely, just like every other Anglo-Indian with the remotest ties to any other country, be it Australia, England, Canada or even the United States.

Elizabeth sighed. That was all they ever talked about these days; any conversation that came up ended with that, the big move— to where, she didn't know—but every Anglo-Indian wanted out of a country they didn't feel they belonged in, for the hope of opportunity.

She had no interest in any of that. She wanted love, passion, the thing that her parents had. Waiting until she was eighteen felt like a lifetime away. Maybe she *was* just too wild. Maybe she just needed to settle down. Maybe it was time to be serious about life. She hoped she would find the right man to share all of that with her. Because according to her sisters, that was all there was to life, finding a good man to marry, and maybe they were right, she conceded.

Elizabeth sighed heavily and pushed herself up. Her mother had been calling her for the last ten minutes and she knew she would be sending a search party out soon. Best go in before that happened. Still, she leaned forward to look down at the ground so far below. She couldn't resist the thrill of it, the danger of being so close to the edge.

She laughed loudly and then sprinted down and into the house. Love would come, she knew it, could feel it in her bones and she couldn't wait.

# Chapter 2 - Before Mike

Elizabeth found love. At the tender age of seventeen. Puppy love, some people called it, but when she thought about it after Mike came along, it couldn't even be described as that.

She always felt a smile form on her lips when she thought about Andy. Andy, whom she had barely noticed as she passed the toy store every morning on her way to work. Andy, who had been watching her from the boys' school across the road as she walked out of the gates of her own, every day, he told her later, for the past year, until he began work at his father's toy store.

"He's still staring," said Carolyn when Elizabeth had gone into the store to search for a gift for her cousin, Sadie, a year younger than her, and someone Elizabeth gravitated towards because she, like Elizabeth, was an embarrassment to her family for her inability to grow up as quickly as they wanted her to. Elizabeth was fond of Sadie, whose family didn't have much money for extravagant gifts and Elizabeth always put a little of her pocket money aside to buy something for Sadie on special occasions. She rarely went into the toy store for anything, but something this day drew her in. Perhaps it was the boy's smile that shone through the glass of the window, an invitation to come in.

"He's not staring," replied Elizabeth, but she glanced his way as she walked behind a selection of frisbees and peeked through one of the shelves. When she caught his eye—yes, he was staring at her—he looked away quickly and Elizabeth felt her cheeks redden. She saw him turn hurriedly to place something on the counter. She took the opportunity to size him up. He was good-looking and fair—her mother would approve—a little lanky, but as her mother would have said, a strong jaw. There was something else too. He had kind eyes, that flickered her way again. They were a light brown and tilted slightly downwards at the edges. She wondered about him. She knew who he was; in this town everyone knew who everyone was, and Andy was the son of a merchant, a quiet, reserved boy, who didn't get into any

19

trouble, got good grades and made his parents proud.

"Now *you're* staring," said Carolyn, giving Elizabeth a nudge.

"He is interesting," said Elizabeth.

"Is he? But is he your type?"

"I don't have a type," retorted Elizabeth, then stopped. She bit her lip in thought. "What is my type?"

"Dale—athletic, womaniser. Joey—party animal. And don't forget Tom who is Joey and Dale both thrown into one."

"They are the only three boys I've ever dated," Elizabeth said, a little indignant. "That doesn't make it a pattern."

"Well, this one is none of them. This one ... *you* will break *his* heart."

"I've broken other hearts, including Dale's and Tom's."

"But they will recover. Don't mess with Andy," said Carolyn quietly.

Elizabeth and Carolyn left the store without purchasing anything, but the next day Elizabeth went back by herself. And the next. She would never make the first move. What if he had a girlfriend? Surely not, with the way he kept looking her way. Yes, she was used to this attention; however, it was usually a one-way affair. She wondered if she should have felt something more, a jolt of electricity perhaps, that would alert her to her true match. She had felt jolts before, when she kissed Tom and Dale and Joey, but she knew from the beginning they were no love matches for her. Maybe if, no, *when* she kissed Andy, she would feel it.

She flicked through a book, not really noticing the title, wondering why Andy had to be so patient. Her mother would definitely approve. As much as Elizabeth tried to hide her dalliances, word always got back to one of her parents and Elizabeth would look down at the floor while being scolded about the proper ways of young women.

"Are you looking for something in particular?"

Elizabeth jumped and cleared her throat. She hadn't heard Andy come up behind her. "No," she replied, putting the book back in its place. "Something for a sixteen-year-old girl." She moved slowly, running her fingers along the shelf. "I'm still not sure."

"Sixteen-year-old, did you say?" He looked dubious, after all this was a toy store, not a lot of gifts for young ladies. Elizabeth frowned and he quickly changed tack. "Have you got any options?"

"No. That's why I keep coming back." She had to make sure he did think she was proper, that she wasn't returning to the store just for him.

"Oh." His voice dropped but it had a teasing lilt. "I thought you kept coming back so you could see me."

Elizabeth looked at him in surprise. It was completely unexpected. "That is presumptuous," she said. Sure, she was used to men making passes at her but they usually came from men about town, those who were more on the cocky side, the ones she was usually drawn to, not from someone like Andy, good-looking, sure, but who seemed slightly timid, a gentleman, someone who still doffed his cap to a lady.

Andy lifted his eyes to hers and she saw a little coat of vapour appear above his upper lip. He was nervous. She tried not to smile. "But maybe you want to see me again?" he said, wiping away the moisture that had lumped itself into a droplet at the side of his mouth.

Elizabeth found herself nodding. She picked up a book and sashayed to the counter.

Andy was a dream catch. Her mother adored him as did her sisters and even Fred enjoyed a game of badminton with him on a Sunday afternoon. Andy had big ideas. He would one day become manager at the toy store and eventually, his father would make him partner. He was an entrepreneur and Elizabeth tried to ignore the fact that his dreams didn't stray too far away from their little town. It had been a year since the family had gotten excited about the move to Canada. The process was slow and the excitement had, by now, dulled. It was pointless to wait in anticipation for something that could happen in two months or in two years. Elizabeth never did have that kind of patience.

"Marry me," said Andy, dropping to his knees one afternoon after he had driven her to the beach, an hour away from home.

It had been a sunny morning and they had picnicked on the sand. Elizabeth lay on her towel, reading a book, when a sudden gust of wind picked up the umbrella she was under and within seconds, she felt heavy raindrops soaking her skin. She screeched and began to gather her things, Andy running behind the umbrella. Together they stuffed everything into their basket and sheltered beneath a tree, waiting for the rain to pass before they attempted to ride home on his scooter. She stayed in the comfort of his arms until she felt him moving about behind her. She turned to see what he was doing when he held out his hand, a little diamond band in it, and he asked her the question. "Andy!"

"Will you?"

Elizabeth hesitated and didn't know why she didn't scream 'yes' right away, what held her back, but she knew what she had to do. "Yes," she said with more confidence than she felt. It had been just under a year and she knew this was coming. By the way her mother winked when Andy left the house last Saturday after having a private word with her parents on the patio, she knew what their conversation had been about.

"That's exciting," said Carolyn when she confided to her about what she suspected the next day as they walked to work together.

"Yes, it is, isn't it?" Elizabeth fiddled with the third finger on her left hand.

"You don't sound excited." Carolyn frowned.

"Oh, I am," she replied, not sure exactly how excited she was. Did she want to be married? Every woman wanted to be married, didn't they? But did she want to marry Andy? She loved Andy, with his warmth, his caring nature, always going out of his way to make her happy, comfortable, to give her what she wanted. Yes, he was a dream catch, she knew she had to snap him up. "I am," she said with more certainty than she felt.

As she lay her head against his back on the way home, the rain pattering at her face, she thought about how happy her mother would be. Then she frowned. Her father, not so much. He had higher hopes for her.

"You can be whatever you want to be," he had said one evening when she had an unusual minute alone with him.

"I don't know what to do with my life," she said. "All I want to do is sing."

"Then do that. You have much talent, so much to hone. You are an artist," he said and smiled at that. Elizabeth nodded, knowing he was taking some credit for that talent; her father was a spectacular artist, spending much of his spare time, which admittedly wasn't much, sitting in the paddocks on the surrounds of their town, painting scenes of children, of lovers, of the reds and greens and yellows that sprouted around the fields, that changed hue depending on the time of day or the weather. Elizabeth joined him sometimes but her patience was not as strong as his, and not getting the effect she wanted immediately, she'd get frustrated and give up. "You also have a well-developed brain," he continued and she looked up in surprise. She had never gotten very good grades and believed her parents thought her a bit dumb. Her father smiled at her expression. "Lily, all you need is a little stickability. You have so much going for you. You can do it all if you wish, but for a future, pick one. If you want to sing, then sing."

"But is that a career?" Elizabeth wasn't sure that it could be one. "Besides, Mother has been talking marriage and I don't know ..." She paused. "And I'm still only seventeen!"

"You have finished the tenth standard. You can begin your Cambridge studies."

"Mother thinks I should be getting ready for marriage. Since Bryan and Tessa got engaged."

"And what do you think?" He always threw the ball in her court, never made an answer easy for her.

"To be honest, I was a bit surprised about their engagement. With all the talk of leaving, going to Canada ..."

Her father nodded slowly. "Yes, that's taking a little longer than expected. But it will happen." His voice was soft and Elizabeth felt sorry for him.

She changed the subject. "I think Andy may ... you know."

"Has he dropped hints?" Her father raised his bushy eyebrows in alarm.

Elizabeth took a deep breath. "Yes, I think so. He tried to ask me what sort of gemstone my favourite was. Then he wanted to know where I pictured myself living, in the city, in the town ..." She chuckled but her father's face remained austere.

"Do you see yourself married to him? To have a future with him?"

"Yes, I think so," replied Elizabeth. "Mother loves him, sometimes I think more than me," she said with a giggle. "He's sweet and he's good to me."

"That's the most important thing," said her father. "But are you in love with him?"

Elizabeth reddened. She never imagined talking to her father about these things. "I know he will give me a good life," she said.

"What should I do if he asks me?"

"Lily, you're nearly an adult. You can do whatever you want to do. Heck, you did so even before. But just make sure that you're sure."

She was sure. She clutched to his waist tighter behind him and felt his hand grab hers. Yes, this was her future. The one who would make her happy.

There was an excitement in the air. Wedding plans were underway for the moment Elizabeth was to turn eighteen and she got a job at a telephone company, trying to help Andy save enough for the type of wedding he knew she would want. "I want big," she'd said when he asked her and she tried to ignore the droop of his lips at that. She knew that children would be the next thing on the agenda when she was a wife. There was no point in continuing her studies and trying to work out a career; there would be no time for one. She hated the fact that she had succumbed to what her sisters wanted her to be, but why be rebellious for the sake of it? She was a woman and she had to begin to behave like one at some stage. Marriage may as well be that stage.

And marriage with Andy would be good. He was kind, mature. She and Andy enjoyed each other and he was always the perfect gentleman, never pushing himself on her, even though at times, she wished he would. They would go out together and spent many an evening in the company of their parents, her playing the piano and singing and him watching her with an almost spiritual devotion. They were, everyone said, the perfect couple.

# Chapter 3 - Meeting Mike

*The lights reflected off the beads of the makeshift chandeliers, throwing down little circles of colour on the white tablecloth in front of her, that danced to the vibration of the music that blared from the stage. The band was in its element, the guitarist, John Jacobs, in a frenzied movement on his knees, the singer, Loretta Davis, belting out 'I Wanna Hold Your Hand' and the keyboard player, Teddy Walters, grinning at the movement on the dance floor. The doors had been thrown open, the chill of winter kept at bay by the heat of the New Year's Eve revellers, the crowd heaped into the town hall, the prospect of the new year, the hope of change and not the least, the dance, keeping the townsfolk energetic. Every eye turned to the door at the sight, Elizabeth, the wild child, finally tamed by love. Mrs Paterson smiled and nudged at her husband. She felt she was partly responsible in the transformation of this butterfly from an unkempt juvenile. Her lessons on Shakespeare must have played a part in her stance. Mr Weatherby squared his shoulders in pride. She must have learned her posture from his gymnastics instruction. The town wanted to take credit for the beauty that Elizabeth had become. But someone else noticed. He saw the heads turn just as his did too.*

Elizabeth sat beside Andy, her feet tapping vigorously to the music, her neck still clammy from the previous dance, but Andy wanted to take a break and she reluctantly trailed behind him off the dance floor. She smoothed her pink ballooned skirt and straightened the lace on the edges of the straps of her blouse. She glanced back towards the floor, wanting to get back on there; she could see Fred jiving with Marcia, his sweetheart, grinning maniacally as he gripped her by the waist and swung her high into the air. Elizabeth wanted Andy to do that with her. Since she had been Andy's girl, she hadn't danced with anyone, had refused all offers for a dance by other boys, only on occasion sharing a waltz with her father or her brother. She wanted to accept, so very badly, especially when a young man nodded respectfully to her rejection and promptly hopped on the floor with another girl. Especially the ones who could dance! Oh, how she wished she could be the one flying through the air as she used to be.

Andy was not fond of dancing. He wasn't terribly good at it, she realised, when he finally yielded to her insistence at a dance early in their relationship. He had been clumsy and stepped on her toes too many times, once even dropping her to the floor in an awkward turn. She tried to teach him, tried to get him on the dance floor and lead. Even her father had tried to show Andy some steps, the jive, the waltz, knowing how much Elizabeth loved to dance. But she knew it wasn't his thing, that when he did dance with her it was to make her happy, so she didn't push. She sat with him, watching others, as she did now, tapping her feet on the floor, drumming her fingers on the table, moving her bottom on her chair.

She looked to Tess who was looking bored, her hand in Bryan's, her eyes on Elizabeth, a slight frown on her face. Elizabeth smiled at her and she looked away. Elizabeth could never understand why her sister didn't like her, and she was tired of trying to impress her. Her eyes moved to her parents, also on the dance floor, her father's arm wrapped protectively around her mother, who was swaying, a respectable distance away from him, but her eyes on his. She sighed; she wanted that, their love. Even after twenty-five years, they were in love. She could see it in the way they looked at each other, the little things they did for each other, the gentle way in which he spoke to her, her response, sometimes not so gentle but warm, loving.

She felt Andy's arm drop on her shoulder and was surprised by her reaction, an ever-so-slight irritation; she couldn't understand why. She turned to him and noticed his eyes start to droop.

"Do you want to leave?" she asked, hoping he would decline. He had worked half a shift during the day and could be tired, but he was an early bird at the best of times.

"No, of course not. It's not yet twelve," he said, stifling a yawn and looking at his watch, clearly unhappy with what it displayed.

"I am happy to leave if you want to," Elizabeth replied. "It's fine. I'm getting tired too." She began to rise from her seat.

"Elizabeth!" a voice boomed from the speakers. It was Teddy Walters, the keyboard player. "Where are you off to?"

Elizabeth turned to the stage where Teddy was motioning for

her to come up. "I'm leaving," she mouthed.

"Not without a song," he said into the microphone and the rest of the band were beginning to chant her name.

Elizabeth felt the stir. The heady feeling she got when she was on stage. She was asked to sing at every party or dance she attended and she had been told enough times that she had the voice of an angel. At least that was completely her own. She didn't have to live up to her sisters or compete with their looks and their proper ways. When she sang, no one could ignore her, and when she was in the spotlight, she gave way to her prim manners. She let loose, moving and shaking like a well-trained entertainer, those on the screen whom she imitated, and those on stage.

"It's getting late, Teddy," Elizabeth shouted and reached out to Andy, who was already in the process of getting out of his seat. When she turned back to Teddy, he was already off the stage and heading towards her, a look of determination on his face.

"Well, I can't let you go without a song." He grabbed her hand and she looked back at Andy, who was sitting back down, a smile of resignation and pride on his face. She was his girl, and everyone wanted her; it was enough to keep him at the dance at least a little longer.

The crowd had joined in the chant, urging her on. She did as a proper lady was supposed to do, protested slightly, until little by little, everyone in the room was calling her name. She felt the buzz, the electricity, and she followed Teddy through the tables and onto the stage. She was glad for the beads that her mother had sewn on her collar. They would twinkle in the gleam of the lights.

"Connie Francis?" Teddy asked. She nodded happily. 'Stupid Cupid' was her favourite song and she stood at the microphone waiting for her cue. Her voice flowed out easily and Elizabeth felt her body come alive, the tingle that emanated from the tips of her fingers to her toes. She danced and jived with Teddy as she sang, avoiding looking at Andy. He wouldn't be too happy about her dancing with another man, but right now she was her own. On that stage, she was not going to answer to anyone.

At the end of the song, she was sorry to put the mic back on its hook, but as she did she heard the chant of the crowd again. They wanted more. She looked at Andy now and his previously droopy expression had vanished; he had a light in his eyes that now popped out of his head, nodding, encouraging her to continue. She looked at Loretta, the singer, who was sidling off the stage, waving at her, glad for the reprieve. Three songs later and she knew it was enough. She could go on forever but she was thirsty. Her body was tingling and her throat was dry, but she was on a high.

She almost skipped back to her table, her cheeks flushed, smiling at her audience, who applauded her efforts and reached their hands out in congratulations. At least that was something her parents had never complained about, her voice, how she drew people in, how her voice sounded like a bell, how she was praised for it. Her eyes fell on her father, whose chin was high, his mouth curved upward, his shoulders square, and she felt a twinge of joy that she could at least make him proud in some way. She turned back to the stage to wave Teddy a gesture of gratitude, but as she did, something caught her eye and she looked back to it.

There he was, a man she'd never seen before, leaning against the edge of the doorway, his head cocked to one side, his eyes amused, laughing, set in her direction, his mouth twisted in a peculiar smile. A jolt hit her and she stumbled, a number of people nearby jumping up to steady her. She nodded her thanks and apologies and straightened herself, her eyes immediately returning to the spot where the man stood, but he wasn't there anymore and she felt a panic rise up to her throat. Her eyes scanned the hall frantically, a knot forming in her belly, a terror that he had been an apparition. She almost breathed an audible sigh of relief when she caught sight of him in the distance at the bar and checked herself. He was ordering a glass of something, she couldn't tell what, his head turned from her. She took a breath and felt her way back to her table, her eyes glazed, from the singing or from the sight of him, she didn't know. She reached her table and quickly sat down, trying to still herself, not hearing the murmurs of 'good job' and 'well done' that echoed around the table.

Andy smiled at her adoringly and murmured, "That's my girl."

"Very nice, Elizabeth," said her mother, who had just returned from the dance floor with her father. She sat down and turned around to acknowledge the talent of her daughter from the neighbouring tables, smiling and nodding with pride.

Elizabeth barely noticed. While she usually sucked every inch of praise her mother doled out to her, right now she was oblivious, her eyes trained on the man at the bar who was now surveying the room—searching for her, she hoped. Short black hair, thick, coiffed on one side, dark skin, not too dark, sideburns not too long, eyes that were dark, intense, full lips that sipped at his glass filled with a dark liquid. He was not tall, not short either, but his shoulders were straight, his chin high. He had an air of something ... arrogance?

He was looking at her and Elizabeth didn't realise for how long until he raised his glass to her, his mouth curving into that enigmatic smile again. Her face flushed and she quickly turned her head from him, embarrassed with her reaction. Her stomach was churning now and she could almost hear her heart beating; it was bumping hard and fast against her chest.

"Are you feeling okay?" Audrey, who sat beside her, was looking at her closely.

"I ... I'm fine. I'm just parched," she replied, reaching shakily for the glass of water and putting it to her lips.

She felt Andy's arm flop over her shoulder, pulling her to him. She flinched and tried to smile up at him but found the gesture irksome and was surprised at herself. While before she revelled in his affection, lately, and especially right now, she found it bothersome. She slowly turned back to the room to look around as if observing the goings-on, but she knew she was searching for him again. She found him still standing at the bar and her heart skipped a beat. He was still looking at her but this time, she boldly kept his stare, even though she could feel her cheeks heat, not a warmth from the energy that had been coursing through her body from the singing and dancing on stage, but hot, near feverish. She fisted her palms, realising they were clammy, and she looked down at them. What was happening?

She was blushing! She didn't blush! Hardly ever! Elizabeth was used to boys looking her way. She had more than her share of attention from the opposite sex. Her curiosity had been piqued some years before and she'd often sneak away to watch the boys training, studying the way they moved their limbs as they raced each other, or played cricket or hockey. She would lean against the fence, mesmerised, watching, learning how to move like them, how to interact with them, how to compete with them on the same level. She hated that she was expected to do what a woman did: stay at home mending, trying to look pretty. That was not for her. She wanted to be one of those boys.

She had always seen them playing their games in the street and had finally plucked up the courage to ask them to join in, which they allowed after some snickering. But they were aware that she was Mr Drake's daughter and not just them but the whole town's respect for her father was immense. She had played her heart out, raced down the street with them until they respected her for her ability, not just because her father was Mr Drake, and every afternoon when she got home from school, she became a regular fixture in their games, throwing her satchel on the ground and rushing to play, not bothering to change out of her uniform. Carolyn sometimes joined in but eventually tired of the strenuous nature of the play and took to sitting on the sidelines, fanning her face with one of her books, her skirt raised well above the knees, her long legs stretched forward, her toes pointing out. Elizabeth didn't take notice. Carolyn was becoming like her sisters, and she was not ready to give up her fun, not yet. When she met Andy, Elizabeth felt she needed to be the woman her mother wanted her to be.

But she wasn't feeling anything of the sort when she raised her eyelids to peek at this man, her eyes fixing on his, and he now lazily looked away and sauntered to a table a little distance away, where he took a seat next to a woman whom she had also never seen before. Elizabeth looked at his company, a sultry young woman, her long reddish hair in a braid that fell over one side of her very ample breast, who put her black gloved hand on his forearm as he sat down. Elizabeth now felt something else. She wanted to strangle that lovely woman and she grimaced at her response.

Elizabeth felt herself being watched and turned to Audrey, whose narrowed eyes were staring intently at her, her fingers drumming on the table. She looked away, worried that her sister could read her thoughts.

"Should we leave soon, honey?" Andy was tapping her shoulder. "You don't look so great."

'No!' she cried too quickly and checked herself. She cleared her throat. "I mean, it's only proper to wait until midnight, since we've waited already." She pulled at his wrist to look at his watch: 11.24 p.m. "We can wait until twelve, it's not long away." Andy nodded in resignation, stifling another yawn.

She wished her heart would stop thumping so loudly, but she couldn't resist looking at the man again. He wasn't looking at her anymore, his eyes were fixed on his companion and he was laughing at something, a lazy laugh. Elizabeth felt annoyance and turned her attention to the conversation at the table, but about what any of them were talking, she would never know. Minutes ticked by and she could stand it no more. She needed to move, to do something, anything to rid herself of how she was feeling, the irritating lump in her throat, the temptation to keep looking his way.

"I need to go to the ladies' room," she said to Andy, who raised his eyebrows. "Powder my nose." He nodded and she got up. As she did, she saw Audrey rise from her seat, but Elizabeth quickly darted away, and hoped desperately that she would not be followed. She took the route that went directly past the table *he* was on and with her head held high, she glided past him. She got to the powder room in one piece but her nerves were shot. Now what? She flopped down on the settee, feeling foolish, and dropped her face in her hands. What on earth was wrong with her? She had never felt so excited, so exhilarated, so ... desperate! She smacked her fist on the cushion and got up and shook herself off. She was being stupid! She checked herself in the mirror and pinched her cheeks, something she usually did to give them a bit of colour but she realised they didn't need reddening. Her face was shining, her eyes sparkling and she frowned at her reflection.

"Stop it!" she told herself firmly. "Get back out there and be with the best guy in the world. And enjoy it!" She took a number of deep breaths and began to feel better, more confident again. What on earth was wrong with her? *For goodness' sake! This is not the first guy you ever laid eyes on. Whoever the hell he is, bugger him!* She nodded at her reflection with determination and stepped out of the room.

A hand clutched at her arm and Elizabeth looked up, startled. *Him.* The relief and alarm she felt simultaneously completely engulfed her and when he dragged her down the hallway towards the kitchen, she followed obediently, weak and exhilarated, floating in a dream. He drew back the curtain that concealed a hubbub of activity, waiters and cooks hurrying to get out the last bits of coffee and cake to the revellers, loud voices yelling in urgent tones, none of which registered in Elizabeth's brain. She found herself pulled into his arms in a crevice in the larder wall, a darkness surrounding her; the only things that she focused on were his eyes, brown, almost black, gazing at her with a fierce want. A thrill of fear ran down her spine but she wasn't frightened of him; she saw her own face reflected in his eyes, the same need, as if she would die if he didn't kiss her.

Then he put his mouth on hers.

She had read those romantic novels where women's legs give way from passion, and how they lost all composure, but she had never understood how any of that felt. She had kissed Andy more than a decent unmarried girl should and it had been fun; she'd even been tempted to go further but put down the whole romantic notion to nothing more than a farce. She thought those stories were exaggerated to keep women reading. But now! Now, she felt as if she were drowning in him, a slow, terrifying swirl of waves that threatened to pull her under. The taste of whisky, she knew it from the trace of her father's glass on an occasional Saturday evening, the same cologne that Andy used, the one she detested, now stung in her nostrils, and she had never loved it more. And his lips, so gentle, so forceful, so smooth, so sweet. He knew what he was doing; she could tell he had done this a lot. The kiss seemed to last forever and yet, all too soon, she could hear her name being called.

"Liz? Are you in there?" She could hear Audrey from the direction of the powder room. She tore her lips away from his and looked into his eyes, his smiling eyes, a knowing smirk that told her he knew that she wasn't as prim and proper as she pretended to be. She remembered herself and stepped back, drew her hand back and slapped his cheek with all her might. Then she turned her back on him and marched away. Audrey caught sight of her coming from the other direction to that of the powder room and looked her up and down, her eyes narrowing.

"Where have you been?" Audrey demanded.

"Nowhere. Just come on, Audrey, let's go," Elizabeth mumbled, trying to slow her breathing.

Audrey didn't look convinced but reluctantly followed Elizabeth. She paused and glanced behind her and Elizabeth looked at her in time to see her catch her breath. Elizabeth turned around to see *him* leaning against the back wall.

"Elizabeth, what are you doing?" Audrey whispered loudly.

Elizabeth spun around and kept walking towards the hall. This was not where she was going to talk about it; she had to gain control of herself again, to figure out what was going on in her head, why she was using all self-control not to turn around and throw herself in his arms again.

By the time she reached the table and took some time shuffling into her seat, she had managed to refocus on the people around her. Her parents, both still panting slightly after their strenuous turn on the dance floor, Molly and Tess, their heads together, gossiping about someone at the next table, Fred getting up to ask Marcia for another turn on the dance floor. Audrey stood behind her and she tried to avoid turning her way. Her throat was dry and she grabbed the glass from the table, dropping water over her chest as she took a big gulp.

"Are you okay?" Andy was looking at her, concern written on his face, and Elizabeth knew hers was flushed. "Do you want to go home now?"

Elizabeth shook her head tightly, unwilling to let any words come out of her mouth, but she felt the irritation bubble up in her again at the sound of his voice and she wanted to scream. For the first time since she'd been Andy's girl, she felt trapped.

Andy had trapped her! She clenched her teeth, knowing that none of this was Andy's fault. He had been nothing but wonderful but her skin prickled at his touch and not in a good way, a feeling of resentment towards him creeping up on her and she stared down at her dress, despising herself for how she felt.

*It's okay. I will sleep on it,* she thought. *This will pass.*

# Chapter 4 - A Perfect Couple

After that first night of their meeting, Elizabeth and Mike spent every waking hour together, barely able to keep their hands off each other. Mike was something else, nothing she had ever seen before and certainly nothing she had ever felt. Everything that came before may well not have even happened. It was like she was reborn. He was sophisticated, suave, knew what to say, but it was more than that. He made her weak, made her knees tremble at the thought of him.

The day after they met, for some reason, she knew he would find her. She had gone home after the dance, let Andy kiss her goodnight and yawned, faking tiredness when Andy made a move to come into the house with her. She hurried to her room before Audrey had the chance to catch up with her, got undressed and hopped into bed. She wanted to think about him, wanted to savour that kiss, to relive her trembling limbs when he had held her. A sliver of guilt ran through her again but she dismissed it. Guilt was not going to get in the way of this immaculate feeling, like she was rising above her bed, floating somewhere between the earth and the stars. His eyes, penetrating hers, something in them—lust? Not just lust. There was something, some animal chemistry; she could not name the feeling.

Elizabeth got up early the next morning, having barely slept. She wanted to get out of the house before anyone else arose and she wanted to avoid Andy who was probably going to be coming over. He did every day and since it was New Year's Day and he was not working, he was sure to want to spend the day with her. She remembered something about them doing something, but her mind was so flustered, she couldn't exactly remember what.

"Where are you rushing off to so early?" Doris was just coming out of her room, her hair in the rollers she'd put in the night before.

Elizabeth was ready. "Meeting Carolyn for breakfast," she said and dashed out the front door before her mother had time to

34

respond. No one was having breakfast that early on New Year's Day but Carolyn had missed the dance so she hoped her mother would create her own narrative or else Elizabeth would have to create one by the time she got home.

The street was quiet, she could hear only her footsteps on the gravel path, and she wrapped her arms around herself, wishing she had put on a thicker coat. She looked about her, wondering if she should be wandering the streets at such an ungodly hour on such a day. A couple of houses had their lights on, the early risers, Mr and Mrs Halpena, the nosy neighbours who spied on Elizabeth and told tales; down the street, she saw the porch light of Prashant Valma, one of the teachers at her school. She liked Mr Valma; he was soft-spoken, encouraged her to excel in her art classes, but he seemed such a lonely soul that Elizabeth would sometimes take her lunch to his classroom and have it there so he wouldn't be sitting at his desk alone at lunchtime. He never did chat much to her but she sensed that maybe he felt her presence and enjoyed the silent company, confirmed when the bell rang and he nodded with a little smile.

Where Elizabeth was going, she had no clue, but before long, she was standing outside the gates of the dance hall. What was she expecting? For the bold young man to materialise, sweep her off her feet, and take her away from everything she knew and thought she loved? How stupid was she? She looked down at her watch. It was barely past 9:00 a.m. now and nothing was opening around her, not even the *bunya*, who usually opened at 6:30. She felt a little shiver run down her spine and frowned. She was never scared of anything. Was it because she was alone in the street, not a human in sight? She heard a car in the distance and squeezed herself between the posts of the gate. She knew almost everyone in town and she would look daft standing in the middle of the street on her own. Whoever it was would have a field day explaining and gossiping about her to her mother. She peeped out and watched the car go past. She recognised it as her Aunt Dimple, the biggest gossip of them all. She pulled herself back and crouched down.

What was she to do now? She felt annoyance with herself. She should just go back home and sneak back into her room. What had she expected to find anyway? That man waiting for her on the steps? She thought about his eyes again and closed hers, her body reacting to the memory. How she wanted to be in those arms again.

She felt her stomach lurch, her body trembling. How was it that he had that effect on her? No one ever had; she never thought one person, one interaction could make her feel like this.

"Hello there," came a voice and Elizabeth jumped up and found herself staring into those same eyes. For a split second, she thought she was still in her daydream, but she could feel her heart beating so hard and fast, she thought she would collapse. She saw his lip curl. That teasing smile again.

"Hello," she croaked, trying to regain her composure by straightening out her skirt, the blue one of Audrey's she had stolen from her wardrobe this morning, the one that clung snugly to her thighs. She put her hand to her hair to pat down the strays that she knew were blowing into her eyes but as she did, she found his fingers on them instead, moving them softly to one side of her forehead. His touch was like fire and she flinched.

"Sorry," he said, pulling back his hand. "What are you doing here all alone in this deserted street?" He waved his hand about him.

"I ... er, I left something at the hall and I was hoping to get here before it opened so I could get it." Elizabeth could always come up with ideas on the spot and she was glad she had somewhat prepared for this one. She had no idea if she would see him but she knew it would be better to be ready.

"Oh?" He leaned against the wall. "What did you leave?"

"My compact," she said.

"And it was so dear to you, you had to get it first thing this morning?"

Elizabeth felt the bristles on her arm rise. He was teasing her. "I can come back later," she said, taking a quick glance at the door she knew was not going to open anytime soon. She began to walk in the direction of her home and felt his hand take hers—a bold move, which she found quite thrilling.

"I'm Mike," he said.

"Elizabeth," she replied, not trusting herself to look at him.

"We can get some breakfast if you haven't had any yet?"

She turned to him now, leaving her hand clamped in his. "What do you want from me?" She was surprised at her own question.

He smiled now, fully, his white teeth baring against his lips. "Good girl," he said. "Straight to the point. No games." He leaned forward and put his lips close to her ear. "I like that."

Elizabeth didn't know how to respond but she felt a rush of heat at his breath on her ear. "Um ..."

"Come with me," he said and walked her in the opposite direction of her house.

# Chapter 5 - Can't Live Without ...

"What do you want from life, Elizabeth?"

Elizabeth sank back into his chest, watching the sun go down over the hills. She had just spent the most magical day with Mike. They had spent the morning walking the outer streets of Derrum, quietly getting to know each other. She told him about her family, and he told her about his love of flying. He was in the Air Force and couldn't look at any life that didn't involve being in the air. The way she felt today, she could completely understand this concept. She couldn't remember too much of the conversation but felt every move he made, from when his hand let hers go and moved to her waist so that he could move her past a narrow alley, to when he slung it loosely around her shoulders. She should have protested, she knew that, but she didn't, couldn't. They walked back to his base, where he brought out a brown paper package and a scooter and with a wink, told her to hop on. Elizabeth was not scared for a minute. She jumped on the back, hitching up her skirt, and put her arms around him. It had been a relief to be able to do that after the whole morning of wanting to ravage him but carefully containing herself. She had leaned her cheek into the leather of his jacket and breathed deeply. She wanted to savour this moment just in case it was the only one she had with him. Then they had ridden to the hills. When he parked on the side of a muddy path, Elizabeth pried herself from him.

"What's that?" she said, nodding to the package that he had pulled from the case in the front of the scooter.

"Food," he said, and leaning slightly forward, retrieved, from where she didn't know, two bottles of cola.

"Very nice," said Elizabeth. Her cheeks were flushed and her knuckles were numb from the cold and she rubbed them against the sides of her thighs.

"You're cold," he said with a frown and edged towards her.

"I'm okay," said Elizabeth. She certainly didn't want to look like a damsel in distress but when he put down the package and the drinks, she felt her heart flutter and looked at the ground. She felt his fingertips under her chin, raising her head to his, and before she knew it, even though she somewhat expected it, his lips were on hers.

There they had sat, a tangle of mouths and arms and hands, for hours; the sun had risen high in the sky and had begun to droop to the edge of the town and the package had lain next to the scooter, untouched. "Let's eat something," he said finally, pulling himself from her and leaning over to retrieve the package.

Elizabeth didn't care if she died of starvation, she didn't want to leave his touch but she nodded. "What have you got?" The touch of intimacy makes one more comfortable and Elizabeth rummaged in the brown paper bag, finding four sandwiches and two apples.

"Got to be healthy," he said. "Jam sandwiches and cheese sandwiches."

Elizabeth laughed. "Healthy? Okay." As she tucked into one, Elizabeth became self-conscious. She watched him eat his sandwich neatly but heartily and nibbled slowly on her own. He took a giant swig of one of the bottles and Elizabeth sniffed the air. "Is that ..."

"This one is yours," he said, handing her one of the colas.

"What's in yours?"

"Oh, there's cola in it," he said with a little smile. "Would you like a sip?"

Elizabeth pursed her lips. She had tasted alcohol before, wine mostly when her parents had toasted an occasion, but it was usually a little taste, and she didn't really care for the bitter flavour. She saw another smile dance on Mike's lips, a smile of challenge, and she took the bottle from him, slinging her head back and taking a swig. She felt the liquid fill her mouth and swallowed. It stung a little but she pulled a face and handed it back to Mike. "I don't care for it," she said, taking her own bottle to drown out the flavour in her mouth.

Mike leaned against a tree and Elizabeth crawled up to him, fitting herself in the curve of his body. What did she want out of life, he had asked. Before this day, before last night, she had wanted the world. She had wanted to study, she had wanted to sing, she had wanted ... to be Andy's wife.

"I don't know what I want," she said softly. "Not anymore."

"You're young," he said. "Eighteen?"

Elizabeth nodded, wishing she were older. "You, Mike?"

"Twenty-three," he said.

39

"And how is it that you have the day to spend with me?" Elizabeth asked, wanting to change the subject of their ages. He seemed so worldly, knew what he wanted from life and she didn't even know what she wanted to do the next day.

"I'm playing hooky," he said and laughed when she raised her eyebrows in alarm. "It is still New Year's Day," he whispered.

"The best day of the year," sighed Elizabeth and looked towards town. When the tall trees over Derrum turned a dusky purple, Elizabeth knew they had to return. She would have to face the music in whatever form that came.

Mike dropped her at the end of her street where she'd asked him to. She reluctantly got off the scooter and stood in front of him. He took her in his arms. "My girl," he said and kissed her deeply.

"Will I see you again?" she asked, not sure if she wanted to hear the answer.

"How's tomorrow?" Elizabeth couldn't stop the smile that spread over her face. "Same time? But how about I pick you up from here instead? It's a long walk to the dance hall."

Elizabeth blushed. "Not very long, but yes. I'll wait for you."


Mike deflowered Elizabeth on the third evening in the back seat of the Ambassador he borrowed from the base and she thought it was the most romantic thing in the world. She didn't feel the pain, the discomfort, and she didn't care where they were as long as they were with each other. After that, as they sat on the cold grass, leaning on the door of his car, Elizabeth remembered the woman who had sat with him at the New Year's Eve dance. Gosh, that seemed like forever ago and it had only been a few days.

"Who is she?" Elizabeth asked.

"Who?"

"Your date. At the dance."

"A friend," he replied, and reached into his pocket for his cigarettes. He offered her one.

Elizabeth hesitated and then took it. She had smoked a couple of puffs that were offered to her by her friends but had never liked the taste or the smell, but on Mike, it was divine, and she breathed it in deeply when she had snuggled into his neck. She watched Mike as he inhaled and rested his head on the car, blowing out the smoke in little rings into the air. She looked at the cigarette poised in her hand. She lifted it to her mouth, took in a deep drag just as Mike had, felt the acrid fume hit the back of her throat and gagged.

He looked at her, alarmed, and tapped lightly on her back. When she eased up, he laughed. "First time?"

'No!' She felt tears well and squeezed her eyes shut to keep them from spilling. She took another drag and felt the heat pierce her throat. She leaned her head on the car as Mike had done. Then she looked at him, his shoulders resting on the car, his hand on her knee. His eyes were closed, his face turned towards the night sky. He was beautiful, and not just how he looked, with his nose, just ever so slightly large, his chin, strong and masculine, his neck that stretched out, exposing his protruding Adam's apple. It was the way he made her feel, even when he wasn't looking at her, like she was a goddess, the only woman in the world. She reached down and took his hand and felt him entwine her fingers in his. She already knew by now that she was in love with him, only three days after he cornered her at the New Year's dance.

"What about your boyfriend?" His eyes were still closed and it seemed like it was a casual question but the veins on his temple throbbed.

Elizabeth wrinkled her nose. She didn't want to think about Andy right now, not after the last few days. Poor Andy, who had accepted that he wasn't going to get more than kisses from her until they were married. She felt a prick of guilt when she thought about him, which is why she tried not to. He was probably at home right now, wondering what had happened to her when he came to take her out for a stroll to the shopping district, where they would walk up and down the festive streets filled with stalls, a tradition Elizabeth usually shared with her family. But Mike's car had rolled into the street and she had seen it before it even reached her kerb and she was already opening the door before it fully stopped. She jumped in and Mike stepped on the gas and roared away. Andy never entered her mind. "Who? Andy?"

Mike laughed. "You have more than one boyfriend?"

"Oh, Andy." She frowned and held out her left hand and Mike glanced at the ring that wasn't twinkling as brightly as it had done before.

"I was wondering about that little bauble."

41

"I am engaged."

Mike smirked. "Yes, clearly you are."

"I don't want to think about Andy," she said and rested her head on his shoulder.

He turned her face up to his. "Then don't."

\* \* \* \*

"What are you doing?" Tess waltzed into Elizabeth's room and plonked herself on the bed. She was taking off her stockings, getting ready for bed, Mike still swimming in her brain.

"What am I doing?" asked Elizabeth, placing her hand on her hip. She had just returned from her evening with Mike and knew there were going to be questions. The last few days she had barely been home. Between working and Mike, she had not had time with her family. She hadn't even seen Tess since the dance.

"It's all over town. You driving around with that ... that ... *man*." Tess spat out the word 'man' and Elizabeth felt a prick of alarm. *Andy*. What if he heard something ... "What's going on, Elizabeth?"

Elizabeth felt her hackles rise in defence and turned to face her sister. "How is it your business?"

Tess raised her eyebrows and put her hands on her hips, knowing she had Elizabeth's attention. "By the way people are talking, it seems to be everyone's business."

"Well, Father always told me not to listen to the gossips," said Elizabeth, shrugging her shoulders, trying to act nonchalant.

"When it affects your family ..."

"Tell me how it's affected anything."

"Oh," Tess said and nodded sagely. "So there is something for them to gossip about."

Elizabeth knew Tess had tricked her. She sat down on the bed and took a deep breath. She wanted to talk to someone about Mike anyway. And tonight, after she had lost her virginity, she felt more lost than ever. "I love him."

"Who, Andy?" Tess's face softened, which made Elizabeth feel like crying. She didn't reply. Tess got off the bed and walking to the door, closed it. "So, not Andy." Elizabeth shook her head and put her face in her hands. She felt Tess's arm move around her shoulder and she let out a sob. "You want to talk about it?"

Elizabeth couldn't help but stifle a laugh and looked up at her sister, who shrugged. "You came in to get it out of me." She took the handkerchief that Tess offered and wiped at her eyes. "I'm in love with Mike." Tess nodded, encouraging her to go on. "I don't know how it happened. It just did."

"And who is Mike?"

"Oh, Tess." Elizabeth turned around and jumped onto her knees, facing Tess. "He is the man of my dreams, the one I've been waiting for." Tess's mouth pursed. "I know, I know. Andy. But Andy is not the one I want."

"You're to be married to Andy." Tess cocked her head in question.

"I don't think I can marry Andy." Elizabeth looked down at her hands which twiddled with the handkerchief.

"But Elizabeth, you have set a date. There are plans underway."

Elizabeth let her shoulders sag. "I can't."

"Have you ... you know ..." Elizabeth looked up at Tess and she bit on her lip, wondering how much she could trust her sister. Tess brought her hands to her mouth. "Elizabeth!"

"Shh," Elizabeth begged. "Please let me trust you, Tess." Tess nodded. "I don't love Andy."

"Then why did you agree to marry him?"

"Because I thought I did. I don't know. I'm so confused. I just know that I will die if I can't be with Mike."

"Stop being so dramatic," said Tess, an annoyed lilt in her voice now. "But anyway," she said with a sigh. "You love who you love. I can't think of being with anyone but Bryan."

"So you understand?" Elizabeth grabbed her sister's hands in hers, for the first time feeling a connection with her, a sisterly bond she hadn't felt with her before.

"Yes, I do. But you need to make everyone else understand. Because right now, there are people out there with questions. I know Mother is trying not to blow her top with you."

"Do they know? Have they heard anything?"

"No." Tess smiled sheepishly. "There is no gossip ... yet, anyway. I saw you run off this afternoon and when I described the guy to Audrey, she told me about the dance. And she told Mother and

Father too." She patted Elizabeth's hand. "But you'd better do the right thing and let Andy know. He's a good guy. It's not fair to him."

After Tess left her by herself, Elizabeth pondered her dilemma as she twirled the ring round and round on her finger. She couldn't marry Andy, even if Mike were to disappear from her life. She had been unfaithful to him. Besides that, she now knew what it was to feel rapture, to be utterly consumed by someone, and that was so far removed from how she felt about Andy. She was enamoured, perhaps by his nonchalance at the beginning, perhaps by his impulsivity, his indifference to what people thought; maybe it was just him. Maybe she had to see how things went. She let herself fall on her bed and stared at the ceiling. She was seeing Mike tomorrow and she could barely wait.

* * * *

"I have to leave for a while," said Mike.

"When?" Elizabeth swallowed the lump that rose so quickly to her throat.

"The day after tomorrow."

Elizabeth knew this was coming. His leave was coming to an end and he was due at the office in Bombay—when, exactly, he had never let on. He had come to Derrum with a friend because he hadn't wanted to go home; he wanted to be a bachelor for a little while. He didn't expect to spend more than a couple of days there, but meeting Elizabeth had changed everything. But by the end of January, he was due back.

She nodded, trying to imagine life without him. They had escaped Derrum and had gone on a scenic train ride to nowhere really, Elizabeth not caring who saw her and Mike together anymore. She had yet to break it off with Andy, had dropped hints when he stopped by, which he was not picking up, either intentionally or oblivious to them. It had been seventeen days of bliss with Mike, dashing off after work and not returning home until the late hours of the night, successfully avoiding a conversation with her parents for fear of being given an inquisition. But now, she would have to sort things out, with Andy, with her family, and without Mike being around to take her into another world, she wasn't sure she could manage.

"Marry me," he said.

Elizabeth couldn't control the burst of excitement that flooded her body at that moment and ignoring the raised eyebrows of the other travellers in the cabin, threw her arms around him and flourished kisses all over his face. "Yes. Yes!" she squealed, completely forgetting the fact that she already had a fiancé.

Mike squeezed her tight. "And the sooner the better," he said.

"When, Mike? When can I be your bride?"

"Perhaps once you have gotten rid of your other guy," he said, grinning.

"Oh, yes. Andy." She frowned. Damn! She would have to break the news to Andy. He would need to be the first to know. "I will tell him tomorrow." She settled into the crook of his shoulder. "Where will we live?"

"Anywhere I'm stationed," he said.

"I'll be anywhere you are," she said and gazed out of the train window, watching the grey clouds float past.

# Chapter 6 - Breaking Up Is Hard to Do

*He loved her. She was going to be his wife. She would be. Sure, he had heard things. When Fred told him that he saw her with that officer, well ... But it was to be expected. Marriage was a big thing. She was nervous. Don't all girls get nervous before their wedding? He was too, but he had never been so sure of anything in his life. When he first saw her, he knew there would be no one else. A man in a uniform, was that all it took? He would be patient. He would let her get it out of her system. She was in love with him, Andy. No damn stranger, however suave and handsome, was going to take her from him. He was patient. He would wait.*

Elizabeth broke the news to Andy that very evening. After Mike had dropped her home, she went to Andy's house and when he saw her standing there, he pulled her to him. She had seen him on only two occasions in the last two weeks and they had been family gatherings that were crowded, not allowing for any conversation, for which Elizabeth was grateful.

"Can we go for a walk, maybe back to my place?"

"Ma, Pa, going for a walk, back soon," Andy called into the house and shut the door. He moved to kiss Elizabeth on her lips but she turned her cheek to him. Now it would be unfaithful to let him kiss her when she was engaged to Mike. She realised how ridiculous all of it was but she wanted to start life with Mike as a dutiful partner.

They walked to her house, Elizabeth nervously babbling about her work and how the new phone system was bothersome. Andy nodded and squeezed her hand from time to time. When they arrived at her house, Elizabeth led him straight into the backyard, where she felt a shiver in the chill of the evening. Andy took off his cardigan and placed it around her shoulders. She felt a deep sadness for what she was about to do to him, and a twinge of guilt, but her happiness with Mike surpassed all else. She had to rip the Band-Aid off, there was not going to be any pussyfooting around it.

"It's over, Andy."

"What's over?"

"Us. We're done."

Andy looked at her with the saddest eyes she'd ever seen and Elizabeth watched with sorrow as his shoulders slumped. She remained silent as he talked, consoling himself with the idea that this was pre-wedding jitters.

"You're just scared," he said, kneeling on the floor and grabbing her hands with his. "We're still young. We can wait a while, if you want to."

Elizabeth didn't want to wait to be married—to Mike, that was. She shook her head emphatically, trying to remember some inkling of love that she felt for him. But she knew that what she felt for Andy wasn't a fragment of what she felt for Mike. She even felt guilty that right now, as she was breaking up with Andy, she was wishing it would finish soon, so she could go back to Mike, who was waiting for her in their usual meeting spot, the park.

She removed his ring from her pocket and Andy's eyes widened.

"It's not on your finger."

"Because I'm serious, Andy. It's over."

"But why? Because of that guy, the one who you've been running around with?"

Elizabeth was not surprised that he had heard something. She knew he probably would have known about Mike, but he had the decency never to ask her about it. Perhaps he trusted her. And perhaps he just hadn't wanted to ask her about it, because then she may have had to tell him the truth, which wasn't something he wanted to hear. Elizabeth was many things, but she couldn't keep Andy in the dark any longer. "Yes," she said, turning her face from his. Then she realised it was best to get it all over and done with at the same time. Why prolong the inevitable? He was going to find out anyway, and it was best she be the one to tell him about it. "He asked me to marry him. I said yes."

Andy jerked backwards like he had been stung. Elizabeth looked down at him now and felt such a sorrow, her eyes welled. Andy's lips were moving but he wasn't saying anything; he looked like a goldfish.

"Andy, say something," she said after a few very

uncomfortable moments.

Then Andy stood up and took a deep breath. "You will come to your senses."

"Andy, no. I won't." Elizabeth looked to the ground again, wishing this whole thing was easier but knowing he was feeling a lot worse than she was.

"Yes, you will." His voice was getting higher. "You will get over that ... that brute. He will leave you high and dry, that ... that *man*." Andy was not a man who spoke very harshly and it was almost comical to hear him try to come up with the right words without cussing. "You just wait," he yelled now. "You just wait. You will come back to me when he is gone, that man, with his bright stupid uniform. He will leave you, don't doubt me. And when he does, you will beg me to take you back."

Elizabeth's eyes were drawn to a shadow that stood behind the screen of the back door, inserting his presence into the scene. Her father. He had clearly heard the raised voices and felt he needed to be close in case things got out of hand. "I won't, Andy," she said more quietly now.

Andy squared his shoulders. "You will. And I don't know if I would." With that, he jumped up, turned on his heel and strode away, pushing past Elizabeth's father and apologising as he rushed past.

Elizabeth sat heavily on the swing and looked up as she heard her father approach. "You want to fill me in?" he asked gently.

"Oh, Pa," Elizabeth cried, throwing herself into her father's arms. "I just broke his heart."

In early February, when the realisation set in that Elizabeth was never coming back to him, Andy caught the train out of town, leaving a note for his parents. He was going to the gulf. That was where his future lay. He didn't mention the shame he felt in the town when everyone, including his parents, looked at him with pity. It was now Mike and Elizabeth, not Elizabeth and Andy.

And Mike and Elizabeth were the talk of the town! At twenty-three, he was already next in line for captain, was handsome, well-to-do, and she, one of the most beautiful and talented girls in town. And they were madly in love.

Elizabeth's family had concerns.

"Are you sure about this man?" asked her sisters.

"What if he takes you away from here?" asked her mother.

"What happens when we all go off to Canada?" asked her brother.

"Do you really love him?" asked her father. To this Elizabeth nodded emphatically.

Yet the interrogation continued. They barely knew each other. Her mother was worried and didn't want to give her blessing. But for once, Elizabeth challenged her mother and threatened to elope if she didn't have it. Her mother succumbed, but Audrey was not so convinced. She tried to talk Elizabeth out of this crazy plan, especially since they had set the wedding date not a few months away. Elizabeth dug her heels in and declared that as she was of age, she was entitled to choose whomever she wanted and would be married whenever she wanted.

Elizabeth stepped out to the back porch after another argument with her mother and sat down on the step, watching Fred who was strumming his guitar. She leaned her head on the banister and he looked up and grinned.

"What is it, Liz?"

"What do *you* think?"

"About?"

"Come on, Fred," said Elizabeth and scooted closer to him.

Fred put down his guitar. "Do you want me to tell you what *they're* thinking?" Fred jerked his head in the direction of the house where she could hear her parents chattering, more loudly this time. "Or do you want my opinion about your new guy?"

"I guess both?" She shrugged.

"I can't give you advice about boys. I'm too young." He snickered. "But them ..."

"I love him, Fred," Elizabeth said.

"Then I can't give you any advice on that," Fred said. "But Liz, you worry them to death. Poor Dad has lost hair over you." Elizabeth narrowed her eyes now. She didn't like the thought of that at all, especially as she had just recently noticed the little bald patch that had appeared right at the top of her father's head.

"Why?"

Fred let out a hearty laugh. "Oh, Elizabeth!"

Elizabeth wrinkled her nose. "They worry that much?"

"See," said Fred, leaning his back on the step, looking sagely into the distance; Elizabeth marvelled at how well he mimicked his father. "We are all happy to go with the status quo, me included. Do what's expected from us, happy to do it even. But you. You're different. You are wilder. You play sport like a boy, you sing, you dance, you get attention from everyone. You even smack people around when they try to get the better of you."

Elizabeth giggled at this. Just last month when she and her sisters were walking down the street together, a couple of guys rode past them on their bicycles and one tried to grab at their breasts. While Tess and Molly stood there, their hands over their mouths, their virtue more offended than their sense of right and wrong, Elizabeth had chased them, caught up with one of them and punched him in the face until her sisters had screamed for her to stop. The young man yelled his apologies over and over again and ran off down the street, his bike still laying on the road. And all she got for it was a lecture from Tess about the proper behaviour of ladies. Elizabeth had argued at first, then realised she was not going to change her sisters' minds and they were never going to understand her.

"They cannot harness you," said Fred. "And that worries them. That you cannot be harnessed—by anyone." He saw her face crumple. "But they are also proud of you. You stand up for what's right, you see the world as yours to take. You don't give in. And I, for one, think that's a brilliant thing."

Elizabeth smiled. Yes, she was also known for the good things—when she was asked to sing at parties, when the parties stopped to watch her dance, when she caught sight of her father and mother, their eyes filled with pride in these moments. Elizabeth lived for those times when she finally made them happy. Elizabeth looked up at her brother, her eyes like saucers. He was younger and yet sometimes so much wiser; he really was like their father. No wonder they didn't worry about him. "Think about just last year," said Fred and his face broke into a grin.

"Last year?"

"Before Andy." Elizabeth looked at him quizzically. "When you were breaking through the fence to go play with the neighbours, the boys in that school."

"I always played with the boys," said Elizabeth but she knew what Fred was referring to. In the last year, she did more than playing—sports anyway. When she realised she had more power over the boys through the way she talked to them, the way they looked at her, she understood what her sisters carried on about. She smiled to herself. It had been more than a year earlier. And then, her mother found her, after much searching, over the fence, leaning on a tree, Billy, a tall, confident senior, leaning over her, twirling a lock of her thick dark curls in his fingers. There was a lot of yelling and a promise not to tell her father if she promised not to do it again. But then Andy came along soon after and the incident was forgotten—they all fell in love with him. "So what are you saying?"

"That you always do what you want to do, without thinking it through." He raised his eyebrows at Elizabeth's indignant face. "It's not an insult," said Fred.

"So I'm impulsive? Is that what you mean?"

Fred shrugged. "What do I know, Elizabeth? I'm just a kid." He picked up his guitar to indicate he didn't have much more to add and Elizabeth put her hands on her knees and her chin on her hands.

Impulsive ...

# Chapter 7 - The D'Souzas

When Mike came back a few weeks later for a week's stay, bringing her father exotic whisky and her mother and sisters even more exotic perfumes and scarves, he won over the family, only Elizabeth's father nonplussed by his generosity and exuberance.

"Are you sure?" her father asked when Mike left that evening. "What about his family? Are they okay with this?"

"I'm meeting them when Mike comes back next week," said Elizabeth. "I wanted to ask you if it's okay to go to Bombay to meet them." Her father took a deep breath. She continued quickly. "Mike promised that it's all above board. They will have a room for me and everything. It will only be a few days."

"Elizabeth, even if I say no, you will still go, so I won't do that." He sighed again, heavily, and Elizabeth wished her father could see what she saw in Mike. "You have my blessing."

It was a long train ride and the closer they got to Mike's family, the more nervous Elizabeth became. She had stared out of the window while he slept, not even noticing as the throngs of people petered out as the train rolled through the countryside, which stretched from a luscious green to a muddy brown and back again. The country was overcrowded, so everyone said, but during the ride she saw acres and acres of land, alive with wildflowers and grass overgrown, the odd herd of cattle popping up as they neared a village. And she knew they were closing in on Bombay when more people began to appear on the fields near the railway line and on the streets adjacent to the track. She smiled when she saw a bus, a full bus, people bursting out of its doors, a bunch of people on its roof. Just earlier she was sure she heard clattering on the roof of the train just above her. It was not an odd sight to see people catching a lift on a bus or a train and she had grinned. Most people complained about it, thought it was a terrible thing, a dangerous thing and although Elizabeth acknowledged that there was danger in what they were doing, she also loved the randomness of it, the daring of these people.

But that sense of daring was disappearing the closer they got to the station. Elizabeth had initially been excited to meet Mike's parents, his sister and brother, but she was nervous. "Will they like me, Mike?" she asked as they reached the border of Bombay.

"I love you, so of course they will too." He said it with a toss of his hand and Elizabeth wasn't convinced. She may not have known Mike for all that long but she was already accustomed to his gestures, his expressions and both of these right now told her he was not convinced himself.

"What have you told them about me?"

"I told them I met the woman I'm going to marry."

Elizabeth sometimes tired of Mike's brief answers. It seemed like he didn't want to elaborate on anything. She had to push to get anything out of him sometimes. "And did they ask for more? Were they curious?"

"What I do with my life is none of their business anyway."

"Mike!" she exclaimed. "They are your family. I thought you were close with them."

"I am, but they can't tell me what to do or what not to do." Elizabeth didn't like that answer. Would she have to prove to his family that she was worthy of Mike's love? "Don't worry, my love," he said with a kiss on the tip of her nose. "They will love you as much as I do." He turned away but not quickly enough for Elizabeth to notice the crease between his eyes.

Mike's sister, Teresa, met them at the station and they caught a taxi back to his parents' home, Teresa chatting for all of the hour's ride. "Father's going away for a couple of months but he should be back in time for the wedding. Elizabeth, what's your dress like?"

"My mother is making my dress," said Elizabeth with some pride. Doris had already begun measuring taffeta and lace and half of the living room was strewn with material, beads and diamantes.

"Oh," said Teresa with a frown. Elizabeth didn't like the way she said it.

"My mother is a seamstress," Elizabeth said. "She's made all our clothes. I wouldn't have it any other way."

"What about the ceremony? Are there Catholic churches in Derrum?"

"Derrum is a big place," said Mike quickly. "Of course." Elizabeth pursed her lips. She wasn't sure if Mike had told his family that she had to convert to Catholicism to marry him. Her parents had not been happy about it.

"Well, I have my dress ready too," said Teresa. "I can't wait to show it to you." She turned to Mike, asked him about his own wedding attire and as she talked Elizabeth took her in, pretty brown eyes that moved about as quickly as her mouth did. She held Elizabeth's hand the whole time and paused, sometimes mid-sentence, to gush about Elizabeth's looks, to the point where Elizabeth turned away in embarrassment. "We're here," she said suddenly and Elizabeth's heart beat faster.

She was about to meet his mother. Alma.

Mike didn't talk about his family very much but when he spoke of his mother, Elizabeth could almost imagine a halo on the woman. Mike's voice became reverent, his facial features softened and he didn't need to say much—it was clear she meant more to him than anyone. Elizabeth needed Mike's mother to accept her, to like her. She knew once her family had gone away, so very far away, she would need someone to be there. She grappled nervously with her handbag as they made their way to the front door.

Alma welcomed her into their home with a flourish, and Elizabeth could smell the aroma of *biryani* wafting through the house, making her stomach rumble. Alma, small, and more wrinkled than someone her age should have been, put out her hand and Elizabeth, who too soon had leaned in to hug her, backed away, and cleared her throat, feeling the ping of the rebuff reverberate through her chest. Mike's father, Albert, tall, shoulders squared, chin raised, resembled Mike in his stance, but there was a hardness to his features that Mike did not possess. He was clearly a man not to be trifled with even though his mouth curved in a smile and he moved to embrace her.

"Teresa, please show Elizabeth where she will stay," said Albert and Elizabeth followed Teresa down a hall into her room.

"How long are you staying?" asked Teresa and Elizabeth was surprised by the question. She thought arrangements had been made for the week-long visit.

"Um ..." She looked back at  Mike who shrugged his shoulders and she had no idea what the shrug meant. She changed the subject. "Is Joshua here?"

"My wayward brother? No." Teresa rolled her eyes and gave an exaggerated sigh. "Don't know where he is. Could be in Ceylon, could be in Kashmir."

"Will he come for the wedding?"

Teresa shrugged. "Don't know." Elizabeth could see that Teresa wasn't keen on continuing with this line of conversation.

Elizabeth again wondered about the elder brother that Mike didn't talk a lot about. "He's a bit different," Mike said once. "Doesn't have his head on his shoulders." But she had hoped to meet them all on this trip. Rip the Band-Aid off, so to speak.

Dinner had been pleasant enough, Elizabeth answering questions about her upbringing and her family and straight after that, it was time for bed and she was put into Teresa's room, in Teresa's bed. Where Teresa had slept that night, Elizabeth never knew, but she appreciated the gesture. She had lain in bed wanting to go to Mike, knowing she couldn't.

On the way home, after just three days, three very uneventful days, Elizabeth realised she hadn't learned much about any of Mike's family. As much as Teresa could talk, she didn't really say anything very meaningful. She was to be engaged to a wealthy businessman whom, after the pleasantries, was all she talked about. Which was fine, thought Elizabeth, because when you're in love with someone, that's who you only want to talk about. But she hadn't really gotten to know any of them, not really. She'd spent the days meeting a few of Mike's friends, a cousin and a councilman who had come over to have dinner with the family.

Mike's father was certainly a presence, a hush settling over the room whenever he entered, which wasn't very often, and Elizabeth noticed Mike stiffen whenever his father spoke directly to him. His mother was courteous, smiling, welcoming, but Elizabeth found it hard to be at ease with her. And she was yet to meet the 'wayward' Joshua. She wondered even more about him now.

They had been to a club, where Mike spent most of his time schmoozing with his old friends, Elizabeth proudly displayed on his arm. She met a few of his friends, jolly, welcoming people, including Max, one of Mike's good friends, a pilot like himself, who had propositioned her when Mike went to use the men's room. She didn't dare tell Mike. She had already been introduced to his jealous rages as well as his best friend—bourbon. She had become a firm friend too.

# Chapter 8 - Becoming Mrs D'Souza

On a balmy evening in the middle of March, Elizabeth became Mrs Mike D'Souza. The day went perfectly and she had never felt her heart so full as she did when she stepped into the getaway car. Until that moment ...

*What a beautiful couple they were, waltzing off the dance floor back to their places at the head of the room, where they sat at two large white chairs that looked like thrones. Befitting for the two lovers, who looked like royalty.*

*Fred smiled widely but his eyes did not. He wished Elizabeth well and hoped Mike would look out for her, that her wildness would not be dulled by him. Carolyn sat with her mother, happy for her friend and a little sad that she would not be able to enjoy the rest of their lives together. She was going away soon, Australia, and she would miss her friend. Molly looked on and felt her heart quiver. She could never tell Elizabeth that she had a secret crush on Mike the moment Elizabeth brought him home. Oh, he was dashing, especially in his uniform, his starched white suit with all the insignia of who knows what ... oh, it was so wonderful, but she felt a little sliver of jealousy that Elizabeth had caught his eye before she had a chance to win him over with her own wiles. Tess nodded in satisfaction. Yes, she felt she had a part to play in Elizabeth's success, showing her how to behave like a lady in order to snag the right type of man. She looked at Bryan and wished his nose was not as large as it was, that his belly was more trim, like Mike's. Audrey frowned, not quite sure Elizabeth had indeed found Mr Right. Something didn't seem right. She looked at her father, whose expression mimicked her own, but her mother stood beside him, the joy on her face evident. Audrey smiled now. Yes, her mother deserved to be happy and now Elizabeth was not her responsibility anymore, that she had been turned over to a respectable man, she had the right to be happy.*

*She looked so beautiful. Unsurpassed by anyone she'd seen and Doris tried to smile, to be happy for her daughter. But there was something that could not make that smile as genuine as it should have been. Yes, her daughter was in love, yes, she'd taught her to do things that women should do, like knit and sew, to cook and to be pretty, but Elizabeth had too much spirit. No one could break that, not even Mike, as much as she could see Elizabeth loved him. She watched as Elizabeth sat at the head of the table with Mike, like a queen on her throne, her king holding her hand tightly on his knee. There was something about the way he held it, something ... she knew she was being too protective, Elizabeth was now his. He was a pilot, for goodness' sake, had a fantastic job, was from a good family, had women throwing themselves at him ... maybe that was the problem.*

*"Doris," said Jimmy. "Would you like to dance with your old husband?" He held out his hand to her.*

*"Why, yes, young man," she replied and she took it, curtseying as she did, a mischievous smile dancing on her lips. With a backward glance at her daughter, she let her husband lead her to the dance floor.*

As she applied her makeup before the ceremony, Elizabeth paused mid-mascara and thought about Andy. It should have been his day. She wondered where he was at this moment and said a silent prayer for him. A wave of guilt swept over her and she pushed it down. She could never have married him, it was best they both discovered that sooner rather than later. He would have bored her and she didn't know how she could have coped with the tedium of being his wife. Now Mike ... Elizabeth never felt a dull moment with him; waves of excitement rushed through her at the thought of waking up next to him every morning, spending every spare minute in his arms even if they didn't go out all the time—just sitting with him on the front porch, having a drink together, hand in hand—it was all she could ever want. That wasn't asking for much, no. And she was never going to be one of those women who wanted it all. Besides, in Mike, she knew she had it all.

The wedding was the stuff of dreams. It was held in Bombay and many of Elizabeth's friends and family drove or took the train for the trip. No one was going to miss the wedding of Derrum's little devil. Mike's family threw a lavish feast and Elizabeth felt like she was in a fairy tale. She even looked like a fairy-tale princess, her mother hurriedly creating her full hooped skirt with the help of her friends, sewing shiny beads onto the bodice of her dress late into the night for the past month, Elizabeth checking on the progress, trying to keep busy by helping when Mike was out of town.

Elizabeth was concerned about how she would look on the day. She once heard that plain girls made beautiful brides and vice versa, but she needn't have worried, the tiara on the front of her high bun, sparkling with each turn of her head, accentuating the sparkle in her eyes. Gliding up the aisle, kicking up her full-length skirt ever so slightly as her mother taught her, so that she wouldn't step or trip on it, she could hear, rather than see, the gasps that she drew from the upstanding guests. But she didn't take her gaze off Mike, who stood at the altar, waiting for her, his eyes glistening, and his chin jutted forward in pride. Elizabeth didn't even notice her parents, who sat in the front row, her mother crying tears of joy and her father, a slight frown on his face.

At the reception, held at the officers' mess, Elizabeth had a wonderful time. She wished that she could have spent more time with Mike, who was busy entertaining other officers and their partners. She even suppressed a pang of jealousy when Mike kissed Marion, a young wife of Mike's superior, Astor Clarke. Astor himself pulled Marion's arm and took off in a huff while Mike just smirked and seeing Elizabeth's questioning eyes, blew her a kiss. She looked up at her father, whom she was dancing with at the time, and he smiled warmly.

"Just know we are always your family," her father leaned forward, whispering in her ear.

"I know, Pa," she said and pulled him closer, feeling the frailty of the old man.

"I mean it, Lily, our house is always yours, forever."

Elizabeth nodded, hoping her father would put his fears behind him. He hadn't been convinced Mike was the man for her, but then he hadn't been convinced that Andy had been either. He found Andy timid, not one to bode well with the spirit of Elizabeth, the same spirit he knew she still had, even though she had been careful to subdue it. But with Mike, she had met her match and she knew her father still had his reservations about him and although she usually trusted her father's instincts, she couldn't think about living a life without Mike in it. Now, she patted her father's back as she watched Mike in the distance, still schmoozing with the crowd. He was winning everyone over as usual, but he clearly hadn't been able to do that with her father, not even with his lavish gifts. "I know, Pa," she said again, feeling a small stab in the pit of her stomach. She put her arms around her father, a little voice telling her to hold him close, tight, and she did.

The rest of the reception was spent in a frenzied state of booze, dance and laughter. Family and friends wished them well and toasted their happiness. Never was such a more suited couple made, said the partygoers, most of whom were either excited for them or green with envy. Elizabeth didn't care which. It was her night. Hers and Mike's and it was going to be the start of an epic life together. Mike's friends were wonderful and had accepted her so easily. She couldn't have a moment to herself because as she stopped to take a break from dancing, someone else would ask her and she just couldn't refuse, especially when she saw Mike look her way, an encouraging smile on his face.

As usual she was asked to perform a song and she chose her favourite song, which was to become their song, 'Unchained Melody', one they would sing together in laughter and in tears in years to come. She couldn't do more than one, her head was spinning and her throat was raw, but as soon as she left the dance floor, she was twirled around by some other man and off she went round the dance floor again.

At the end of the evening, they waved goodbye to their guests and drove away in the car Mike borrowed from his brother, waving and laughing, Elizabeth's head still spinning and her heart giddy with joy. She was also giddy with the amount of alcohol she had consumed, but she ignored her stomach that rumbled furiously and her head that had begun a slow ache.

She leaned her head back on the seat and laughed breathlessly while Mike stared straight ahead through the windscreen, the dark around them as they flew through the night, eerie and oddly contrasted by the revelling just minutes before. Mike pulled over the car about a mile down the road and Elizabeth turned to him, giggling.

"Can't you even wait until we get to the ..." she began.

The pain seared through her jaw and Elizabeth felt her face slam against the glass of the car window.

He didn't even turn to look at her, his jaw braced as he spoke.

"You embarrass me like that again, I will kill you!"
He put the car into gear and drove.

# Part Two: Innocence Lost

## 1967–1985

# Chapter 9 - That Night

She looked down at the ring, a sparkling brilliant diamond sitting atop a simple band of gold. It was heavy but she never removed it, not even when she went to bed and sometimes woke in the morning with little indents from the ring on her forehead. It was the reminder of her love for a man who amidst the turmoil that her life had become, loved her back with a fiery passion, a fierce adoration, a man who loved her with his heart and hit her with his hands. Each time she threatened to leave him, to go to her family, to tell her father about what he had done and each time, he held her, stroking her wounds with the same hand that had caused them. And each time she believed it would be the last.

He had his own demons, something he tried to fight and something she found hard to understand. She may have been a fighter as a child, even a teenager, but she never encountered violence like this. She had grown up in a home where her parents' respect for each other was paramount. Not a harsh word she had heard spoken between them and always imagined her own marriage would be the same. It had to be, she had seen no different.

Her mind always went back to her own wedding day, a day so full of fun, of love, of laughter, and ended with the same, when he held her close, whispering words of love as they consummated their marriage. It could have gone another way; she knew there were so many things she could have done. For one, she could have gotten out of that car and run back to the reception. She could have hit him back. She could have left the next day. But would she have done anything differently?

She shook her head at the idea. No. She could never leave him. She absently stroked the side of her head, trying not to remember the sound of the window smashing with the force of her skull. She had been so shocked, there was an absence of pain and she had looked down in confusion at the sprinkles of glass that glinted off her satin skirt, sparkling brighter than the beads her mother had lovingly sewn onto it.

"I'm sorry, my darling." She heard his voice falter and suddenly she was in his arms, her head cradled in his chest. The realisation of what happened hit her and she felt the bile in her stomach rise. She tried to move away but his fingers were caressing her hair, his mouth kissing her forehead amid whispers of remorse, and she let herself remain against him feeling the rise and fall with the intermittent heave. "You were so beautiful tonight; you are beautiful, perfect. I couldn't bear those men looking at you." He let her go and put his hands on either side of her face, his eyes wet, looking deeply into hers. "Believe me," he pleaded.

Even though her own tears welled, Elizabeth wouldn't allow them to fall. She lowered her gaze and allowed Mike to straighten the locks of hair that had escaped from the bun that sat atop her head. She could feel that her tiara was lopsided and thought it strange that all she wanted to do right now was adjust it. But she didn't. She let the man she loved so completely soothe her injured head, and more so, her battered ego.

He turned her head to the side to inspect the injury and took out his handkerchief, patting at the wound. That's when she felt the pain, burning from the side of her forehead all the way down to her heart that was throbbing with fury. She heard a sob escape her lips and suddenly she was back in his arms.

"Never again, my girl," he cried into her hair and she felt his kisses over her head, her neck, her shoulders.

Elizabeth clung to him despite her bewilderment and nodded. She knew he never would. She raised her face to his and put her lips to his.

# Chapter 10 - A New Life

"This is beautiful." Elizabeth collapsed on the double bed that was sprinkled with the petals of marigold flowers, her hands stretched out above her head. Even though the resort was walking distance to where Mike's parents lived, they had no intention of seeing anyone in the little time they had by themselves before Mike was to fly away again.

It had been a two-hour ride to the resort and her limbs were sore, cramped in the little car, where she found herself rambling after the incident, about the wedding, about the dresses, about the speeches, about anything that wouldn't let her brain stop to understand what had just happened. She didn't want to think that it had happened. It didn't happen. Mike's hand tightly holding hers told her it didn't. Only when they stopped at Mike's parents' house so they could pick up their luggage and Elizabeth could change out of her wedding dress did she stop to look in the mirror and clean up her bloodied face. She swallowed hard, not allowing herself to get caught up in the sadness of it all. It was her wedding day. She took a deep breath and went back to the car with her husband.

Mike dropped the suitcase on the floor and hauled himself on top of her. "You're beautiful," he said, kissing her forehead, her cheek, dragging his lips to her neck, and Elizabeth tried to push away the thought of what had happened that kept re-emerging in her brain.

"You are," replied Elizabeth as she felt Mike's hand fumble for the buckle on her dress. "But are we going to stay in bed all day or enjoy this place?"

"I vote for bed," said Mike with a sly smile.

"You must be tired from all that driving," she said coyly. "And we have three days. You will be tired of me." Elizabeth laughed but let him continue the arduous task of getting her belt off.

"Never enough of you," he replied and then raised himself off her to focus on the task at hand. "Damn belt," he said and Elizabeth snickered as she watched his face contort while he figured out how to get the latch off. "Aha," he declared when the clasp released and he freed the belt, holding it in the air in triumph.

Elizabeth giggled and pulled him to her. "Good. Now make love to me." She looked into his eyes as he slid the dress from her shoulders and knew that she would love this man forever, and as he bent his head to kiss her neck again, all misgivings about the incident in the car were forgotten.

It seemed that the expense of the hotel, with its great big pool and access to the beach, as well as a thumping nightclub that could be heard through their lovemaking, was all for nought. The closest the two of them got to getting out of the hotel room was when they sat on the balcony when twilight hit the water.

"So gorgeous, Mike," said Elizabeth as the setting sun poured hues of red onto the sea. She looked at him and he was looking at her. She laughed. "Don't you say it."

"But it's true, my darling. Nothing is more beautiful to look at." He lifted his brandy and Elizabeth lifted hers, their glasses clinking together.

When Elizabeth thought about it later, it seemed that even at that moment, it was too late, and when he held out his hand, she took it and knew she always would, dancing in his arms, her head rested on his shoulder, the hardness of his shoulder, the smell of musk, all drowning her in a state of ecstasy. She was dizzy, light-headed, a tingle running through her body, and she wasn't sure if it was the feel against Mike or the brandy that she had helped him finish. And suddenly she was trying to figure whether there was any brandy left. Her heart gave a little thump at the thought, the same time Mike raised a lock of her hair and whispered words of nothing against her ear.

Three full days and three full nights, the most perfect she had ever had and the most perfect she would never have again. Blissful moments, his arms wrapped around her as they watched the setting sun from their balcony, making love on the rug by the fire, passionate embraces as they danced together, Mike watching her in awe as she sang to him, joining in at times as if he knew exactly the accompaniment she needed. It seemed that everything they did was perfect together; they melded like they were one already and had been forever.

And the booze. Never far away, always making things slightly more than perfect, just that little edge that allowed Elizabeth to revel in the dream she felt she was in. She chose to ignore the 'incident', as she called it, and when she fell asleep in Mike's arms every night, a little light-headed, the only thing she allowed herself to think about was the warmth of his body next to her, the strength of his arms around her, his warm breath on her bare shoulder. *This is perfection.*

Going back to Derrum, where they had decided to make their home for now, was just as exciting to Elizabeth. She couldn't wait to be Mike's wife, to cook for him, to clean for him, to be with him, as husband and wife in the two-bedroom flat they rented out before the wedding. Elizabeth and her sisters had gone shopping every day in the lead up to the wedding and had purchased basic furniture—a bed and a lounge setting, which Mike had paid for. "Go crazy," he had said. "Buy what you want. This may not be our permanent home, but I want you to live in luxury." But Elizabeth had not been focused on creating a home yet, her mind had been on the impending wedding and her excitement about her life with Mike.

"We can do it up as we go, Mike," she'd said. "You know, have some basic stuff and then both make it our home."

"You can do what you want with it," he'd said, looking at her in surprise. "I thought you would love to go crazy buying all that girly stuff. I mean, you will be here more than I will."

"What do you mean?"

"I will still have to go away often. I already have several appointments that are set up."

"But Mike, what about our life together? I want time with you."

"We will have time, my love," he'd said with a kiss on her nose. "But I have to bring home the bacon, as they say. This is my job."

Elizabeth knew how much Mike loved his job, how he talked about it, how he flew his plane, the adventures he and his co-pilot had. The first sliver of resentment flickered through her; why, she had hopes of becoming something, perhaps a singer, maybe an artist, even a nurse like her mother, a long-term option, but she knew how unreasonable that was. Mike loved his job but he loved her too and right now, she wouldn't change a thing. "Okay, Mike, but I still want you to be involved in the house stuff."

He'd nodded a little patronisingly and kissed her nose again.

"Well, the first thing I can contribute to is help around the house," he said. "I've already gotten us a maid." Elizabeth wasn't sure she liked the idea, felt that it would be unnecessary. She was fit and capable, but he insisted it would be right. After all, everyone else in their position had maids. "Besides, it would be nice if you had some company while I'm away."

When they returned home from Bombay, Mike dutifully carried her over the threshold and she shrieked with delight. She dragged him straight to the bedroom and made love to him on their un-linened bed. "Christening it," she breathed in his ear after they were sated and wrapped in each other's arms.

When Mike returned to Bombay the next morning, Elizabeth sat on the sofa and looked about the place. No, Mike would not have time to help her. She grinned ruefully. He didn't have any intention of helping her to beautify the place. She felt her heart ache for him already. A week without him. She didn't know how she was going to cope, but she'd better get used to it. Elizabeth was glad her new home was not more than a ten-minute walk from the one she grew up in and felt a ping in her heart. Soon, her family would be gone too.

She shook herself out of her gloom: she was a newlywed, had a new home, everything that she should want. Her restlessness needed to be controlled. She wasn't a young girl anymore, one who could tear about on the streets as she used to, even though those days didn't seem so long past. She heard a rap at the front door and looked up in surprise. Mary, the new maid, wasn't due until the next day.

"How is it being a married woman?" Tess blurted when Elizabeth opened the door to see her sister standing at it with a bowl of sugar in her hand.

"Oh, Tess." Elizabeth took the outstretched offering. "I don't even know how to explain it."

"I want details," said Tess and linked her arm through her sister's. "And quickly, because the parents are not far behind me."

"I miss him already," said Elizabeth, her throat closing.

"When is he returning?"

"A week," sputtered Elizabeth who had already let the tears fall. "I don't know how I'm going to cope."

"That's what we're here for," said Tess. "Now, chin up. There's a lot to be done." She looked about her. "You clearly didn't think about much after the wedding, did you? Well, when he gets back, this is going to be a new place." Elizabeth smiled at the enthusiasm of her sister. It was infectious. "But first," she said. "Where is your kettle? We need tea."

At least she had thought of that. "Black tea though because we don't have milk. Haven't been out shopping since we got home."

"Oh," said Tess with a wink. "That way, is it?"

The family came and talked and laughed, reliving the wedding, how mad Aunt Harriet danced the whole night not realising she was missing a shoe, how the party carried on after Elizabeth and Mike had driven away into the night. Elizabeth swallowed at that one, realising that everyone had been kicking up their heels while she was in that car with Mike. She breathed away the memory, guilty for even letting it enter her mind again.

Audrey, Tess and her mother took Elizabeth to the linen store and she enjoyed arguing with them about some of their choices. Elizabeth again was relieved that they lived nearby so that when Mike was out of town she would have company and something to distract her, at least for now. She came home with bags of shopping and after she let herself into the house, she dumped them on the floor and sat on the sofa, the emptiness of the house enveloping her. She looked at the time: 9:30 p.m. No, she couldn't go to bed yet, she was too jittery. Besides, the thought of going to bed without Mike made her chest hurt. She stood back up and went to the kitchen. She may as well start there. She turned on the radio her father had given her, tuned it to her favourite station and went about setting up the house. At 3:30 in the morning she dragged herself to bed. And at 4:45 a.m., she was still staring at the ceiling.

"Oh, Mike," she cried to herself. "I miss you so much."

She knew this was something she would have to get used to. She knew the man she had married, and his job, one that he loved, which required him to be away for long amounts of time. And she knew her family would not be around for too much longer. She sighed, wishing it were an option for her and Mike to go with them to Canada. She pushed the thought from her mind. It would still be more than a few months before they got the paperwork okayed to take off. She would deal with whatever came then. Maybe she would suggest a holiday to visit, maybe Mike would change his mind about leaving too. She hadn't even really had the conversation with him, hadn't had a moment to herself since he came into her life. Now she knew she would have to prepare for many a lonely night.

She tossed and turned and eventually gave up on the idea of sleep and went into the living room, picking up a book she had taken to Bombay, but had never even thought about. Sleep finally found her on the sofa, the book already read halfway through. The second night panned out the same and even though she kept busy decorating her house throughout the day, at night, she was restless. She took to sewing the curtains her mother had bought her material for, hemming the new lace tablecloth.

Mary, the new maid, was young, probably just over sixteen, Elizabeth surmised, and she told Elizabeth that this was her first full-time job. She would need to be shown the ropes. Elizabeth pursed her lips at that. "We can learn together, then," she declared, feeling more confident than she felt.

"But I can cook well, Miss," Mary said, a little apologetically.

"Well, that's good," said Elizabeth with a laugh. "Perhaps you will teach me."

Elizabeth looked forward to seeing her maid, who arrived every morning on the dot of 7:00 a.m. and left at 5:00 p.m. every evening, relishing the chance to be busy, and even though Mary claimed not to have been experienced at the job, the house was always spotless and Elizabeth helped her with the cooking, enjoying the new food she was experiencing, writing down recipes as Mary cooked. And when she did leave, Elizabeth felt so alone, sometimes walking over to her parents' home or Carolyn's, not relishing the return to her own lonely one.

Several nights later, Elizabeth had gone into the living room with her book, frustrated by her insomnia. She looked up towards the bookshelf and spotted Mike's whisky sitting on it. She raised herself off the sofa and picked it up, giving it a sniff. It smelled like Mike and she inhaled again deeply. She had just received a letter from him, telling her he missed her and she was all he was thinking about and could not wait to return to his wife. She liked that—his wife—and re-read the letter over and over again. She had it in her hand now, preparing to read the words she knew by heart, written by his hand. She brought out a tumbler and poured a little of the whisky in it. She just wanted to smell it, to feel as though Mike were close to her.

By the time she fell asleep, Elizabeth had downed more than four pegs and she woke in the morning to a nasty headache and ran to the bathroom, feeling what she had drunk come back up. She spent the day in bed, hoping she wouldn't have any visitors, but as luck would have it, Carolyn stopped by at eleven in the morning.

"Miss," Mary was saying again and again, and Elizabeth buried her head deeper into her pillow. "Miss, please wake up?"

"What is it, Mary?" Elizabeth didn't remove her head.

"Your friend here to see you."

"Who?"

"She said her name is Carolyn."

"Nooo," said Elizabeth, feeling that if she moved an inch, her head would explode.

"Tell her I'm busy," Elizabeth said.

"Why are you fobbing me off?" Elizabeth heard Carolyn's indignant voice in her room. It was too loud for the way Elizabeth was feeling.

"I'm a little tired," said Elizabeth, irritated by the intrusion, but brought her head out from under the pillow to see Carolyn standing above her, hands on her hips. Mary was nowhere to be seen.

"Why?" Carolyn sniffed at the air. "It smells like a bar in here."

"And how would you know what a bar smells like?"

"I know enough," said Carolyn, and Elizabeth realised her gaffe. Carolyn's mother had found a man, not one who looked after them but one who took her mother's hard-earned money and drank it away.

"Sorry," said Elizabeth. "I just had a little drink last night ..."

"By yourself?"

"You wanted an invitation?" Elizabeth wasn't sure if she was being sarcastic or serious.

"No; well, maybe." Carolyn laughed.

"I just miss him so much, Carolyn."

"How long now?" Carolyn sat on the edge of the bed and Elizabeth raised herself up with some effort.

"Six days," said Elizabeth with a heavy sigh. "It's just dragging."

"Can't you go with him next time?"

"And be where? While he flies away." Elizabeth laughed. "No, thank you. Besides, I don't think that's even possible if I wanted to." She got up and put on her dressing gown. "But I must get up and do something, I guess."

"What's on for today?" Carolyn sounded way too chipper for the way Elizabeth's body felt.

She wandered into the living area and looked around at the house, already impeccable, the curtains curved into their pegs, the silvery thread shimmering through the lace ones behind them, shining a white light through the room. She moaned. There wasn't much left to do. She shrugged. "How about we sit outside on the terrace and reminisce about our youth?"

"We are still in our youth," said Carolyn with a smirk.

"Well, humour me," said Elizabeth. "This has been the longest week of my life."

# Chapter 11 - Part of the Family

"I don't think they like me, Mike," said Elizabeth, pulling at her skirt to make it appear longer by lowering it over her knees. It didn't help that it was made of dyed calico and kept bouncing back up.

"Of course they do," he replied and grabbed her hand.

Elizabeth tried not to roll her eyes. His mother barely kissed her on their wedding day; even Teresa, who had been so chatty when she'd first met her, seemed to have her nose out of joint for some reason. She suspected it was because she was not the maid of honour—but she had been one of her bridesmaids; Elizabeth thought that should have been enough, especially considering she had only met her the once when she had been to Bombay. But she hadn't expressed her concerns to Mike, and why should she? He adored his mother and sister, they couldn't put a foot wrong in his eyes, but Mike was very careful about his father and whenever she tried to talk to him about what bothered him, he shut down, closed off from her, lips pursed, eyes narrowed. It brought her back to that moment in the car and she decided he would confide in her when the time was right.

"They didn't want you to marry me, did they?" she said softly. She'd realised by now that they had expected Mike's latest fling to be short lived. He wasn't supposed to marry this one.

Mike chuckled. "They didn't expect us to go the distance, I suppose." He brought her hand to his lips. "But we will, my love. We will show them all."

Elizabeth couldn't help but wonder why there was resistance in the first place, but then she thought of her own father, accepting of her new husband but still suspicious. She had put it down to him being overprotective of his daughter and after their wedding day, she realised he had reason to be. "Well, we have to," she said, smiling, her hand automatically dropping to her belly, which was still as flat as it always had been.

She thought of the day she found out she was pregnant, just

two months after they had been married. She didn't know whether to be alarmed or delighted when the doctor announced she was with child. Her happiness depended on Mike's happiness. Of course she wanted to have children, but so soon? It had to have been a honeymoon baby, but they were still in the honeymoon phase of their marriage and Mike was away more than he had been at home. But when he had come home a week later and she had told him of her condition, he lifted her off the floor and swung her around in delight.

"The best possible news," he cried. "The best gift you could ever give me!" And that's when she realised how much she really wanted to have this baby.

Now here they were on their way to Bombay to tell his family their news and Elizabeth hoped that this would bring them closer to her. There would always be a connection now with them, and her son—she hoped it would be a boy, for Mike's sake—would be their kin too. It didn't help that they were moving to another country too, Australia, and they wanted Mike to come with them. From the little he told her, she surmised it had to have been his resistance at the idea of going with them and rather than blame him, they blamed her. It was easier to blame the outsider. Much later, she would recall this when Mike's brother, Joshua, joked that all the in-laws in the family were 'outlaws'. She had wondered when she was eventually going to meet the wayward brother who hadn't even bothered to show up for the wedding. At least he had sent a very extravagant gift, silk sheets, embroidered with fine silver string, Mike and Elizabeth's name. Mike had tried to hide the smile from his face while he outwardly objected to the wicked gift.

Mike's mother was waiting outside the house when they arrived in the taxi she had sent to pick them up from the station, her hair tied back severely, a white apron over a grey dress, her hands held behind her back. Elizabeth swallowed. She didn't know what to expect anymore. She reached out her hand to Mike and he squeezed it in reassurance. She wished they had gone to a hotel, instead of staying with his family, but Mike was determined Elizabeth get to know them better. "Two nights," she said in a whisper, and Mike nodded without a word.

"Hello, Mike," said his mother, putting out her cheek for Mike to kiss, which he dutifully did. "Hello, Elizabeth." Elizabeth did the same.

"How are you?" Elizabeth asked.

"I'm well, dear," she said with a smile, warmer than any Elizabeth had known to grace her face before. "Now that you two are wed, you may have Teresa's room. She will stay in the living room at night."

"I thought we could have Josh's room."

"Well, that boy came home without warning." His mother shook her head in exasperation.

"I can finally meet him," said Elizabeth.

"Yes, you will." Elizabeth couldn't quite figure the expression on the woman's face, a mix of relief and irritation. "He is out with friends now, but he should be home for dinner."

"Why did he bother?" said Mike under his breath.

"He is your brother, Michael." His mother said it without emotion.

"He wasn't even there to stand up with me at my wedding. Some brother."

"You know how it is ..."

"You mean how *he* is," Mike retorted as he and Elizabeth followed his mother into the house, and she put her hand on his arm to calm him. "Where's Father?" Mike asked.

"He will be home from work soon." Elizabeth felt the stiffness in Mike's arm loosen at that. "You should settle in and come out for tea. Teresa should be home soon too."

"Thank you, Mother," said Mike when his mother nodded curtly. She shut the door behind her and Elizabeth flopped on the bed, relieved they were alone. The tension in the air she just felt between mother and son was palpable and she didn't understand why.

"Are you okay, Mike?"

"I'm fine." He sat beside her and took her hand. "I wish we weren't staying now."

"But aren't you glad Joshua's here too? I can finally meet him."

Mike's eyebrows knitted but he nodded, but before he could reply, a voice boomed from the other side of the door.

"Where is she? Where is my new sister?"

Mike sighed loudly. "Here we go," he said.

\* \* \* \*

Dinner began well, Joshua dominating the conversation, which worked in everyone's favour as Mike's mother and sister were quieter than usual, his father smiling happily around the table. He was in a grand mood and Elizabeth surmised it was because all his family, especially the errant Joshua, were at home.

Joshua had blasted through the bedroom door and even before he acknowledged his brother, had picked Elizabeth up and swung her around. Elizabeth laughed in astonishment and glee. A member of the family who didn't seem to find her presence deplorable. She was being unkind, she knew. She barely knew them and they her. But this reception by the brother that Mike rarely talked about was exciting for her, made her heart soar.

"I'm Elizabeth," she said, a smile still on her face when he finally put her down.

"I know who you are." He took her hands and stepped back to survey her. "Mmmm," he said appreciatively. "No one, not one person justified this." He turned to Mike. "Brother, how did you manage to snag this beauty?"

Elizabeth reddened and turned to Mike, her smile fading. Mike's face was thunder. She understood now his jealous rages, her hands clutched tightly in his whenever they went out anywhere. The only time he let go of her was when she was asked to sing, and there he would be glorying in the magnificence of her voice, readily taking the credit for his wife's talent. But his brother? Jealous of his brother? "Mike?"

"Hello, Joshua." Mike held out his hand for a shake.

"Mikey!" Joshua grabbed Mike into a bear hug and shook him around and by the time he was done, Mike was smiling too, a childish smile, and he waved his hands about, pushing his brother away. It was like he was a child being teased. Elizabeth studied his behaviour. It was odd to see Mike act like a kid, not so in control as he usually was. Joshua let go of Mike and took both of their hands. "Come on. Let's go to the terrace and have a nip before the old man gets home."

Elizabeth thought Joshua was fun; he reminisced about his flights abroad and in India, telling them of the fun he had with the locals, taking them on joyrides and getting into trouble for it. He talked about the woman he had nearly married when he had drunk too much and how she threw all her shoes at him when he realised just in time that she wasn't the woman for him. He asked about Elizabeth's family, threatening to come down to Derrum and sweep one of her sisters off their feet if they had an inkling of what Elizabeth had. He even joked about how he had once stolen one of Mike's girlfriends away from him and Elizabeth tried not to look at Mike's face at that. He slapped Mike on the shoulder. "Saved you breaking up with her, hey? That horse-faced lassie." He guffawed and Elizabeth now did sneak a look at Mike, who was smiling with his mouth, but his eyes were fury. She was beginning to understand Mike's attitude towards his brother a little better. He was the loud, brash one, who did his own thing, without apology or regret. Mike was nothing like him.

She took another sip of gin, the bottle that Joshua had brought out of his room. He'd put his finger to his lips. "Shh. Not for the mother to see," he'd said in a mischievous whisper. Elizabeth thought it delicious, especially when Joshua mixed it with soda and put a slice of lemon in it. After an hour on the terrace, she felt light-headed but it was an enjoyable feeling, like she was swimming, like the tension that had invaded her every pore since she got onto the train in Derrum was draining away.

"I'll be back," said Mike. "Duty calls." Elizabeth giggled, Mike could never have more than two drinks without visiting the men's room. She smiled and held out her hand to graze his as he walked past. He turned back and gave her a kiss on the forehead before continuing down to the house. Elizabeth looked at his receding figure. She could see his mood had mellowed and she loved it when he was a little tipsy, enough to flirt with her, want her.

"Love, that's what they call it."

Elizabeth turned around to see Joshua staring at her, a grin on his face. "What?" she said, realising she had a stupid smile on her own.

"The two of you," said Joshua. "Making me ill." He made gagging sounds.

"Stop it," Elizabeth said with a laugh.

Joshua's expression sobered. "You're good for him, Elizabeth." Elizabeth didn't reply, waited for him to go on. He didn't.

"What do you mean?"

Joshua shrugged. "I'm glad you are not going with them to Australia."

"Your parents?" Joshua nodded and Elizabeth was curious. "Why aren't you going with them?"

"Have you met them?" He laughed and Elizabeth smiled. "They are my parents but I'm glad I don't have to live with them anymore, put it that way."

"Tell me about them," said Elizabeth, peering towards the entry of the terrace, hoping Mike would stay away a little longer. She had never really gotten him to open up about them and Joshua seemed to want to talk about them. He raised his eyebrows at her and she pursed her lips. "I mean, I'm family. I don't know them all that well."

"In a nutshell," said Joshua, also glancing in the direction Elizabeth had, "Mother is Mother, but she has spoiled Mike silly. He really is a mummy's boy." He saw Elizabeth's indignant expression and put up his hand. "I mean, she only has eyes for him. They rest of us are invisible."

"So she'll never accept me fully."

"No," said Joshua thoughtfully. "She will have to accept you and she will. But you two are better off far from them. Like me."

"And your father?"

Joshua's expression darkened. "Father is Father," he said, leaning forward. He began to raise his shirt from the back and Elizabeth wondered what he was doing.

"What do you mean?"

"Father is a cheater and a beater," he said with vehemence. "The further away I get from him the better. Look ..."

"Another drink before we have to go," Mike's voice sailed across the terrace and Joshua quickly lowered his shirt.

A chill went through Elizabeth and she leaned back on her chair.

"More?" asked Joshua when Elizabeth upturned the gin from her glass into her mouth.

"No more, Josh," said Mike.

"But she's only ..."

They were saved by the call for dinner by Mike's mother. None of them had even realised that Teresa and Mike's father had returned home while they had chatted away on that terrace. It had been a very pleasant evening and Elizabeth had hope that this visit may turn out well after all.

Now she watched, more than participated in, the conversation at the table, marvelling at how Joshua managed to disguise the initial tentativeness at the table by regaling the same stories he told them on the terrace, albeit leaving out the more risqué bits, and had questions for everyone—Teresa's new beau, Alma's new maid, whom Alma grimaced at, their father's latest venture and inevitably the move to Australia came up.

"And what about you two?" He turned to Mike and Elizabeth, looking at her hands which fiddled with her napkin on her lap. She knew it was a sore topic and wished Joshua had stayed away from it.

"We have news," said Mike and stood up, picking up his glass of water and raising it slightly. Elizabeth's eyes widened and she felt a bolt in her chest. Now? The rest of the family turned to him, his mother moving to the edge of her seat. "We're having a baby," he blurted.

There was a moment of silence before Joshua was backing his chair out noisily and lumbering over to Elizabeth. His father was doing the same and Teresa smiled almost mechanically. But his mother remained seated, a smile on her mouth but a frown in her eyes. Elizabeth could feel the hugs and hear the congratulations but the one she wanted the most to be happy was Mike's mother, who just sat there and stared. She looked at Mike who was also looking at his mother, a yearning for her blessing written on his face and her heart went out to him. When Joshua and his father were back at their seats, still laughing and congratulating everyone, she took Mike's hand under the table but before she could squeeze it, he roughly grabbed it away from her.

"Dessert," said Alma and left the table. The awkwardness that would have remained at the table was disguised by the chatter of Joshua, and Elizabeth was grateful for it. She smiled shakily at him and catching her appreciative look, he gave her a quick wink.

Mike's mother walked back into the room, a tray filled with an array of sweet cakes in her hands, putting it down in the centre of the table, and then she went about setting down little plates in front of each of them. She took her seat and put her chin in her hands.

"How will you be able to come with us now?" She stared at Mike. It was a challenge.

"I'm not going yet," replied Mike, helping himself to a piece of cake.

"But you said ..."

"I changed my mind." Mike set his jaw tight. Elizabeth turned to him in surprise. What had he said to them?

"But, son," his father interjected. "We applied to go as a family."

"I'm sure it will be fine if I don't ..."

"But this is your chance to ..."

"To do what?" Mike set down his spoon and looked his father in the eye. "I'm doing what I love, I'm married and having a baby."

"But this shouldn't upset things too much," said Teresa. "I'm sure ..."

"Teresa," said her father with a warning glance. Teresa slumped in her chair, frowning.

"It doesn't matter, Teresa," said Mike. "We're not ready to leave here anyway."

"Because of the baby?" asked Mike's mother.

Mike turned on her. "The baby? Your grandchild? Your first grandchild?" He pounded his fist on the table and Elizabeth jumped. "Thank you for your blessing with that."

"But Michael ..."

"We don't need it, Mother," he said, and taking Elizabeth's hand and yanking her out of her chair, he strode out the door, dragging Elizabeth behind him.

* * * *

She knew they were disappointed and she couldn't blame them. They may have given up on Joshua being around them and doing his own thing but they had just assumed Mike would be going with them. But the baby now put a spanner in the works. Bags were already being packed and things in Australia were being arranged. Elizabeth sympathised; her own family were disappointed too that they were not going to Canada with them. Oh, how she wanted to go with them and how they tried to convince her and Mike to join them. But Mike loved his job, his status, his life here.

"One day," he said. "Either Canada or Australia, you can pick."

Elizabeth didn't need the choice. She was already missing her family and they hadn't even left yet. She wanted to tell Mike that one day it would happen, when he was ready and she would go anywhere he wanted, that his family just wanted to be near him. But Mike was in no mood to hear it and she knew better by now not to talk to him about anything of importance when he was in this foul a mood. He went to the side of the house and picked up his sister's scooter, Elizabeth hopping on the back. Mike needed to blow off some steam and Elizabeth didn't say a word when they arrived at a bar.

"I hope it's a boy," he said when the bartender put his whisky in front of him. He raised his glass to hers which was filled with gin, and clinked it with more force than necessary.

"Mike!" a voice boomed and Elizabeth turned to see a group of people approaching them, most of them familiar faces. She had met them at the wedding, she remembered, and was happy that Mike now had the chance to celebrate the baby as he should have with his family. Mike's face lit up and there was laughing and hugging all around after the introductions were made.

Catherine, one of them, joined Elizabeth at their table, while Mike played pool with his friends. Catherine was a buxom girl with reddish hair that shimmered each time she turned her head. She took a sip of beer, which Elizabeth thought interesting, for a woman to be drinking beer, but who was she to judge anything. No one knew how much of Mike's whisky she got through to stave off the loneliness when he was away at work. She turned to Mike, who was looking over at them, and Elizabeth thought she detected a frown, but then he blew her a kiss, which she returned.

Catherine watched her carefully. 'So, you're going to be a mother soon."

"Uh-huh," said Elizabeth, as she sipped on her gin.

"Should you be drinking?"

"It's only a sip," Elizabeth replied, a little irritated with the question. A sip or two every now and again was fine, she told herself, quite conveniently forgetting she had had a glass of gin on the terrace with Joshua. She needed it, especially after the hostility at the dinner table at Mike's parents' home.

"Of course." Catherine looked back at Mike. "You realise that many women want to chop off your head?"

Elizabeth almost choked on the sip she had just taken. "What? Why?"

Catherine kept her gaze on Mike. "Just look at him," she said, and Elizabeth thought she detected a look of longing on Catherine's face. Catherine looked back at Elizabeth and seeing her expression, gave a short laugh. "Oh, no, not me," she said hurriedly. "That ship has sailed. Mike and I have been friends for too long. We never thought about anything like that."

Elizabeth wondered how much truth there was to that and she turned back to watch as Mike downed his ball and looked again at her. She waved at him. "So?"

"He's just, well, he was the most eligible man in town. Every girl and her friend wanted him. Most likely their mothers too." She laughed, a tinkly laugh.

Elizabeth wasn't sure she wanted to hear more, but some sick curiosity got the better of her. "And?"

"Well, you were the winner." Catherine tapped her hands together lightly.

Elizabeth had mixed feelings of flattery and irritation, but irritation won out. "There was never any competition," she said coolly, and setting down her drink, walked up to Mike, who was about to take another shot. She took his cue and placed herself between him and the table. She drew him to her and kissed him deeply, hearing wolf whistles around them. "Let's go home," she said. "And make passionate love."

They were laughing all the way to the bike. He got on and she clutched him around his waist, leaning her head on his back. "To hell with the lot of them," she said to herself and raised her chin to feel the cool evening breeze run through her hair. The last thing she heard was her laugh echoing through the air.

# Chapter 12 - An Accident

There was something cold on her forehead and Elizabeth opened her eyes and looked up at a strange ceiling, white, but with grey cracks snaking their way through it. She put her hand to her head which was throbbing and looked about her. She was in Teresa's bed; she recognised the pink flowers on the quilt that lay over her. Afternoon light was shimmering through the curtains and the room was empty. She tried to sit up but a bolt of pain seized her shoulder and she whimpered and lay back down. Just then Mike walked into the room with a tray and she remembered what had happened. Well, some of it. A thump, a crack and then nothing.

"What happened, Mike?" she asked when he placed the tray on the bedside table.

"Are you okay?" His eyes were red and there were scratches and bruises on his face. Elizabeth nodded, putting out her fingers to touch them. "We had an accident," he said. "Ran into a tree. There was a pothole in the road and I couldn't avoid it."

"Are you okay?" She touched his arms now, his torso, feeling the pain running through her own stiff body.

"I'm fine. You have a bruised collarbone and some nicks on your forehead." He put his hand on her tummy. "Baby is fine."

Elizabeth collapsed on the bed in relief. She hadn't even thought about the baby but now she began to sob. "The baby," she said. "What if ..."

He put his arms around her. "Shhh. It's okay. It will be okay."

"I want to go home," she cried. All she could think about now was her mother, her sisters, her father and her brother, at home, her home, their warm living room. Her mother would be by her side, probably admonishing her for riding in her condition, but her love and care would be paramount. Her father would be pacing, stopping every few moments to stare at her with concern. She wanted to be in a place where she was loved. This was not it.

"As soon as you're okay," he said, patting her hair.

"I'm okay," she said, pulling away and looking into his eyes. "I just want to go home. I need my mother. I need to take care of this baby."

"We'll go. Tomorrow, we'll go."

"Thank you, Mike." She felt like a child being coddled, but she let him take care of her, whisper words of comfort in her ear.

"Rest for a bit more and then if you're up to it, come out to dinner. Or I will bring it in here for you. But it would be nice to spend the last evening with the family. I don't know when we will be able to come back before the baby is born and they may be gone by then anyway."

Elizabeth nodded and let him kiss her and watched him walk out the door. She tried to move again and gritted her teeth in pain. But she wanted to please him. She may not be seeing his family for a while and a little effort on her part would make him happy. She struggled to change her clothes; someone had put her nightdress on her and she wondered who. She hoped it was Mike and not one of the women in the house. She pulled on a loose dress and slipped on her slippers, hoping it wouldn't insult them if she wore them to dinner. She noticed scratches on her legs and touched them lightly. They stung and she jumped in pain but closed her eyes and put weight on the ankle that had been hurting but looked fine. She winced and limped to the door. She could hear voices in the other room and headed towards them.

"Just tell us, Mike. She did it." Elizabeth stopped in her tracks to the voice of Teresa.

"Stop it, Teresa. I don't know what happened."

"You said you were blinded." This was his mother's voice, almost a whisper.

"I said I couldn't see what was in front of me."

"So she must have covered your eyes." Teresa now. "She was drinking. We know. We heard. We hear about how she is in Derrum too. We know she is wild."

"She is who she is. And she's my wife."

"Who was drinking with a baby in her stomach."

"Stop it, both of you." Mike's voice was hushed.

Elizabeth felt ill and didn't want to hear anymore. She backed into the bedroom and sat on the edge of the bed, wondering about what she had overheard. Is that what they thought of her? Wild?

Well, she was known to be wild, but she would never put her child at risk! She stroked her belly and a tear escaped her eye. No, she shouldn't have had anything to drink. "I'm sorry, baby," she said and curled up in bed, determined to be a good mother, to never let any harm come to what she and Mike had created.

\* \* \* \*

"Am I getting too fat?" Elizabeth asked one morning. She was six months pregnant and her belly had stretched right out in front of her. At three months, she had barely been showing and she walked through the streets of Derrum sticking it out as far as she possibly could, to announce to any and everybody that she was to be a mother. Not that the news hadn't already spread through the town, some even gossiping about whether the wedding had been that of the shotgun type. She didn't care; she never did, not really. She just worried about what the talk did to her mother, but her mother was in a bittersweet mood about the whole thing. She wouldn't be in Derrum to share the arrival of her first grandchild. Elizabeth tried not to think about when that day would arrive, the day they would be gone. She was enjoying the moment, being spoilt by Mike and the rest of her family.

Now she stood swaying to and fro in front of the bathroom mirror, gauging the swell of her stomach. "I am, aren't I?" She turned to Mike who was getting out of the shower.

"You're having a baby. You're supposed to," Mike said with a laugh, reaching for the towel.

That wasn't the answer Elizabeth hoped for or expected and she screwed up her mouth. "But am I still attractive to you?" He glanced at her and leaned his head to one side, pretending to scrutinise her physique. "Stop it," she said with a laugh, even as she felt a pang of fear, not quite sure of what his answer would be.

Mike had been spending a lot of time away from home in the last couple of months, not just on trips for work, but evenings at the officers' mess, always some event going on, and as wives and girlfriends were not allowed to attend, Elizabeth spent many an evening reading, listening to music, the temptation to raid the liquor cabinet becoming overwhelming. But then she would pat her belly and smile at the movement, the faint thwacks against the skin of her growing bump, already in love with what was growing inside her, not willing to give in to her urges, despite her mounting suspicions about her husband.

Some nights when Mike let himself into the bed, smelling of whisky, slurring words of love to her, sometimes waking her to make love in the middle of the night, she could swear she could taste the scent of another woman, the faint whiff of a perfume that she didn't herself use. But he was in their bed, making love to her, and how, she thought, could a man be in the bed of another woman and come back to bed his own wife? It was not logical. Yes, she was being unnecessarily suspicious and she cursed Catherine for getting into her head. She, Elizabeth, was his wife, the woman he chose to spend the rest of his life with.

"But I'm no prize right now," she said, almost to herself.

"Stop being silly," said Mike, the slightest irritation in his voice, but she caught it.

Something indefinable had changed. Oh, she still loved him fiercely and not anyone could say anything against him, but she could sense an air of him being too comfortable, too callous with her. He went out more often and didn't feel the need to explain himself and when she asked him about his whereabouts, he shook his head with irritation, as if she had asked him to do something deplorable like clean the toilet with his bare hands. Elizabeth wanted to go with him wherever he went, even in her very pregnant state, and they did go to dances and the odd party, but Mike was out most evenings. When he wasn't stationed elsewhere, he wasn't home anyway and Elizabeth was just as lonely as if he were out of town.

He had been home from this last trip for a few weeks and he was already getting antsy. He didn't seem to be as happy at the office in Derrum as he was when he was away. When he came home and regaled her with tales of his flights, the ins and outs of the Air Force, to which Elizabeth smiled and nodded and added questions, more excited about his zeal rather than the tale itself.

She tried not to think about her father's dreams for her, the dreams she had for herself, being something, all that talent her father talked about, dreams now that would never be, not now that she was a housewife, with a child on the way. She consoled herself that this was what she wanted; she would give up anything in the world for Mike. But lately she had been wondering if it were still the same for him.

Elizabeth went to see her mother after Mike left for work. She didn't want to spend another lonely morning moving around the house, fluffing cushions that had already been fluffed by Mary, or sew or read. It was becoming boring and she couldn't wait until the baby was born so she could shower her love on him every day. She had been spending the mornings at her parents' place more often lately, watching as they talked about their departure, not more than a few weeks from now.

"Shall we take the kitchenware, Mother?" asked Audrey, who was going through photographs at the kitchen table.

"No, I don't think we'll have room for that on the plane," Doris replied, looking around the room forlornly. She turned to Elizabeth. "Would you like them, Elizabeth?" Elizabeth shook her head. She already had a bunch of kitchen and tableware that was still unpacked, wedding gifts, some of which they hadn't even opened. Her mother sighed. "Are you sure you and Mike don't want to move in here?"

Elizabeth had considered it; she knew her mother wanted her to have the house after they left. It was a beautiful house, the one she grew up in, left to her mother by her parents. It had four spacious bedrooms, a large backyard, but it was a little old-fashioned. Water still had to be rung from the well, albeit electronically. But the place she was in, much smaller, had all the comforts of modernity. Tap water, lights that didn't flicker for a few seconds before turning on, a brand-new coat of paint. But they weren't the only things. Mike had warned her that they may not be in Derrum for a long period of time, that his job could whisk them off to wherever he was stationed. And then what would she do with the place? She looked at her mother's expression, which was willing her to change her mind. She would now have to let her sister Dimple and her family move in. It's good, thought Elizabeth. They needed it more than she did. "I don't think I will do it justice, Mother," she said. "I don't know when we will need to move."

"You're coming with us then?" asked Fred, his eyes lighting up.

"No," Elizabeth replied. "But I hope someday ..."

"What about shoes, Mother?" called Molly and Doris turned back to the packing at hand.

She felt a little thud in her heart at their excitement, and wished she and Mike could go with them. But if he was against the idea of going to Australia with his own family, going anywhere with hers was out of the question.

She came home more deflated than ever, knowing how much she was going to miss them being so near. Elizabeth wandered around the house looking for something to keep her mind occupied while she waited for Mike to return home. She caught sight of the whisky sitting in the cabinet while she was rummaging around the kitchen drawer for a pair of scissors. Her hand steadied on the countertop and she reached for the bottle, looking about her, even knowing Mary was out shopping for dinner. She twisted the lid and sniffed gingerly at the nozzle, her skin tingling at the aroma that wafted from it. She closed her eyes, tempted—more than tempted. Whisky was not really her drink of choice but at this moment, it seemed like the most delicious thing in the world. She raised the bottle to her mouth and suddenly a sick feeling tore through her stomach.

Guilt.

She slammed the bottle down and twisted the lid back with force, her teeth clenched, her eyes narrowed, a feeling of despair running through her as she replaced the bottle and slammed closed the cabinet. She poured herself a glass of water and gulped it down, feeling the insipid liquid rush down her throat so fast, she gagged.

She looked at the time again. Half past three. Staying home on a Friday night was not becoming to her but lately, with her burgeoning belly and Mike's work, there wasn't much choice. She was getting fidgety though. She just wanted to forget the smell of that bottle and do something fun. She prepared dinner with Mary and when Mike got home, they ate together and went to the terrace as they sometimes did on a cool evening, Mike taking a glass of whisky with him.

It was a beautiful evening and the wind rustled through the trees that reached just beyond the handrail of the terrace. Faraway voices could be heard and the sound of Mary singing a Hindi song wafted up to them from below. Elizabeth began to hum along softly and Mike, after a little while, began to whistle to the tune.

"Let's go out," she said suddenly.

"Now?" he asked.

'Yes, now. It's Friday and we haven't been out for a while."

"You went out today. You had Carolyn over yesterday."

"But with you Mike." Elizabeth pouted. "You're leaving for Delhi in two days. Let's go out before I really can't move around much," she said, looking down at her stomach.

Mike leaned his head back and looked to the clear sky above him. Elizabeth knew he was softening, but she already knew that if she persisted, he would resist. They had been married just a few months and she already knew how far she could push him. He frowned but then turned his head towards her and grinned. "Okay," he said. "Let me finish this." He raised his glass to her.

"Ooh," squealed Elizabeth. "I'm going to start getting ready." Mike laughed at her enthusiasm. "Which wig should I wear tonight?"

"What's wrong with your own hair?" Mike looked up at her in question, his face screwed up.

"I like to change it around a bit sometimes."

"You have too many of those things."

"Yes, and I can be whomever you want me to be." She leaned down and kissed him, quickly disappearing down the stairs before he changed his mind.

She put on her earrings and her dark red wig with cascading curls that dropped below her waist. Even though her hair was nearly as long, the time it would take to set her hair like that would be too much. She was excited. A night on the town, at the club maybe. Some singing, lots of dancing; well, as much as her body would allow. Oh, to dance again. Her toes curled eagerly at the thought.

"Where are you going?" Mary popped her head into the dressing room.

"Maybe to the club," said Elizabeth smiling through the mirror at Mary. "Don't stay up." She sometimes wondered why Mike had asked Mary to become a full-time maid. She didn't need to be babysat just because she was pregnant. But Mary was more than happy to do it. She had her own little room and sent all of her pay to her family, who lived close enough to be able to see often.

"Shall I get a taxi?" asked Mary.

"No, I think Mike will probably want to ride." Mike took every opportunity to ride while he was home. His motorbike was his other passion.

"Will he drink?" Mary whispered.

Elizabeth frowned at Mary. "Now, Mary, you know better than to ask."

"Yes, Miss," Mary said and backed out of the room looking ashamed. Elizabeth didn't like to admonish the maids, but sometimes they did overstep. Mary was still young, so Elizabeth understood that she didn't quite know her place, that what happened between their employers, even in front of them, was not something they had a say in. When she lived at home, in her parents' home, Elizabeth always played with the maids as if they were her siblings and never thought to treat them any other way, even when new staff came in, replacing those she had grown fond of, and her parents encouraged it. But now, living with Mike, things needed to be different. She was the mistress of the house and Mike had not been happy when he had come home and found Mary and Elizabeth sitting together at the dining table drinking tea. He didn't understand that Elizabeth was lonely but he did give her a lecture on keeping a healthy distance from the help.

Elizabeth sighed as she saw Mary's shadow disappear, wishing what she'd said hadn't sounded too harsh. She looked back up at the mirror, adjusted her wig, bared her teeth, wiping them with her finger just in case lipstick had smudged onto them, and grinned, her mood rising again. She was going on a date with her husband.

The evening was beautiful, a light breeze tunnelling past, as they rode through the emptying streets, people hurrying home with smiles on their faces, anticipating the weekend and whatever it may bring. Elizabeth leaned her head on Mike's back, her arms wrapped around his waist, and closed her eyes, focusing on the feel of his leather jacket, the buzz of the bike beneath her. She hadn't felt this excited, this eager for a while. They neared the club, out of which the sound of the music was already drifting and as they hopped off the bike, Elizabeth could see that Mike was ready to party. He kissed her on the cheek and put out his elbow for her to take, which she did. His face now smiled widely as he led her in, pride written all over it. She knew how much he liked to show her off, and was happy that he still did, even with the bump she carried in front of her. As usual, a crowd of people gathered to them offering them seats at their tables, and Mike accepted that of Admiral Dinay, his senior officer, who ushered them to his table.

The band was playing a jive and before Elizabeth could sit down, Mike was already dragging her onto the dance floor. As always, the crowd parted for them and Elizabeth revelled in the clapping and cheers. She and Mike seemed to be made for each other, even on the dance floor; the first time he had pulled her onto the dance floor early in their relationship, she could see he was a masterful leader, and she easily followed his moves, inserting her own style that matched his perfectly. They had already entered a couple of local competitions, never having to practise and winning each time. The trophies were proudly displayed on the mantel in their home. Even with her oversized belly, Elizabeth shook it up and Mike grinned with pride as he swung her about and Elizabeth, still unwilling to relinquish her heels, dodged and strutted to the beat.

When the jive died down and the band began a more relaxed song, Mike drew Elizabeth close to him and whispered in her ear. "Remember the day we met?" Elizabeth nodded, slightly puffed, but she was so very attracted to him and she could feel her body shiver in his grip. "When you just couldn't stay away from me?"

"You mean the other way around," she said, raising an eyebrow, but a warmth coursed through her veins.

"You're the only woman who's ever done that to me," he said softly and inhaled the scent of her hair. "Are you wearing that wig again?" he said suddenly.

'Uh-huh,' she said, burying her head in his neck.

"Let's go home," he said, his hand lowering to the small of her back, and she nodded, even though they had barely been there a half hour, but she wanted him badly now. He grabbed her hand and led her to their table to collect her purse but Mike paused when they heard Elizabeth's name called out from the stage. Elizabeth groaned inwardly.

"Let's escape," she whispered reaching out to clutch her purse, but Mike was already pulling her in the other direction and she plastered a smile on her face and let him lead her to the stage, where the band leader was already holding out his mic for her.

After belting out two songs, she begged off, but Mike was already chatting to some of his friends by the bar, so Elizabeth sat back down and looked around for any friends of her own. There were, of course, none. They were at the officers' mess and the only people there were officers and their wives or girlfriends, most of whom didn't seem to warm to Elizabeth. *It's too soon,* she thought. *We've only been married a few months.* She chided herself for feeling resentful.

She looked at the table which was filled with drinks of all kinds and wished she could have some, but she had promised herself, not when she was pregnant, and the thought of Catherine and her judgey words stopped her. She tapped her feet on the wooden floor and before long, Admiral Dinay came to the table with his wife, Lulu, who actually donned a tiara.

"How are you holding up, my dear?" said Lulu, a sympathetic look on her face.

"I'm okay," said Elizabeth with a sigh. "Apart from my aching feet."

"Yes, all that dancing will do that," said Dinay with a wink. "But you two know how to create a sensation."

Elizabeth blushed. "You have been dancing up a storm yourselves." Elizabeth had noticed the older man swishing his wife about on the dance floor and couldn't help but admire the man who seemed to defy his age. She guessed he was around his fifties and his wife certainly looked about the same.

"Yes, well, as long as these old legs can hold up, I will be making sure we use them," said Lulu with a laugh. Elizabeth was already warming to these two whom she had only met on a couple of occasions. "How far along are you, my dear?"

"Not even a month to go," said Elizabeth and felt a little kick. She smiled down at her belly. But she knew it was impolite to keep the conversation on oneself. "What about you, Lulu? Do you have children?"

"No, my dear," said Lulu. "We didn't get that lucky." Elizabeth noticed that her husband took her hand at this and she wished she had thought of something else to say, but Lulu gave her a placating smile. "Besides, we have been on the move for most of our married life. It's no life for a family, but that's what it is."

"It must be hard to not have one place to be, you know, a place to call home?" said Elizabeth, suddenly aware of that's how her life may turn out to be.

"Well, in a couple of years, we will have to settle down." Dinay seemed happy to join in the conversation again. "But for the moment ..."

"Darling, this is my favourite song!" Lulu jumped up and grabbed Dinay by the hand.

"Are you okay by yourself, my dear?" asked Dinay.

"Yes, of course. Go have a ball," she said and he looked at Elizabeth apologetically as he was dragged off to the dance floor by his already dancing wife.

Elizabeth watched them dance together and let her hand rest on her chin. She liked this couple, who actually took the time to talk to her. She hoped that at their age she and Mike would be just as close and in love as they were. She sighed and looked around for Mike. Her back was already beginning to hurt from sitting down, even though she had a number of offers to dance before the admiral and his wife had come to sit with her, but after her wedding night, she dared not accept their offers. She understood the jealous rage that could take Mike over and didn't want it to rear its ugly head again.

She twisted around to rub her lower back which was really beginning to ache now and she looked around for Mike, slightly annoyed that he left her by herself. It wasn't unusual when he had his friends around him, especially that slimy Timothy who leered at her incessantly. She wondered why Mike never punched him in the face. She sipped at her soda, her eyes searching the hall, but she couldn't see Mike anywhere. *I'm not a wallflower,* she thought angrily, and besides, the ache in her back was worsening. It was fine while she was moving about but now, sitting in the same position, she couldn't bear the ache and she was ready to go home. She sneered at herself. She and Mike were usually one of the last to leave a dance but now, well, her body told her otherwise.

Moving around the tables and the dance floor, where she smiled and shook her head at more offers to dance and sing, Elizabeth still couldn't find Mike so she went outside to where they had parked the bike but apart from a few people, who were necking against the wall, she couldn't see him. She was glad for the cool night air and wanted to remain there but a queasy feeling hit her stomach and she needed to sit down. As she was returning inside, she caught sight of the back of Mike's purple shirt, but as she was about to call to him, she saw a movement behind him. A woman, in fact, the wife of his friend Jerry. She was leaning against the wall, baring her gleaming teeth in a laugh, Mike leaning into her.

Elizabeth froze and she experienced a sensation that she couldn't quite describe. A raw animal instinct, a tightening in her chest, her stomach, the desire to attack the woman, to pull the hair out of her scalp. The woman's eyes caught Elizabeth and her smile vanished as she tapped Mike on the shoulder. Elizabeth clenched her fists, trying to gather every ounce of poise she possessed. She was not going to lose her cool. She took a deep breath and raised her chin, as she watched Mike turn around and throw her a sheepish grin. He said something to the woman and walked lazily back to her.

"Let's go," he said, and grabbing her hand, moved towards the bike.

Elizabeth got on the back and looked away from the woman. *He's going home with me,* she tried to tell herself with some conviction, but her heart was thumping almost out of control and she clung to him in rage as they made their way home.

"Why were you talking to her?" asked Elizabeth as they got ready for bed. The passion she had felt on the dance floor not more than an hour before had subsided, and although she wanted Mike's arms around her, to hold her and tell her she had misconstrued what she had seen, she wanted the truth. She knew he would get angry, but she was not going to be one of those wives whose husbands just did whatever they wanted while they looked the other way and made excuses for them.

"She was just talking about Jerry," Mike said, but his voice always grew high when he was caught in a lie. He was still quite drunk, but he turned towards her and gave her a kiss on her shoulder. "Goodnight, darling," he said and pulled himself under the covers. End of conversation.

Not for Elizabeth. She pulled the covers over her but remained sitting. The fury which she had been holding in was brimming at the surface and she couldn't let it go. "Tell me the truth, Mike," she said and crossed her arms against herself. He didn't answer. "Mike," she insisted and before she knew what was happening, she felt his fist against her cheekbone, almost jerking her off the bed. She turned to look at him as her hand went to her face but he was already turning around again.

"Why couldn't you just leave it alone?" he muttered and Elizabeth stared at him in shock, her eyes stinging with tears, her cheekbone smarting from his knuckles. She stayed in that position for how long, she didn't remember, but when heavy snorts escaped his mouth, she realised he was asleep! She dropped her head on her pillow and refused to let herself cry.

Elizabeth remained in bed the next morning, allowing Mary

to serve Mike his breakfast; she feigned sleep when she heard him rise, but she hadn't slept all night. The bruise on her cheekbone still stung and she just wanted to stay in bed forever. When she heard him leave the house, she crept out of bed and looked in the mirror. She gasped. It was a whopper! It wasn't just discoloured, it stuck right out of her face and she could see that she was going to have a black eye, purple lines already snaking their way to the bridge of her nose.

After she bathed, she tried to cover it up with makeup and thought she had done a pretty good job. She didn't want to think anymore about what had happened. It was only a slap this time, she thought, not letting herself believe that it meant more than that. When she began to tear up again, she decided she needed to do something, get out, busy herself so as not to think about what had happened, There was no point going over and over it all again. What would that accomplish? Maybe she should have just left it alone. Maybe Mike was just upset that she was suspicious over nothing. But she knew better; her heart may have been soft but her mind knew better. She grabbed her sunglasses on the way out and called to Mary that she would be out for a while.

Where she was going, Elizabeth didn't know, but before long, she was at her parents' house. She had been visiting there often, helping them pack, discussing the trip, where they would be staying, what was the first thing they would do when they got there. For Molly, it would be to buy new shoes, warm boots, with fluffy tops. Elizabeth found herself smiling at that now and suddenly she found her lips quivering. She would be alone. Sure, there were cousins and aunts and uncles around, but her family, her home, the place she felt most comfortable in, would be gone. In less than a week. She hadn't felt the emotion so acutely as she did now and she let her hand touch her cheekbone and winced with the pain. She was glad it was a sunny morning, a good excuses for the sunglasses, a designer pair Mike had gotten her on his travels.

She stopped at the front door and hesitated. What if they could tell something was wrong? Tess opened the door as she reached for the handle.

"Lizzie!" she cried. "I was just about to head out to your place. I need a handbag I can take on the plane. Tell me you have one."

"You have lots of handbags," said Elizabeth in puzzlement.

"But go to my place. Mary will let you in."

"Are you okay?" Tess narrowed her eyes and tipped her head to the side.

"Yes, of course. Go on over." She quickly moved past her and into the house, wondering if coming over was a mistake. She could hear movement all over the place already. Preethi, the maid, was cooking, Fred was strumming on the guitar and she could hear her mother chattering with Molly in her bedroom. Elizabeth felt her throat clog. Home. Not after the next six days. She went in search of her father who she knew would still be having his mid-morning coffee in the backyard as he did on his days off. He heard the door of the house open and looked up.

"Lily," he said with a smile.

"Hey, Pa," she said and after giving him a kiss, sat on the chair beside him. "You wish you were still working, don't you?" she said with a chuckle.

He sighed deeply. "I'm just trying not to get in anyone's way," he replied and put up his hands.

"Yes, best to stay out of all their way. Too much woman stuff going on in there."

"I'm no help at all," he said sadly.

Elizabeth put her hand on his and tried to suppress her feeling of sorrow. "I'd better go see if they need anything," she said and went in to see if she could be of any use. Her mother set her to work packing photo frames and she was glad to have her hands busy, while Molly chatted on about this, that and the other. She had lunch with her family and then everyone was scattered again. Elizabeth went out to the front yard and sat on the porch floor, swinging her legs over the edge as she used to as a child. She was still a child, with a child in her. She put her hand on her belly and tears sprang to her eyes. Mike. He promised. He swore he would never raise his hand to her again. Now he had, and Elizabeth wasn't sure he wouldn't do it again. It wasn't even calculated. It was a loss of control, a reaction. What life was she bringing this child into?

"Don't go back," her father's voice said behind her. She hadn't heard him come out. She quickly wiped away at the tears, glad her sunglasses were back on. She'd had to take them off to eat lunch with the family as it would have seemed too odd if she left them on, but she'd kept her head lowered for the most part and thought it had gone unnoticed as no one said anything.

"Pa, what do you mean?" she tried to lighten her voice.

"We can wait for you." Her father, with some effort, lowered himself on his haunches. "Come with us."

"I can't do that."

"Yes, you can. We can delay. We can wait for you. In fact, why do we have to wait?"

Elizabeth sniffed. "If you haven't noticed, I'm about to drop a baby."

"Lily," he said soothingly. "You can still fly, I'm sure. If not, I can stay back, wait for the baby to be born ..."

"I can't, Pa." She knew what her father was saying, that he would stay back to protect her and right now Elizabeth wanted to go with them, desperately, but she knew she couldn't.

"It's not too late, Lily." Her father put his arm around her and she leaned into his safe shoulder. "He's not a man if he lays his hand on you," he said quietly.

She knew better than to deny that Mike had hit her. "I can't leave. Look at me. I'm having his child. He will never let me go." She had a thought. "But he's leaving tomorrow for two weeks. Can I stay with you until he leaves?"

Her father squeezed her shoulders. "This house is yours, always. Even though Dimple is staying here when we go, she knows that it's yours."

"Oh, Pa! That woman!"

"Now, now, Lily, she is your mother's sister. We offered it to you but you didn't want it, remember?"

Elizabeth screwed up her mouth. "It's fine, Pa. I like where we are. Besides, it will be strange with all of you not in it." She got up. "I'd better go find something to help with," she said. "I'll be okay, Pa. Hopefully when the time comes, we will join you all again." She said it with more confidence than she felt and giving her father a kiss, she headed inside.

It was in the late evening as Elizabeth was helping to set the table for dinner when a commotion could be heard from the front of the house. Molly, Tess and Elizabeth all froze and looked at each other for a second, and then they were all dashing to the door where they saw their father, the little man that he was, holding Mike against the gate, his hands around his neck.

"Please, sir," Mike was shouting.

"Stay away from my daughter, you animal," her father said, his voice low and controlled.

"But I love her." Mike was cowering.

"Love? You call that love?"

"I'm sorry. I was just so ..."

"Pa, stop!" Elizabeth rushed to them and pulled her father off Mike, who shook himself off.

"She's staying here," her father spat at Mike.

"Elizabeth," said Mike, his pleading eyes boring into hers.

"Give me a moment, Pa," Elizabeth said quietly.

Her father threw Mike a look of disgust and strode into the house.

"I'm sorry," said Mike, getting on his knees and Elizabeth sank to the ground.

"You did it again," she said sadly, taking his hands.

"I don't know what came over me," he said, wrapping her in his arms and Elizabeth put her head against his neck. She knew she was going home, her home with Mike. "I love you, my girl, I love you," he cried and spread little kisses over her face, her eyes, her mouth and she drank it all in, his love for her in how he made her feel, in his arms, in his words.

Elizabeth stood up. "I'll let them know I'm leaving," she said wearily and walked back to the house, leaving Mike at the gate.

She couldn't look at her father, who stood against a wall, his arms firmly crossed over his stomach, and went about saying goodbye to her mother and sisters. Fred had gone out some time earlier and she was glad he wasn't home when Mike had come over. When she went to her father and kissed him goodbye, she squeezed his hand. "Thanks, Pa."

"He will do it again."

"I love him, Pa," she said and gave her father a quick hug. "And I'm about to have his child."

She went back to the gate where Mike was still waiting and they walked home in silence. After pouring Mike a drink, they both sat together in the moonlight and soon, they were laughing and flirting and making love.

Mike left for Delhi the next morning.

The next week, her family left for Canada.

97

Elizabeth was alone.

# Chapter 13- Loss

The pain came in the middle of the night, heavy and strong. Elizabeth had been having contractions through the day but when Mary had called a rickshaw and had taken her to the hospital, she was sent home. "At least two days," said the doctor after examining her and Elizabeth was relieved. Mike was due back in two days, a week before the baby was actually due and she hoped he would arrive in time for the birth. She sent Mary to the telegram office to let Mike know the baby was coming sooner than expected, so he knew to get back as soon as possible. She spent the day in discomfort, shifting her position and shifting again, moving about to alleviate the pain, and when Mary offered to spend the night in the living room, she gratefully accepted. It was nearing summer and the heat was already stifling and she lay on the sofa in the living room, much cooler than the bedroom, where she dipped a towel in a bucket of water and spread it over her forehead, letting the ceiling fan cool her.

The pain was excruciating by the time Elizabeth rose to get ready for bed and she knew the baby wasn't going to wait. She sat down again. "Get a taxi for me, please, Mary," she said, as the maid sat nervously by her side holding her hand.

"Yes, Miss," said Mary, but Elizabeth was squeezing her hand so tightly, she couldn't free it. "Miss ..." Mary cried, as Elizabeth felt a burst of liquid between her legs.

"Too late, Mary," groaned Elizabeth. "You will have to go get Dr Jaree from his house."

"Too far!" cried Mary.

"Get into a taxi, Mary," said Elizabeth more sternly and held the urge to push that had been cramping her belly for hours now.

Elizabeth and Mike's child was born in the middle of the night when Elizabeth was alone, and when Mary arrived with the doctor, she was trying to grapple with the bloody red thing that was spread out in the middle of the living room floor. She didn't need the doctor to tell her that the child didn't make it, and she lay still, while the doctor did what needed to be done. She pushed out the afterbirth in silence, not feeling the pain. She was numb.

When Mike arrived home two days later, he already knew what had happened as another telegram had to be dispatched; Elizabeth didn't want him coming home to find a childless wife. For those two days, Elizabeth sat in bed, eating quietly what Mary served her, not taking visitors or mail. She saw the telegrams, from her parents, friends, Mike, all piled up on her bedside table but she couldn't look at the notes of condolence, the pity that was laid out in the words of the well-wishers.

But when she saw Mike burst through the door, his face white, his hair a mess, she burst into tears. "Mike," she croaked. The first words she had uttered in two days.

"My darling, my baby," said Mike and rushed to the bed, pulling her to him. In his chest, she wept for her baby, which was still at the morgue. "Shh, shh," he said and stroked her hair. "I still have you," he whispered. "That's what matters."

\* \* \* \*

*She had been worried for Elizabeth, for Mike too. She could see that things were not going well. After the death of their child, Elizabeth had not been the same. She wondered how long she would work for them. It had been a long time now but they weren't a normal husband and wife. The miss was kind to her and sir was as well but they were strange. Had strange habits. They were habits she'd rather not be around. It wasn't just cooking and cleaning with these two. It was dealing with those habits, hiding stuff. But they paid well, and honestly, she was lucky to be in their keep. She had a place to stay, food, and the money they paid her went to her family. And they were good to her. When her little brother got sick, Elizabeth was at her hut, in the middle of the village where no employers came, and she came with hot food bought from the restaurant and medicine too and put a few rupees in her mother's hand. Her mother told her she was lucky; the woman her mother worked for sometimes beat her with a broom and her father, who sat around all day playing cards and drinking, didn't care. Mary nodded to herself. Yes, she was lucky.*

"Another peg, please, Mary," slurred Elizabeth. Mary looked

at the bottle in hesitation and Elizabeth was irritated. "Don't worry, I'll get it myself." She got off the sofa and fell back into it.

"Maybe time for bed, Miss?"

"I'll decide that, Mary." Then seeing the scared eyes of Mary staring at her, Elizabeth softened. "Just one more, Mary, and I will go to bed, okay?" She saw Mary relenting and smiled. Perhaps it was time for bed; she could barely stand. She laid her head back on the cushion and closed her eyes. The image of the baby came to her. It did every time she closed her eyes, but now, three months later, she could do it without crying. Her heart tightened, her belly ached with the emptiness she felt, but she didn't feel it as acutely as she once did. Of course the drinking helped. It always helped. It numbed the pain in her chest, it dulled the ache in her heart and it made her feel less desolate.

Mike had been amazing, had cancelled his next trip and stayed home with her for the first month, had let her have a drink with him, had looked after her, but sooner or later, she knew he would have to get back to work. She slowly began to take calls from the neighbours, her aunts and cousins and Carolyn, and replied to the messages of condolences from her family.

Mike's brother Joshua came over one afternoon with a bouquet of flowers and it didn't take a genius to see that the rest of Mike's family blamed her for the death of her child. There was no correspondence from them except for a get well card from the whole family and Joshua looked embarrassed when she asked him how they were. "Same as always." He shrugged and despite herself, Elizabeth was nonplussed. She was beginning to understand that she couldn't please everybody, and she knew she was never going to be their choice for Mike.

When Mike left, promising her a quick trip, she was lonely, the enormity of it all hitting her when she was by herself. Mary hovered near and Elizabeth appreciated it, but she needed Mike, more than ever. And when she wandered into the kitchen one evening after Mary had returned to her own home for a night, she saw it, knowing it was what she had come to seek. She didn't hesitate this time; she grabbed the bottle and took a long swig, letting herself slide to the floor, putting her head back to feel it go down. It wasn't smooth, it was harsh. She didn't like straight whisky but that was all there was. She looked at the clock—9:00 p.m.—her head already getting lighter, and looked at the remains of the bottle. There wasn't much left, less than a quarter and she knew that just wouldn't do. She cursed the fact that it was late and Mary was gone for the night, but she got off the floor and putting on her shoes, grabbed her purse and headed to the street corner, where she hailed a cab and headed to the liquor store.

The next morning was one of the worst of Elizabeth's life. She had drunk herself into a stupor and found herself on the living room floor, being roused by Mary who had let herself in early. She raised her head and a dizziness hit her and she found herself heaving vomit all over the front of Mary's chest. Mary fell back in horror, but Elizabeth had to give her credit. She raised herself back up and rested Elizabeth's head back on the floor.

"Stay there, Miss," she said in a calm but quivering voice.

"I'm sorry," Elizabeth tried to say but felt the puke surge back up through her oesophagus. This time Mary, with her hand still on Elizabeth's head, deftly dodged the projectile and let it spew past her.

"Stay down," said Mary a little more forcefully and Elizabeth obeyed. Mary disappeared while Elizabeth thought she was dying. Her head throbbed, the room spun and even though bits of vomit were still left her mouth, she remained on the floor, her sticky hair splayed around her. Mary returned with a bucket and a pile of towels and she wiped Elizabeth's face before cleaning the space around her. Elizabeth looked at the girl, who seemed to have more control of the situation than she did. "Any more coming up?" Mary asked.

"I don't know," said Elizabeth helplessly.

"Can you sit up?" she asked and Elizabeth just stared at her. She really didn't know if she could. Her chest burned and her stomach churned. "How about we try?" said Mary. Elizabeth, with Mary's help, raised herself to a sitting position. She gagged and Mary put the bucket in front of her and held her hair while Elizabeth let out more of what was in her, which by now was just bitter, yellow bile. When she dry retched, feeling like the whole of her face was being pulled out of her head, Mary held on to her back. "Okay, Miss," she said gently. "I drew you a bath. That will make you feel better. I will make some fried eggs. It will help."

"I can't eat anything," Elizabeth wailed.

"You have to. Even if you throw it up again."

Elizabeth wondered how Mary knew so well what to do and let herself be helped up and led to the bathroom, where Mary gently undressed her and helped her into the bath. She washed her hair, soaped her body and Elizabeth allowed her to, feeling like a child but appreciating the assistance. Elizabeth felt a little better after she got out of the bath, at least strong enough to get herself to the bedroom.

"I'm going to make the eggs," said Mary and disappeared, but right now, Elizabeth just wanted to curl up and go back to sleep.

"Mary," called Elizabeth and the girl turned around. "I'm sorry," she said and smiled sheepishly as Mary nodded. "I think I've learned my lesson. I will never touch it again." She wondered about the sad smile that came from Mary's face.

"I know, Miss," said the girl and left the room.

* * * *

David was born a year later. A healthy boy, chubby, cheeky, and Elizabeth thought her family was complete. She thought of her dead daughter so much in the past year that she almost resented David for being born whole, complete, healthy. As she cradled her son, she thought of how he was going to change the world; she didn't know how but when she looked into his dark brown eyes, almost black like his father's, she knew she could never love anything as much as that child. She silently thanked the Lord that she had somewhat resisted the alcohol when she found out she was pregnant again.

It was a difficult thing to do and the first few months after the birth of her stillborn baby, Elizabeth was in a state of numbness. She knew she needed alcohol to numb the pain she felt when she caressed her empty belly and readily took the antidote to her pain, especially when Mike was out of town, which was more often than not. When he was home, he was caring, helpful, took her out to dinners, even let her have a nip of brandy with him, but when he was gone it was more than a nip she took. Mary never said anything and Elizabeth tried to ignore the sullen face of her maid whenever she was asked to fetch a bottle of gin from the liquor store.

When she became pregnant, she knew she would have to give up the booze again and she was bitter. She had not touched alcohol for the duration of her first pregnancy, at least not after the Catherine incident, and yet there was no baby. What was she giving it up for?

So she didn't. Just a peg here and there to take the edge off, to keep from becoming too anxious. Loneliness didn't help. Carolyn was busy helping her mother and her mother's new husband prepare for their move to Australia and apart from the nosy aunts and cousins, she didn't have anyone to trust, anyone she could be herself with. She missed her family so much and every now and then reminded Mike that the opportunity for them to move to Canada was still open. Mike didn't indulge her train of thought and she held out hope that he would consider it one day, soon.

Mike vowed to be the best father ever when his children came into the world and when David was born, he was smitten. Every moment Mike spent at home was spent on cooing and cradling the child. A big party was thrown for his christening, with all of Mike's friends and all of Elizabeth's family invited. His family came down from Bombay to celebrate with them. They brought gifts for David, cute baby clothes, rattles, and gushed over him, and Elizabeth was pleased they had taken an interest. She saw Mike's eyes light up when his mother and Teresa spent the evening cooing at David while his father watched from afar, disapproving eyes when David spurted up milk all over Teresa's blouse. Teresa laughed it off, gave the baby a kiss and went off to clean herself but Elizabeth didn't miss the scared way Alma looked at him. A sliver of anger ran through her gut. How could Mike's father be angry about a baby regurgitating his food?

"Spare the rod and spoil the child," he said one day when Mike was cooing over David's crib. It came completely out of the blue but Elizabeth started. Was that his way of telling Mike how to discipline his children? She didn't know what that was supposed to mean, especially when the baby was just that, a baby! She noticed other things on that visit. Whenever both his parents came over, Mike was stiff, acted differently, not scared, but more alert, ready for battle, if that was the correct phrase. But when Alma and Teresa came by themselves, he was his usual self, smiling, relaxed, talking more. She wondered what his relationship had been like with his father when he was younger. And more to the point, what it meant for their own little family.

The family spent three days in Derrum and when they left, straight after the party, Elizabeth felt like she was making strides in gaining their affection. Even Alma gave her a hug that lasted more than a second. Mike went to Bombay often to see them but never invited Elizabeth to go with him and he returned happy that he'd seen them, yet irritable. She wondered often what made him tick, what made him the way he was, how he could lose his cool so easily, yet be so loving and affectionate. When she tried to talk with him about his parents, his childhood, he dismissed his past as just that, his past. She realised his father was mostly absent, a tough, unbending man, who disciplined his children with the rod. His mother, aware of her husband's philandering, made up for his strictness by going completely the other way and Mike and his sister were spoiled by her. Yet none of that seemed to come her way. But Elizabeth couldn't blame his mother; she had taken Mike away from his family, moved his home base to Derrum. They must miss him a great deal.

When the party was over, Mike sat amongst the mess, a glass of brandy in his hand, while Elizabeth and Mary tried to tidy the place. "Sit with me," called Mike, who didn't look like he was ready to retire to bed. "Mary, go to bed," he called. "Finish in the morning." Elizabeth looked at him and smiled. He seemed to be the happiest man in the world and she put down the tray she was about to wash and went over to sit with him. "Have one with me,' he said, pouring her a drink.

Elizabeth felt her tastebuds tingle. She had not had a drink for a week, the last time Mike was out of town. Carolyn had convinced her to go to a party of one of her friends, and Mary had happily offered to look after David. She had drunk a little too much, but knowing Mike was arriving back the next day, Mary helped her with her hangover by making one of her horrid-tasting concoctions, which never seemed to work anyway. She didn't count the little sips she took of Mike's whisky when he wasn't home, filling up a bottle just a little with water; Mike never seemed to notice.

She didn't like the taste of brandy, but she didn't care. "Yes, okay," she replied, excited to be sharing time and brandy with her husband. It was late into the night when they retired to bed, Elizabeth's head spinning.

"We are leaving for Bangalore next week," said Mike, when he had rolled off Elizabeth after a drunken bout of lovemaking.

Elizabeth wasn't sure she heard right. She sat up, feeling a rush of nausea. "We're going to Bangalore? For how long?"

"We'll talk about it in the morning," he said with finality and she wondered why he even bothered to mention it now. She lay down and closed her eyes. Sleep came more easily than she thought it would.

"At least a couple of years," he said the next morning at the breakfast table when Elizabeth came out of the bathroom, having had a long bath. She was glad David was beginning to sleep through the night and last night was a night she needed sleep. She realised she had more brandy than she had thought.

"Bangalore?" she asked as Mary tucked David under her breast and he nodded without looking at her. "Why?"

"Work," Mike said and got off his seat.

"But there's no one there," she said.

Mike practically pulled David off her teat and cradled him. Elizabeth wiped her breast and looked at him questioningly. He was cooing at his child, and Elizabeth had to smile. He became a big baby himself when he was around his son.

"Mike?"

"Oh don't worry, we don't have to leave until Saturday."

"Saturday?" said Elizabeth, stunned. "That's only a few days away. There's so much to do."

"Alex Macau found us a house. It's on a hill; he was going to take a polaroid for me, but I trust him." Alex Macau was a colleague of Mike's, one that Elizabeth had little time for. He had tried to come on to her a couple of times at parties and dances and Elizabeth avoided him like the plague and she definitely didn't trust him. She felt like he was a bad influence on Mike. "He's leaving with Blanche next week." Mike sniffed the air and held David, whose expression was changing rapidly, out at arm's length. "Mary!" he called. When Mary came running in, he wrinkled his nose in disgust and let her take the baby.

"Oh, Mike, I could have done it," said Elizabeth, who was also a little relieved. She was sick of breastfeeding, tired from sleepless nights and Mary had been such a blessing, taking every chance to play with the tot, while Elizabeth could grab a moment to nap. She needed to have this conversation now though. "But there's so much to do, to pack. What about ..."

"I told you we were going to have to do it at some stage," he said, going to the bar and pouring himself a brandy, which Elizabeth looked at with envy but perplexed because Mike may have liked his booze but not usually at nine in the morning.

"But our family, our friends ..."

"What friends? Those people who just use you? They only come to you when they need something. When your mother sends you things from Canada, then they see the postman and decide to visit."

"That's not fair," cried Elizabeth. "There's Carolyn ..."

"That one is the worst. Wasn't she meant to be going to England anyway? When is that happening?"

"Carolyn is my best friend. And it's Australia. And anyway, you're right, she's leaving in a couple of months." Elizabeth was sad to think about Carolyn leaving. Apart from the few friends she had, who were not very close to her, Carolyn had been around forever, even when the baby came and Elizabeth felt she was boring. She was always the first one Elizabeth would go to, especially when her own family had gone away, but Mike was right: Carolyn had been busy lately and she had not really seen her friend very often,

"Well, that's far from the point anyway," he said with a wave of his hand, a dismissive gesture she was used to but not fond of. "We have to go. I'm leaving the day after tomorrow and you can come up on Saturday. It's settled."

Elizabeth was far from happy. She didn't want to go. As it was, with Mike travelling so much, she was lonely. She didn't know anyone in Bangalore, but she knew he was right. The family she did have here didn't have a lot of time for her, except when Mike was around. She had been to her old home, now Dimple's, exactly once, and she had not felt welcome there at all. Of course she saw them on occasions, but she knew they were judging her, for Mike's roving eye as well as for her having a drink or two. Maybe it would be good to go somewhere new but she was afraid. She had lived here her whole life and it was familiar. She knew every street, every corner, every shop, every bar ...

By the time Mike left, two days later, everyone in town knew Elizabeth was leaving and they all came over within those days to farewell her.

"Remember, this is your home," said the now sweet Dimple. 'You are always welcome.'

Somehow it sounded very different to when her father had said it, not so very long ago.

# Chapter 14 - Bangalore

When Elizabeth and Mike returned to Derrum nine years later, she came back with four children, not just the one she took with her. There was now Robert, born a year and a half after David, and Faith and Genny, less than two years apart, and she never realised how fiercely she could love anything, even as much as Mike. David was a timid boy at first, but once Robert, Faith and Genny came along, he turned into a doting brother, albeit somewhat shy with strangers. Robert was fierce, tough, the brawn of the family. Faith was what her name implied. She was the faithful daughter who stayed awake long into the night with Elizabeth, who read to her, and she followed her mother everywhere she went. Genny tried to stay awake, not wanting to miss out on anything that happened, but sleep was too powerful for her and many nights, when all the children ventured into Elizabeth's bed when Mike was away, Genny was the first one to fall asleep.

Elizabeth had mellowed by the time she left Bangalore, knew she was a different person these days, a woman, and at twenty-nine, her optimism about life had waned. When she rode through the familiar streets of her childhood, her heart depressed in her chest. She could still see herself tearing through them, boys hot on her heels. She could still picture her sisters tottering on their heels, as she trailed behind, to the shop down the street.

She asked the taxi driver to detour past her parents' old house and she asked him to slow down as they drove past. She swallowed, a wave of nostalgia hitting her as she pictured her mother on the porch calling for her to come into the house, her father behind her mother, grinning to himself. She opened the window of the taxi and smelled the heat of the tar on the road hit her nostrils and she took a breath. Maybe this was what she needed. To go home. She just wasn't sure that Derrum was her home anymore. She didn't know where she belonged.

Elizabeth didn't like Bangalore, perhaps the sultry weather mirroring that of her hometown the only similarity. Mike's friend

Alex, who with his wife, Blanche, had been residents of the city for a few years, took it upon themselves to introduce Elizabeth and Mike to the hoi polloi of the city. After her initial shock of the move, Elizabeth was excited, not just brought on by the birth of her children but the promise of a new life, one that perhaps entailed Mike being a more present husband. However, her hope that Mike would become the husband she knew he could be was not burning so brightly.

The womanising began the moment they arrived in Bangalore, Elizabeth left to take care of David, while Mike went out, almost every evening with his friend Alex. Luckily, Mary had been convinced to go with them and she was a big help with the care of David as well as the new arrivals. With Mary around, Elizabeth knew that when she did go on a bender, the children were always well looked after. Elizabeth smothered them with love, took them out to the park, cooked with them, and Mary took it upon herself to do those things when Elizabeth was not feeling bright and bubbly after having a drink the evening before.

The next few years passed in a blur for Elizabeth. Between nursing her newborns and running around after the others, she was left exhausted. Mike was rarely around, this new job taking him away for weeks on end. But when Mike was home, it was undeniable the love he had for them, to the point that Elizabeth almost felt left out. He was always playing with them—never changed a nappy or fed them, but when those things were dealt with, he always had one of them in his arms, and David was always at his heels.

Apart from her children, it was an uneventful nine years, not a lot changing in the relationship between Mike and her. The beatings continued but not too regularly and never too viciously. Elizabeth learned that the less she provoked him, the less he gave her. She was being a good wife and mother and her drinking, well, he wasn't around enough to know how much she drank. Elizabeth was lonely and spent much of her time not just sipping out of Mike's bottle of whisky anymore, but now buying her own. She was not going to make excuses for it anymore, but she trained herself to have just enough to take the edge off and not get paralytically drunk as she had before.

But Bangalore, for the most part, was tough, the business of life leaving Elizabeth exhausted, the children bringing joy and laughter into her days, the days that Mike was away. Which was often. Even when he was not at work, flying off to who knew where, he spent the evenings after the children had gone to bed out with his friends. Elizabeth had lost some of the fight in her, perhaps because she was so busy, so tired all the time. And she craved a drink so badly by the end of the day that it was a bit of a relief that Mike was not around to keep an eye on the level of her drink or to argue about whether she should have any at all. She had become deft in sneaking her drinks, topping up the bottle, buying her own and hiding it in outlandish places, behind the toilet bowl, under the side steps of their house, sometimes even under her underwear in the bottom drawer of her bedside table.

She learned to curb the guilt she felt when she put the bottle to her lips. He should feel guilt, not her, she reasoned and let the familiar scent of Chanel N° 5, a perfume she detested, run through her brain, the smell of which Mike sometimes rolled into bed with after a night out with his friends. She knew he was cheating, it was hard to ignore, not just the perfume, but the looks, the sympathetic faces of Mike's colleagues and their wives when Mike did take her out for a dance or a party. She even suspected Blanche, the wife of Alex, when the woman just stopped coming over to see her a couple of years after they had moved to Bangalore. It seemed coincidental that Alex stopped visiting as well and when they bumped into them at a get-together, Blanche pecked Elizabeth on the cheek lightly and swung away to talk to another couple. Alex didn't even bother to greet them.

Elizabeth didn't confront Mike. To provoke him was just asking for trouble.

Besides, what was the point anymore?

# Chapter 15- The Return

*She watched from the window as the taxi drove up. It was something she did after the school children had gone home for the day. It was a sad time for her. She enjoyed teaching them, playing with them, reading with them, and then she was alone. She only had them for a couple of years and they were gone. She shouldn't get so attached to them, she knew, but she couldn't help herself. She opened the curtain a little more and cocked her head as she watched a woman step out of the taxi. She was slim, her back straight, her neck even straighter, a bun balancing on the crown of her head. Suddenly the other doors of the taxi opened and out streamed a bunch of children, all running for the front door of the house next door. Margie raised her eyebrows in delight. She knew a family was moving in and others in the street all wondered who would be invading the space that had lain empty for almost three months. She saw another woman, clearly a live-in maid, also come out of the cab and the woman and the maid, along with the driver, emptied the trunk of the car. Four suitcases, large ones. She didn't know how all that even fitted in there. The woman turned her head towards her house and Margie backed away from the window, hoping she hadn't been caught observing them. She peeked out again and saw that the woman had turned back and was helping the driver and the maid take the suitcases into the house. Then she followed the driver back to the car and paid him, watching as he drove away. She turned around again, looked about her, up and down the street, and folded her arms, rubbing at them. She looked scared—not scared really, more unsure, anxious. She looked towards her house and hesitated. Margie took a breath. She had to go to her, make her feel comfortable, find out if she was okay. She didn't see a man depart the taxi and she wondered if there was a man. Then there was a movement at the house and Margie turned to see one of the boys approach the woman. Her demeanour changed immediately; a smile lit up her face, all traces of her trepidation now gone. Margie would have to give her time to settle in before she*

111

*welcomed her to town. Perhaps tomorrow morning.*

"Welcome to Derrum," called Margie, leaning on the wooden fence that separated their homes the day after Elizabeth and the family had moved in.

Elizabeth glanced over at the woman with the warm smile that dimpled her cheeks and walked to where Margie's heavy frame rested. "Hello," she said holding out her hand. "I'm Elizabeth. Oh, and I'm not new to Derrum."

"Oh?" Margie took the offered hand and crinkled her eyes. "I thought I knew everyone in town by now."

"I've been in Bangalore for a few years."

"Oh, *that* Elizabeth," said Margie with a raise of her eyebrows.

Elizabeth twisted her lips in a wry smile. She had been gone so long and yet people were still talking about her, and not in a good way, she guessed. The children came running out and hung to their mother's dress.

"Well, hello," said Margie, looking down at them. "There are lots of you!"

Elizabeth introduced them and Margie smiled and shook each of their hands in turn. Then Margie pointed to a little blackboard that stood on stilts just in front of her porch. "I run a nursery. Are your children going to Xavier's?"

Elizabeth looked at the sign that said *Nursery to Second Standard.* "The girls are about that age," she said, her eyes lighting up. It would be so easy, she thought, but she wondered if it were too easy. Margie looked like Mrs Claus; even her clothes were colourful, her voice light and fun, but what if this woman were a terrible teacher?

"I come with references," said Margie with a curl of her lip and Elizabeth flushed.

"I'm going down to enrol the boys tomorrow at Xavier's but I can talk to Mike about you."

Margie laughed. "You let me know," she said. "And if you need anything, you know, a cup of sugar ..."

"Thanks," said Elizabeth, feeling a warmth from this stranger. It was good to be home.

Margie was a Christian woman, who spent much time with Elizabeth discussing passages from the Bible. She was a strict teacher who Elizabeth could see was having an impact on her girls from the moment they entered her little school. Faith and Genny were excited to go to school every day, almost flushing their breakfast down their throats in their eagerness to go next door, and came home in the afternoon displaying their new-found knowledge of the alphabet, stories from Aesop and drawings, which Elizabeth displayed on the fridge. Margie was fun too, and when Mike was out of town, Elizabeth spent many evenings in the company of this jolly woman, sipping tea and cakes, the children running around their legs, and there were moments when Elizabeth was alone that the thought of alcohol didn't rush to her brain.

Elizabeth thanked God for Margie. She really had been a godsend. Not just because of the fact that it was all so convenient, but her kindness, her willingness to spend time with Elizabeth and the children kept Elizabeth sane, making her life easier, the alcohol more easy to resist. Even Mike liked Margie and that was surprising as no friend that Elizabeth made seemed to have a positive impact on him, except for Blanche, and she was positive she knew what had transpired to make that friendship fall apart.

"So what's next for Mike?" Margie asked one afternoon when Elizabeth leaned over the fence to greet the girls after their school day.

The family had been back for three months and she had seen Mike for perhaps a third of that. "Back in a couple of days." She sighed. She should have been happy but she knew it would not be for long. "And then ... who knows?"

Margie harrumphed at that. Elizabeth frowned. Mike may be a lot of things but it wasn't up to anyone else to remind her of them. As it was, she had to ignore the snipes from neighbours and friends that referenced Mike's infidelity, even in the short period of time they had been back. She didn't need to hear it from Margie.

Instead she chose to focus on her children. When David showed an interest in Mike's guitar, she taught him to play and sang along with the girls trying to follow along. In the evenings, while David sat with his eyes creased, focused on the chords, his teeth biting his tongue, reminding him so much of her brother, she read stories to Faith and Genny, and smiled as Robert pretended to play with his trucks, instead listening in. When they tired of the books they had, she made up stories, tales of wizards and elves, tales of romance and glamour, and she would inevitably bring out her Bible, from which she said there were much better stories than any others.

When the children were at school, Elizabeth took to helping Margie, who only had a handful of students. She tidied up the little living room which doubled for a classroom, sometimes did readings and on breaks, sang to the enthralled little children. She loved doing it and having seen what the girls were learning in that little school, she was satisfied.

And in those gaps, when she was lonely, when she craved her husband, Elizabeth went to town, re-formed the friendships she had broken when she moved. She wished Carolyn was still in Derrum and although she kept in touch with her via mail, long, wistful letters filled with memories and news, she missed her friend more than ever now she was back in Derrum. Some of her old friends from school would call in on her, her cousins and aunts coming by to visit and even though she tried to ignore it, she realised it was more for what they could get from her—'just a couple of rupees for sugar', 'could you spare a fiver for flour?' and Elizabeth would fish out the required amount from her purse. It wasn't just money either, it was things.

"How beautiful that princess figurine looks, Lizzy," said her Aunt Dimple. "How nice it would look beside my ornamental dog, you know the one, on the hall table ..."

"Liz, where did you get that scarf?" Dimple's daughter exclaimed. "It's beautiful." She ran her hands over the silk scarf Elizabeth had bought on a trip to Goa.

Elizabeth would always give them whatever they asked for and they knew when to coax her out of anything—when Mike wasn't home. In fact, people rarely visited when Mike was in town, his motorbike in their driveway alerting them to his presence. He was not as giving as Elizabeth and regularly scolded her for being taken advantage of by fair-weathered friends.

But what hurt was the gossip, the words she heard repeated back to her by those same friends.

"Did you hear, Elizabeth?"

"I'm just telling you because I care about you."

And other words, sometimes whispered even in her presence. "Did you hear she sent her servant for two bottles? Two!"

"Martin saw her staggering into the Muscat's bar."

The same people, all of them. She held her head high, tried to ignore it, hoped she could be above it, but it stung. They were not lying.

Not Margie. With Margie literally next door, Elizabeth felt she had found an older sister and she loved sitting on the porch with her, watching the street children play with her own, throwing marbles, playing hopscotch, racing each other down the road while they chatted about nothing in particular. She thought about her sisters, how she resented them for their knowledge of life; she recounted stories about how they teased and tormented her but now it was with a sense of nostalgia. She wished they were still here, that one of them, probably Tess, could pull on her pigtails and call her names. How simple life had been then. She talked to Margie about her mother, who wrote often, sometimes sent parcels, which Elizabeth would distribute to her friends, the few that popped by from time to time.

"Please don't offer me anything," Margie said when the postman delivered a parcel wrapped in brown paper with overseas stamps emblazoned on the front and Elizabeth looked at her with eyes wide. Margie narrowed her own. "The crowds will sense it," she said and returned to her sewing. Elizabeth put the parcel in the house. She wanted to wait until the children were all at home before she opened it. There was always an excitement when they opened the parcels together; her mother always sent something for each one. Elizabeth returned to the seat on the porch and picked up the dress she was hemming.

"Dimple is your aunt, is she not?" Margie said.

"Yes," Elizabeth said. She was wary of Dimple and her daughter and had discussed Dimple with Margie before.

"Yes, well, you can't choose your family, can you?"

Elizabeth silently agreed and mourned the departure of her family even more. She picked at the thread which hung from the needle. "I need to get more," she said and went inside. At the sewing box, she patted the shawl her mother had made for her on the day of her wedding. She kept it in tissue paper, never wore it, afraid it would be ruined. She felt a stab at her heart. She missed her mother so much. Her father had passed just a year ago and how she wished she could have gone to see her, to be with her, to mourn with her. But it could not be done. She missed her father too, was alone when she got the telegram, had cried into the night, didn't even have a drink to calm her as Mike was in town. He had come home and tried to comfort her, had taken her in his arms and soothed her. Then he let her have a nip of brandy. She had more and he let her. It had ended badly, needless to say. It always did.

She pulled out the thread, glad that she had something to do with her hands to take the nerves away. She and Margie sewed clothes for the old-age home and when they delivered it, the matron asked if she could entertain the elderly, so she took the chance to sing, sitting at the piano and belting out songs. She enjoyed it, it kept her busy and she felt useful, always coming home elated at the response, the smiles on the people's faces and how they tapped their toes to her songs.

For that short period of time, Elizabeth was happy. She had been surrounded by people for most of her life but she had always felt so alone, so different somehow. Being with Margie made her feel like she had someone and she'd often forget that feeling in the pit of her stomach, that want, that need, that thirst. She was in her hometown, she had a good friend and felt like she was contributing to the world. Her children were happy and healthy and Mike, well, Mike was Mike, but he was loving and caring when he was home. And she still loved him like nothing else.

Yes, she was happy.

# Chapter 16 - The Picture

## 1978

*Eight by six centimetres, with a thin white edge, it sits in a frame almost double its size, a pastel green frame that pales in comparison to the black-and-white photograph within it.*

*The photograph contains a moment in time, as all photos do: a couple on the dance floor, the man in profile, unbuttoned collared white shirt with black pants, the bottom of the photo ending just above his knees, the woman, in the middle of a turn, her arm bent, her head atilt, black curls flowing beneath a broad-brimmed, white-laced hat. She is wearing a light, high-collared dress with small dark spots, but not polka dots, small flowers instead. Her hands are gloved, white. The man is gazing at the woman with what looks like a smirk, but looking closely, you can see it's more like pride. She in turn is smiling, not directly at him, but in a flashy way. She knows she makes him proud.*

*The photograph is so closely shot that one cannot see much more than the couple, but a young boy is caught in the background just behind the arm of the woman, his eyes watching them, his smile wide. They seem to be the centre of attention and, in fact, they are. They are in the middle of a dance competition and they will win. But she will never dance again, not like she did that night.*

"Never cry when someone is leaving the house. It's bad luck and something bad will happen to them." Elizabeth took Genny's cold little hands in hers and rubbed at them, feeling the soft chubby fingers clutching at her own. She prised them out and turned around, walking, no, almost running so she didn't have to think about her daughter crying behind her. The others had just hovered, knowing that no matter what they said, she was still going. But Genny still tried, her wide tear-filled eyes pleading with her not to go. In years to come, she would be reminded that they were the first words her daughter remembered, ingrained in the memory of a five-year-old, the night she left the house on a motorcycle with a man that wasn't her husband.

Elizabeth and Mike had been to a dance, the Anglo-Indian Dance-Off of 1978, and had arrived home with the trophy. She placed it along with the others, a smile of satisfaction on her face. She could still feel the effects of the gin, and her body was crying out for more, but she knew it could wait. Then she turned around and kissed Mike, who was standing behind her.

"Two glasses, Mary," he called as he pulled her into his arms. She grinned and her mouth watered. She had played the good wife, had made him proud and he was rewarding her with what she craved.

"Let's wake them first," she said, still buzzing from the win.

"Get them up," Mike bellowed and she crept into their room, turning on the night light. She stood for a moment and watched her girls both asleep on the same bed, Faith, her perennial frown on her face even as she slept, and Genny, her arm stretched out over Faith's shoulder, and she smiled at their closeness. They looked so serene, she considered putting out the light and creeping away, but Faith's eyes fluttered.

"Mummy?"

"Shhh, your sister is asleep," Elizabeth whispered, but as she did, Genny's eyes began to flicker too. But Genny opened her eyes only for a second and they closed again. Genny could sleep through anything, but it was Faith who usually stayed up late, and had clearly been waiting for her parents to arrive home.

Elizabeth leaned against the doorway and smiled at her daughters, and in a moment both were already scrambling out of bed.

"Did you ..." asked Faith, her hands together in anticipation.

"Yes, we did," she said as she felt the girls' little arms go around her.

By the time they got to the living room, David was already shuffling in, wiping the sleep out of his eyes, and she could hear Robert in the bathroom. She smiled. Mike had woken them too. They wanted to share their elation with the children. Mary was already warming up hot milk for them, even though she clicked her tongue at them having something to drink so late in the evening.

"The gin, Mary," said Elizabeth and tried not to notice as the children looked at each other in alarm. Mary's face creased, and she stood there a moment longer before she moved to the bar to pour the drink. Mike was already sipping at his bourbon.

David placed himself on the floor at his mother's knee, Faith and Genny were on either side of Elizabeth, squeezing together on the small sofa, while Robert sat on the arm of his father's chair. They waited for Elizabeth and Mike to recount the events of the dance.

"I was a little worried, Mike," said Elizabeth. "Aruna was really determined this year. Patty said she and Jai had been practising for weeks."

"Still not long enough to beat you and me," said Mike with a sneer.

"You're always the best, Daddy," said Faith.

"Yes, we are," said Mike, giving his daughter a broad smile.

"And you even bet on it!" Elizabeth exclaimed. "I thought I was going to faint after that jive."

"It was a sure thing," replied Mike with a wave of his arm. Elizabeth knew how much Mike loved to gamble but she knew better than to ask how much he'd won. He was sometimes secretive about the oddest things. Mike and Elizabeth were the clear winners, as they had been for the last two years running. Elizabeth had even managed to win a competition in Bangalore when she had been eight months pregnant, not allowing her stomach to stop her winning streak.

"Did Daddy throw you in the air, Mum?" asked Faith.

"Yes, everywhere, but I always landed," said Elizabeth.

"When's the next one?" asked David.

"In a few weeks," said Elizabeth. "Mike," she said turning to him. "Will you be in town?"

Mike shrugged. "Don't know."

"Are you going away again, Dad?" said Robert, who usually didn't have much to say, but Elizabeth knew he was not happy when Mike was away. She looked slyly at Mike, who also liked to keep his schedule a secret, why, she couldn't fathom, but she saw his eyebrows flatten.

"So let us tell you all about it," began Elizabeth taking the focus off Mike.

The children listened with oohs and aahs and after their story, Mike suggested a sing-song. The guitar was brought out and David asked if he could play it, and together Elizabeth and Mike belted out their favourite songs from Elvis, Patsy Cline, the Bee Gees, while the children listened in rapture. It wasn't often they enjoyed the togetherness, the happiness of their parents and they tried to stretch it out for as long as possible. Even Mary sat in the doorway, humming to the music, a little smile on her face, a small crease between her brows, nevertheless.

"Okay, time for bed," said Mike to the children with a little wink at Elizabeth, whose stomach still reeled at the idea of his hands all over her.

The children protested. "Not yet ..."

"Just one more ..."

"I'm already awake now ..."

"Time for bed," said Mike a little sternly and Elizabeth put a hand on his arm. Although he never touched the children other than in affection, she knew they were scared when he raised his voice.

"Come on now," said Mary, pulling up Faith by the hand and reaching for Genny who was yawning.

Mike moved to the sofa and Elizabeth rested her head on his shoulder, wishing it could always be like this, that there were never fights or anything else that came between them. "One more?" he asked and Elizabeth nodded. Her head was already spinning but it wasn't often that she sat with her husband late on a Saturday night, enjoying his company, happy together.

"All out," he said, returning with just one glass, only half full.

Elizabeth swallowed but she was happy to have him just sit there with her and as he flopped into the sofa beside her, she nestled her head into the crook of his neck. "It was so wonderful tonight, Mike."

He grinned. "Yes, a good night." He turned to her. "You're really beautiful, you know that?"

"Stop it," she said with a swish of her hand.

"You put everyone to shame."

"Now I know you've had too much to drink," she said and regretted it the moment the words came out of her mouth. He never liked any reference to his drinking, even though he was quite happy to refer to hers. She quickly changed tack. "Caris and Tony asked us to their place next weekend," she said as she stroked his hair.

"That man gives me a headache," said Mike. "Make an excuse."

"But it would be nice to go. You're not leaving for at least a couple of weeks, right?"

His eyes narrowed. "Why do you want to go so badly?"

"Because they are our friends." Elizabeth could already hear the tone of Mike's voice change, ever so subtly. "And they have been asking us to come over forever. I'm tired of making excuses."

"Maybe you're just waiting to spread your legs for him." Mike slurred now, his voice hardening, and she was always astounded at how quickly his temper could change.

"Oh, Mike," said Elizabeth, realising it was already too late. "Let's go to bed."

"Why now?" His voice was now raised higher and Elizabeth rose, but he pulled her back down on the sofa. "The thought of that man turns you on?"

"Be quiet, Mike, the children," said Elizabeth gesturing to the bedrooms.

"Why are you changing the subject? Have you got something going on with Tony? That shrivelled old idiot." His hand was already tight on her wrist.

"Mike, he is your friend," said Elizabeth, trying to calm him but knowing they were not the right words. "I would never do anything ..."

"So if he wasn't my friend?"

It was too late to stop anything. It had gotten past the point of no return and Elizabeth steeled herself for what was to come. But by now, she was also angry. This was an ongoing accusation and she was fed up with it. "Maybe that's you, not me. Maybe there's some reason you don't want to see Caris." As she said it, she knew she had hit the mark but it wasn't jealousy she felt. Mike's face went blank and for a moment, she was scared. "Mike, let's go to bed, please." She hoped for a miracle that she knew was not to come and tried to squirm out of his grasp.

Mike let go of her hand, took a swig of his bourbon and looked at the glass, still half full. He raised it above his head and smashed it down on the glass table so hard, the table smashed, shards of glass flying in every direction. Elizabeth froze and before she knew it, she felt herself fall to the floor, a striking pain bolting through her head. She squeezed her eyes shut, and put her hands over her head to shield from the barrage of strikes that were to inevitably come.

"Sir!" she heard Mary cry and opening her eyes a squint, she saw as Mike grabbed the keys of his motorbike and stormed out of the house, slamming the door behind him.

She closed her eyes again in relief. It could have been a lot worse and she let out a little sob. It was always like this and even during their celebrations earlier, they all knew what would ultimately happen; it was why the children had tried to prolong it as they did. It was just a matter of time, but sometimes their love for each other lasted longer than all the other things they also felt for each other and each time they always hoped that it would be different. But with whisky or gin or whatever other drink was involved, it was inevitable that the evening would take a horrible turn, although the word 'horrible' was tame for some of the things they could say and do to each other.

Elizabeth sat up and felt Mary's hand help her to a stand. She shook away the hand and gave Mary a nod. Mary left the room and Elizabeth stood and stared at the shattered table, watching the dark brown liquid which was dripping from the metal posts. *What a waste*, she thought absently as her eyes moved to the empty bottle that sat on the floor. She put her hand to her head and looked at her fingers which came away red and sticky. "Mary," she called and looked up to see the children standing at the door, each one with a different expression on their faces. David, apprehension, Robert, anger, Faith concern, Genny, fear. But there was no surprise in any of them and Elizabeth sat down and spread her arms out, the children all clambering into them. "Watch the glass," she warned as they all looked searchingly at her face, her body, trying to decipher what was safe to touch.

Mary came back into the room with a mop and a broom and went about clearing the mess. "Mary, I need you to do something for me," she called, and with some effort, she stood up and led Mary out of the room.

At least there was no major external damage this time, except for a red blotch on the side of her face, next to her ear. She came back into the room and sat heavily on the sofa. Faith began to pick up the pieces of glass that were shattered on the linoleum floor and Elizabeth smiled at her, leaned forward and gave her chin a squeeze. Genny jumped on her mother's lap and drew back. The smell of alcohol, which she already knew well, assaulted her senses, but she didn't want to offend her mother by showing her distaste. Instead, she put her head on Elizabeth's chest and Elizabeth tried to comfort Genny by stroking her hair. David and Robert hovered near, one sitting by her feet and the other, the one who really objected to their drinking, slightly further away. Even in her fuzzy state of mind, she saw it all, felt for them. But they had each other and she needed to calm herself, take stock of what had just happened, unfrazzle her nerves.

"It's all right," she said to them. "Go on back to bed now, it's late."

"We want to stay up for a bit," Faith said.

"Just a little bit," Genny put in.

"Are you okay, Mum?" Robert stood at the window, intermittently glancing out into the dark night while the others cleared up around her, David moving the table to the side of the room.

"I'm fine," she said. "But tonight you must go straight to bed, okay?" She hated seeing their sad faces filled with concern, not just for her but for what may still happen.

"Where's Mary?" asked David.

"On an errand," replied Elizabeth in a tone that implied there would be no further explanation. Her children knew that tone and each with a kiss on their mother's cheek, lingered back to their rooms. Elizabeth's heart hurt for them. They had been in this situation a hundred times; she knew they would wait until they heard her go to bed before settling down. She always peeped in before she did and their little heads would bob up and down at the sound of her voice. She could see this time that Robert was not so sure this would happen. That boy had a sixth sense about him. She knew he would be alert, waiting for anything to happen.

She sighed. Any number of things could happen. Mike could return, Elizabeth may leave, other visitors may arrive ... At least this time their father had left without leaving their mother battered and bruised, save for the gash on the side of her head, but he could very well come back and she hoped she would be gone by then. She could feel her resolve wavering. She wanted to go to her children, or maybe go to her room, call out for them, let them cuddle with her until they fell asleep. But she was agitated, the clenching of her hands showed her that, the way her lip trembled, the way her chest heaved. She knew she couldn't stay. She needed it.

"Where is Mary?" she whispered to herself between gritted

teeth.

Elizabeth picked up her purse, checked to see if there was any money in there. Not a lot but enough for a couple of drinks. Perhaps it wasn't too late and Devron would come to pick her up or even get what she needed. But Devron never had any money and she knew she would have to buy him something too for his trouble. She wished Mary was convincing enough. Devron, a man she had met at the bar, wanted more from her but she just liked his company and his ability to drink with her. She toyed with the handle on her purse and set herself back down on the sofa to wait for Mary to get back. Crossing her legs, she patted down her dress, and winced from the pain that emanated from the bruise on her thigh, still fresh from two days ago.

Now, she looked at the time, wondering what was taking Mary so long. Her thoughts returned to Mike and she said a small prayer for his safety. He had drunk quite a lot and had taken the bike. But he was a skilled rider. He had taken her on rides, even when they had both been drinking heavily, and they managed to get out of situations, even if they had crashed a couple of times.

*It hasn't been that long since the last time,* she thought idly, wondering why he had lost his temper so quickly this time. Usually after his begging, pleading and words of unstoppable love, he held back for a while. But two days? She tried, through the blur in her mind, to think what it was that set him off the last time, but she couldn't quite remember.

She heard the motorbike and got up, heading to the door, but before she could close it behind her, she felt the tug on her skirt. Genny stood there; behind her were Faith and David and just behind him was Robert, his eyes like thunder.

"Go back to bed," she whispered, bending down unsteadily, and took Genny's hand. "I will be home in fifteen minutes."

Genny clung to her legs, crying. "Don't go, Mummy."

"Mary is with you, Faith and the boys ..." She looked up at the children and Mary, who was gathering the children around her, avoiding Robert's steely gaze. She knew he was challenging her. "I won't be long. Fifteen minutes," she reiterated. "I will be here when you get up in the morning. Go on, have a good sleep."

The others came around and kissed her, the ritual whenever someone was going out, but Genny still clung to her, crying, begging her not to go. This was when she bent down and told her daughter those fateful words.

"You must never cry when someone is leaving. It's bad luck and something bad will happen to them."

Then she left.

# Chapter 17 - Recovery

She always wondered why she said that. Maybe it was to stop Genny from crying, so she wouldn't feel so badly, maybe it was to appease herself; the temptation to stay with her child was almost as strong as the temptation to leave. But she knew she wasn't going to be very long. Devron waited at his bike, just outside the gate, and she was just going out to get some more alcohol. The liquor store was probably closed by now, but she knew the owner lived in a little apartment just above it. She had coaxed him out before and she knew he would come out again. Devron, always ready to help, always ready for a party, kept his eyes straight ahead. Seeing the commotion would only remind him of his own family, who sat home waiting for him every night.

As she mounted the bike, she tried not to look back at the door, where Mary was trying to usher in the kids, but she couldn't help it and she turned away quickly.

She never knew until much later the weight of those words and she never knew what it did to her daughter to hear them. So much time would go by before Genny could truly tell her the guilt she had felt for crying, for allowing her mother to go into the night after bringing her bad luck.

As Elizabeth lay on her cot, her body in a cast, she thought only of her children. Being without them for so long was excruciating, more unbearable than the pain in her body. Mike told her they had come to see her the day after the accident, but she was already in surgery, and now they were gone. Packed away to boarding school, because their mother was stupid enough to go for a ride on a bike with a man who wasn't her husband. She tried to remember how it happened, but the last thing that she could recall was Genny's little arms reaching for her.

"You didn't even make it to the shop," Mike said when Elizabeth asked him about it.

"I don't remember anything," Elizabeth said sullenly.

She was out of surgery now, her vertebrae fractured, her little toe nearly torn square off. She was told she may not walk again, but she knew better. She was tough, an athlete, strong and supple. She trusted her body but preferred not to argue. She would show them. She would get her strength back, get her children back. She was fuming when Mike told her what he'd done. A boarding school! With strangers!

"Why couldn't you leave them with Mary until I was better?" she had asked, her eyes wide in shock.

"Because Mary couldn't look after all of them. I had to let her go."

"You let Mary go?"

"There's no need now." Mike was nonchalant.

"But she's part of our family. She would have looked after the children until I got home."

"We couldn't risk that."

"Risk what?"

"We didn't know if you were coming home," said Mike, a controlled patience in his tone.

Elizabeth felt a flutter in her chest. They, her children too, thought she wasn't going to make it? She squeezed her eyes shut. "How long have I been here, Mike?"

"Nearly three months."

Elizabeth's eyes sprang open and her jaw dropped. "The children have been in that place for months?"

"They're okay," he said, placing his hand on hers. "Teresa helped to get them into the school in Bombay. St Martha's. It's a good one." Elizabeth wondered what he had told his family about what happened. Teresa, who had married a jeweller now, divided her life between Melbourne and Bombay and Elizabeth rarely saw her but Mike visited her a few times a year when she was in India. So she had taken it upon herself to relocate the children, without the consent of their own mother?

"I'm going to get them out," Elizabeth said, maddened that he had let his sister do this. But when she tried to move, she felt a searing pain bolt up her spine. "Ahh," she cried and Mike jumped off his seat.

"Liz, Elizabeth!" he cried. "Doctor!" he yelled towards the

127

door.

Elizabeth couldn't contain the flood of tears that fell from her eyes and Mike held her hand, kissing her hair, her cheeks. "You will get home soon, my love," he said.

"Will I walk again, Mike?" The pain that came in waves reminded her of how badly her body was broken.

He didn't answer.

Elizabeth didn't need an answer. She had her own; she would do it. She didn't need anyone to tell her she would get her life back, her body, her children.

Not even Mike.

When Elizabeth was better, she left the hospital and went home, to an empty house, so lonely without the children; it fuelled her. She worked hard, so hard it nearly killed the spirit that she had recovered. And she prayed. She had faith that she would heal. She tried to avoid anything that looked remotely like alcohol and Mike helped with her recovery when he was around. But Mike was also gone for most of the time. Her cousin Sadie checked in on her once in a while and Margie often popped in with soups and pastries.

"I'm going to put on too much weight, Margie," she scolded, when Margie came into the house carrying a tray of cakes.

"Then you will turn out like me!" Margie gave a hearty laugh and Elizabeth couldn't help but laugh with her. Margie sat with her and read with her, talked with her and sometimes brought her brother Jacob over, a new face with new stories. Jacob was also a physical therapist and he gave her pointers on how to exercise properly without hurting herself. She liked his company and that of Margie, whom she wept to about the absence of her children.

But she was glad for Mary, her faithful Mary, who she promptly reinstated the moment she returned to her house. Mary who helped her with her moods, her recovery, sat with her while she cried in pain.

"You can do this, Miss," Mary would say and Elizabeth looked towards the cabinet, the bottle of whisky laughing at her. Mary's eyes travelled to the cabinet too. "No. Without that. You can do it without that."

"I know," Elizabeth would reply, saliva flooding her mouth at the thought of it. Then her mind would go to her children.

She missed her life. Her husband, the laughter, the drinking, the parties. She missed her family, her father whom she would never see again, her mothers and sisters who were building a life for themselves in another country. How she needed them now.

But most of all, she missed her children. She was unable to see them. The drive to their boarding school was more than eight hours away, a distance her body could not bear. There was no phone in their house and she wrote letters every week, none of which were answered, and she wondered if they even got them. But she got news of them from Mike, who did visit them regularly, stopping in to see them on his trips into and out of town. She resented him for having that luxury and sometimes begged him to take her too.

"Please, Mike," she pleaded.

"You're in no state," he said patiently.

"But it's not too far," she insisted.

"It's a long drive and you can barely walk, my love," he replied and she saw his eyes shiny with tears. "And do you want them to see you like this?"

She knew she didn't. How would they react, seeing their mother hobbling on crutches or a walking stick, barely able to hold herself straight? What would that do to them? What would it do to her? She was determined they would not see her in this state, that she would be standing and walking straight when she finally had her children in her arms again.

She worked harder.

"You will hurt yourself," said Jacob as she leaned on him in exhaustion.

"I can do this," she would snap, trying to ignore the burn of her bones as she tried to walk the small distance between the house and the fence between her and Margie's house, Margie standing on the other side, encouraging her on.

Every day she tried but got only a half or third of the way and when she collapsed in Jacob's arms, she'd sob in exhaustion.

"Rest now," said Jacob.

"No," she'd reply, more determined.

"Yes, get to it, Liz," yelled Margie, and Elizabeth would grit her teeth and let Jacob help her onto her feet again.

Jacob was around often now and she relied on him to visit and help with her recovery. However, on the days Mike was home, he knew not to show his face anywhere near their house.

"Who is that man?" Mike asked one day when Jacob, going into Margie's house, nodded to the two of them as they were getting into a taxi on the way to a hospital check-up.

"Margie's brother," said Elizabeth with a curt nod back at Jacob.

"Does he live with her?"

"No, I think he comes to visit her sometimes," Elizabeth said, trying to sound casual.

If Mike knew that Jacob helped her, that he was her friend, she would never see Jacob again. Mike shrugged and put out his hand to hold hers and she was satisfied that he was satisfied. She was relieved Jacob hadn't tried to come over and introduce himself to Mike. He had obviously been prepped by Margie that Mike was not a man who would take kindly to Elizabeth having visitors, especially of the male variety. But Elizabeth liked Jacob. As it was she was devoid of company except for that of Margie, Mary and on the odd occasion, her cousin Sadie, who lived too far a distance to walk over very often, especially now that she had her own family to contend with. So Jacob was a welcome companion.

She missed Mike more than ever. Since she'd been out of the hospital, he had become the caring, kind, attentive man he was when they had first met. He brought coffee to her in bed and even got up in the middle of the night to help her to the toilet and in the evenings, he walked with her to the front gate and back or they sat together watching television or playing card games. There wasn't much in the way of lovemaking but they hadn't been as affectionate with each other as they were in a long while. She anticipated his returns now with bated breath.

On a dry evening, Elizabeth sat on the porch enjoying a sunset. It had been a harrowing day of therapy, not helped by the heat, and Mike was to return that evening. Elizabeth had walked down the street, all the way up to the post box and was excited to tell him how far she had come. Mike was going to be home for at least two weeks, which meant she wouldn't be able to see Jacob for all that time and she felt something like a loss. Margie, having just waved goodbye to Jacob, sat with her.

"Tell me more about Jacob," said Elizabeth.

"You know him well enough," said Margie, fanning herself

with a magazine.

"Do I?" replied Elizabeth. "I know he helps me, I know he's your brother. That's all I know."

Margie turned to her with narrowed eyes, her magazine paused mid-wave. "Why do you want to know anything more?"

Elizabeth wasn't sure. She knew she loved Mike as fiercely as ever, but there was something so caring about Jacob, something endearing about him and after four months, she looked forward to seeing him more than she knew she should. "Well, he's my friend, I guess ..."

"You have enough friends, Liz," Margie snapped.

"Do I?" Elizabeth paused. "No, I don't. Everyone I thought was my friend has gone." She remembered the parties she threw not so long ago, the lavish dos that people flocked to her house for. Luncheons, dinners, booze flowing, lobsters wasting ... After the accident, not one, save for Sadie, had come to see her. A card here and there, but not much else.

"I don't think it's a good idea for you to be *friends* with Jacob." Margie stuck out her chin. Elizabeth knew that look, that disapproving expression.

"Why not?"

Margie paused and fanned her face from the evening flies. "How long have you been off the drink?"

Elizabeth usually loved Margie's candour, but she thought the question intrusive. She twisted her mouth in annoyance. She didn't tell anyone, not even Margie, that she had been at the cabinet on a number of occasions. Only Mary knew she sometimes still sipped at Mike's scotch. At times, Elizabeth asked Mary to buy her a bottle, having put away a little extra money from the grocery budget that Mike left her. She wasn't telling Margie any of that. She didn't need a lecture. She was not getting roaring drunk as she used to. It was just a little here and there to take the edge off, those days where she felt like she couldn't take the pain anymore, not just the physical pain but the pain of being alone, of not having Mike home, of not having the children around her. No, Margie was better off in the dark. "Not since the accident," replied Elizabeth.

"Then it's better that Jacob is not your friend."

Elizabeth cocked her head. This required further explanation. "What do you mean?"

"Jacob is what you call a recovering alcoholic," said Margie. "It would do no good for you two to be more involved with each other."

"That's rich!" exclaimed Elizabeth. "You're the one who introduced us."

"Yes, to help you recover and that's it."

"I like Jacob," said Elizabeth softly.

Margie swung her head towards Elizabeth with some vehemence. "What do you mean, *like*?"

"Not like that," said Elizabeth defensively, but she wasn't so sure anymore. She looked forward to him coming over, to him helping her out of the house; she enjoyed him being a literal crutch for her. She enjoyed his gentle persistence, his whispers of 'you can do this', 'just one more step', 'well done, Elizabeth'. It was comforting, reassuring and was not designed to make her feel like a child. She felt his concern for her was genuine, her improvement a joy to him.

She saw a car drive up and all thoughts of Jacob vanished. Mike was home! How she wished she could jump out of her chair and throw herself into his arms as she used to. She felt tears well and squeezed them away. She leaned forward and raised herself off the armchair slowly. Mike had been away for four weeks this time and when he almost ran to her, she allowed herself to fall into his arms.

# Chapter 18 - Jacob

It had been six more gruelling months of recovery, months she went without seeing her children. She couldn't understand why Mike didn't bring them home for the term holidays, or just bring them back altogether.

"They are spending the holidays with Teresa," he would say without further explanation. When she pushed, he would snap at her. "You are in no position to look after them!"

With that she couldn't argue, but the children weren't babies. They didn't need to be picked up or fed or bathed, and Mary was always around, but when it came down to it, she knew she was scared to push him, to provoke the tempers that had now returned and always seemed to be brimming close to the surface. It was routine now, when she said anything untoward, for him to slap her, or shove her, always careful not to incite her injuries.

This was the time, she realised later, when she began to resent him, to realise there was no excuse of raging jealousies or flighty tempers, that his attacks were not just a loss of control, that they were controlled, calculated even. His loving attention quite out of the blue turned to annoyance, irritation at her inability to do the things she normally did, like walk up to the terrace with him or ride on the back of his motorbike. The coffees in the morning stopped and more often than not, after he returned from his working day, he went out with his friends, coming home late into the night after Elizabeth had retired to bed.

"My uniform is creased," he yelled one morning when he was running late for work. He was a punctual man, never late for anything and she knew this was what had made him agitated.

Elizabeth came out of the bathroom. "Mary ironed it last night," she said.

"Mary isn't the one who irons my clothes. You do it," he snapped.

"I was resting last night," she said. "My back ..."

"When are you going to get over that?" he replied. "It's always something. It's been months now." He shook at the shirt on its hanger.

"I'll do it now," she said, taking the shirt from him. As she reached for it, he shoved her backwards, throwing her to the floor. She fell on her hip and winced as a bolt of pain shot through her thigh.

"I'll do it myself," he said without a glance in her direction, taking the shirt to the laundry room.

Elizabeth gritted her teeth, had to hold back from retorting. A sudden shiver ran down her spine. What if her father could see her now? On all fours, succumbing to the abuse of a man he'd warned her about. How she had let her father down. She rolled to her side and leaned against the wall, bringing her knees to her head. "I'm sorry, Pa," she said softly.

"You can come to live with me," Jacob said one afternoon as they walked down the road, her on a walking stick, Jacob's arm on the small of her back.

Of course Elizabeth had thought about it. She and Jacob had become good friends and although she didn't fully explain the extent of her circumstances—to do that would be disloyal to Mike—she did have to explain some of her bruising that was not caused by the accident and he was smart enough, had seen enough to know that even though she was injured, they were not injuries caused by walking into walls and falling down a set of three steps.

She also knew by now that Jacob was in love with her and as much as she liked him, she couldn't feel for him how she felt about Mike. "I can't leave Mike," she said flatly.

Jacob didn't try to convince her. "I just want you to know that my home is always open to you. In any circumstance."

Elizabeth smiled up at him. How she wished she could love him, this kind man with hair that greyed around the nape of his neck and the sides of his face, his caring brown eyes that looked at her with love, not a carnal love but a pure love. He would care for her like a man should, would give her the world. It would be so much easier. But apart from being so irrevocably in love with Mike, there were other things to consider. Four of them. Mike would fight her for them and he would win. In this place, it wouldn't matter that she was their mother. She would lose everything that mattered to her.

"I know," she replied. "What about you, Jacob?" She changed the topic. The poor man must be sick of listening to her woes, putting up with her outbursts when she was in pain. His patience seemed unlimited.

"What about me?" he asked but she felt the tendons on his arms stiffen.

"You were a surgeon."

"A long time ago," he said and she looked at his face which held a faraway look, his brow creased, his eyes troubled.

"Tell me, Jacob. What happened?"

He heaved a heavy breath. "You may not look at me in the same way," he said with a forced laugh.

She was not going to be cut off. "You have children."

"I do," he replied and paused. Elizabeth remained silent and nudged at his ribs with her elbow, willing him to go on. He cleared his throat. "What has Margie told you?"

She snickered. "That you were a surgeon and you have two daughters."

He laughed at that. "Well, I won't bore you with the details. Yes, I was a surgeon, worked at a private hospital." His face bore no expression. "Had a wife, two beautiful daughters, adults now with families of their own, I imagine happy ..."

"You don't see them?" Elizabeth's breath stuck in her throat.

He shook his head but his countenance didn't change. He stared straight ahead. "No." He stopped.

Elizabeth remained silent. She wanted to know more but understood how hard it must be for him to tell her about himself. He was the one who was strong for her. They walked a few more steps and there was an awkward silence. "It's okay, Jacob, you don't have to go on."

He looked down at her with a sad smile and she tucked her hand through his arm. "Well, I've begun, so you may as well know it all. To cut a long story short, I couldn't cope with the stress of it all, physical stress, emotional stress. Long hours at work. I wasn't strong enough. I neglected my family." He took a breath. "I drank. A lot. Then I drank some more. Made mistakes. Lost my job. Then lost my family."

"Oh, Jacob, how?"

"Marcia could not deal with it all. She took the children to her parents in Kashmir and told me in no uncertain terms that she never wanted to see me again."

"You let them go?"

"At the time, all I could see was the destruction my life had become. I drank until I was in the gutter, quite literally." He shrugged. "Then Margie came looking for me ..."

"How long ago was this?"

"Some eight years ago," he said.

"And then?"

"Margie pulled me out, took care of me, sent me to rehab with the help of her nuns ..." Elizabeth snickered. She had seen the little band of nuns that gathered at Margie's house for prayers twice a week. Little women who were covered in white, their heads bowed to the ground at all times. Jacob chuckled. "You've met them, I see." Elizabeth nodded. "Well, they got me into a place. Set me up at an AA meeting place."

"And that's all it took?"

"Oh no, my dear," said Jacob. "It took another four years before I could completely let go of the booze; sorry for that very vulgar term, but that's what it is. It's a demon that won't let you go."

Elizabeth swallowed, realising how much she could use some of that demon right now. "But you defeated it."

"Yes, eventually," he said. "I got back on my feet, got a job at a private hospital as a physical therapist, as you well know, and the rest is history."

Elizabeth was curious. "But the alcohol, Jacob. You don't want to drink anymore?"

He guffawed. "My dear, you know how much I would kill for a drink right at this moment? But I know I can't have it. I have my life, I have my job and one day I will go back to my children and beg their forgiveness. For one more chance to be back in their lives."

"Why haven't you done that already?"

"Because I'm still not ready to face them yet."

"You're hiding." It wasn't a question.

"Yes, I guess you could call it that."

"How old are you, Jacob?"

"Now there's a question," he said. "Nearing forty."

"Go get them, Jacob," she said, swiping a tear out of her eye.

"Get them back."

"Now, after all that, would you like to see what I got for you?"

"Yes," said Elizabeth in excitement. Jacob sometimes brought her favourite *burfee* or a special lunch when he came to visit with Margie. "What is it?"

"I hope you're hungry," he said as they made their way into Margie's gate.

They were getting close, too close and she knew how he felt about her. If Mike was home, Elizabeth sometimes saw him arrive and shook her head at him. *Don't come today.* She could see his face drop and felt her heart do the same. She felt the emptiness of his absence. She looked forward very much to his weekend visits. He had been instrumental in her recovery, not just her physical recovery but her mental one as well. She was beginning to feel whole again but she knew she needed to set Jacob straight.

She mulled it over that night. She needed to talk to him, let him know that there was no chance for her to be with him. She wondered if she had led him on in any way. Perhaps she had, but she had been desperate for a friend. A friend. Was he just a friend?

"Mary," she called. "Could you please see if Jacob could come over?" Mary made a face and left the room. She knew Mary disapproved of her friendship with Jacob but Mary didn't dare say anything to her about it.

"What's the matter?" Jacob rushed in. "Are you okay?"

"I'm fine," she said and motioned to the seat beside her. She had broken hearts before. This time shouldn't be any different but she just hoped his friendship was stronger than his desire for her. "Jacob." She took his hand and saw his brow furrow.

"What is it?" His voice was a croak.

She felt ridiculous now. Imagine telling someone not to love her. He probably didn't! What vanity to think he would want her for more than friendship. She had needed him, he was there! He was a good, kind man, that's all. "Nothing," she mumbled and felt a flutter in her chest. Maybe she wanted him to want her. His eyes, as they gazed into hers, revealed his desire. Did hers show the same? She reached forward and put his head between her hands. Before she knew what she was doing, her lips were on his. He responded with such urgency, she knew she hadn't imagined anything. She pulled away.

"I'm sorry," she said.

He stood up. "No, I'm sorry." He looked about him as if searching for something. "I have to go," he said and walked hurriedly out of the room.

Elizabeth banged the sofa with her fist. How could she wreck this, this ... whatever this was? Why couldn't she have just left things alone? Now she had probably lost her friend, probably broken his heart and by the thump of her heartbeat, her own in the process. "Mary," she called and Mary materialised beside her. "Please help me to bed."

She spent a sleepless night cursing herself but to her surprise nothing had changed. Jacob was at her door at 11:00 a.m., a smile on his face, ready to take her for her walk. He didn't say a word about the incident and she didn't either, happy for things between them to return to the status quo.

# Chapter 19 – Boarding School

Elizabeth steadied herself. She needed a drink but didn't dare touch any for the past three days. Apart from the fact that Mike had been home, she was preparing to see her children and she didn't want to give Mike any excuse to leave her behind. And her head needed to be clear. How she needed a drink, just a sip to calm her battering nerves but she held off, knowing a sip or a slug wouldn't be enough. She would have to be strong on her own, let her mind and body deal with it.

After changing her clothes a number of times, she settled for a high-collared white blouse and a pair of brown flared pants.

"Come on, taxi's been waiting," Mike called with impatience. She took another look in the mirror and took a breath. She was ready. Ready to see her children.

She ached on the drive there, her back stinging from the pain, her foot in agony from being cramped in the back of the taxi. Mike wanted to surprise the children with her presence and watching his face, so animated while he talked about them, so filled with excitement, kept her mind off her pain. It was so nice to see him in a good mood, hanging on to her hand as they watched the fields of Bombay go past and into the distance. She remembered back to the day, a day very much like this one, when they were riding past some of the same fields, the day he put that ring on her finger. That day seemed so far away now, so very different. Had she known then what she knew now, would she have said yes? Would she have agreed to spend the rest of her life with him? She glanced at Mike and felt her heart depress. Yes, she probably would have.

When they arrived at the gates of St Martha, Elizabeth suddenly felt like her insides were going to fall out of her and she held on to the cuff of Mike's shirt.

"What if they don't recognise me?" she asked, her voice quivering.

"Don't be silly," he said dismissively. "Of course they will."

"Don't leave me alone, Mike."

"I'm right here," he said, patting the hand that was still clinging to his shirtsleeve. He paid the taxi driver and led her to the gates, which were opened by a woman who Elizabeth found looked quite familiar.

"Isn't that ..."

"You remember Greta? She came to our wedding." He gave Greta a warm smile and Elizabeth tried to ignore the sense of familiarity she felt move between them. "Greta, do you remember Elizabeth?"

Elizabeth smiled but she wanted to tear Greta's pretty green eyes out. She knew this was not the day for petty jealousies though and tried to stand straighter, feeling her back pinch.

"Elizabeth," exclaimed Greta and took Elizabeth's hand warmly. "Come, I'll have the children brought down." She motioned to another woman standing nearby and led Elizabeth away from Mike, who was moving in another direction, where, she didn't know. "He's going to get the boys," said Greta, as if understanding Elizabeth's hesitation. Elizabeth did not want to be separated from Mike. She needed him, for moral support, and in all honesty, for physical support. She walked slowly with Greta to what looked like a playground. How she wished she had a drink right now, how she wished she could have given her recovery another few weeks. She was not ready! What would they find? What would they remember? What ...

Then she saw them, her girls, bounding towards her, Genny's hair in pigtails, Faith's hanging loosely round her shoulders. With all the strength she could muster, Elizabeth stood upright and shrugged Greta's arm off hers. Her heart filled and she began to move towards them. Suddenly they were upon her and she fell to her knees, opening her arms for them to clamour into.

She hugged them tight, her head nestled in their hair as they cried into her ears.

"Mummy, you came."

"Mummy, I missed you."

"Let me look at the two of you," said Elizabeth and pulled them away. "Wow, who are you people? Look at how big you've become!" She really couldn't believe it. Genny was definitely taller and Faith's face had become thinner. They had changed. More than six months can do that to children. How much she'd missed!

They led her to a bench and they sat together, Genny and Faith regaling their stories of their friends, their subjects, their teachers. She wanted to ask them if they were happy, but she couldn't do it. She didn't want to hear the answer. If they were, it would mean they didn't miss her, that they could live without her and if they weren't, it would make her worry and guilt-ridden. But they seemed happy and healthy and they had each other.

Then the boys were there and there was more laughter and tears. It felt like the time went by so quickly, and too soon it was time to go home. Another eight-hour ride back to Derrum.

"Can we stay with Teresa?" she begged Mike. "Just for a night? So we can come back tomorrow? I mean, it seems so far to come for such a short amount of time."

Mike shook his head. "They aren't in town," he replied. "And I have to go on a trip pretty much straight after we get home. We will just have to go home." Elizabeth's lips quivered and she looked at him, hoping for some semblance of humanity for her plight, her not having seen her children for so long. He looked down at her forlorn face and softened. "Let's stay at a hotel."

The drive home to Derrum was sombre, Elizabeth sobbing most of the way home. They had stayed at a hotel and had gone to the school the next day, picked up all the children and took them out for the day. They went to a park, had lunch at a restaurant and when it was time to return the children, Elizabeth begged Mike to take them home with them.

"Not yet," was his only reply.

She wished she had fought harder but when Mike's mind was made up about something, it was hard to change. She used to, at times, be able to coax him into things. Not now. She sat looking out the window into the darkness, the pain in her body excruciating, but all she could think about was what Genny had said to her when they were saying goodbye.

"I'm sorry, Mummy."

Elizabeth had bent down again and looked her daughter in her tear-filled eyes. "Why?"

Genny threw her arms around Elizabeth. "For making it happen. I did it."

"What?" Elizabeth whispered. "What did you do?" She

looked at the other children who just stood there looking down at their feet. Faith shrugged.

"The accident. I did it. I cried so I made it happen. You told me it would happen and I still cried." Elizabeth could feel her six-year-old child's little body heaving against hers and felt a gush of tears spring from her own eyes.

"You didn't," Elizabeth cried. "My darling, you didn't. It was me, all me."

"No, it was me," Genny insisted and Elizabeth squeezed her daughter with all the strength she could muster.

She let the tears slide down her face again. All that time, Genny had felt responsible for the accident, had lived with the guilt of what she'd thought she'd done. Elizabeth hated herself for it, hated herself for everything she'd allowed herself to become. When Mike tried to put his hand on her knee, she grimaced. It was him too. She felt disgust for him, for them both and clenched her hands into little balls, thanking God for the pain she was in, her penance for the plight of her children.

When Mike left for his trip, two days later, two unbearable days, she caught a rickshaw and headed straight for the bar.

# Chapter 20 - Checking In

## 1981

*The driver rolled his eyes and pulled over. Always the same, he thought, annoyed at the holdup. He glanced at his timepiece dangling from the rear-view mirror and was irritated again. They would blame him; they always blamed the darkie. He peered in the mirror and looked at the woman. She was quite beautiful, her hair rising into a high bun, her cheekbones giving her an air of royalty. Anglo-Indians—they always had that look, that way of acting, like they were better than the darker people. He looked at the timepiece again and back at the woman, whose eyes were now larger, a deep crease between her brow, mascara running down the sides of her face. Even through his irritation he felt his heart soften and he pulled up the parking brake, at the same time opening the door of the van. Picking up his pack of bidis which lay on the dashboard and whistling to the little mongrel that was sitting in a towel by his feet, he headed out for a break, the grey-and-black terrier dancing behind him.*

She tried but failed. She almost made it to the gates, but her heart nearly stopped and Jacob, seeing her distress, poked at the driver to pull over.

Elizabeth clung to Jacob's chest and he whispered to her while she cried softly, blobs of mascara staining his white linen shirt. She thought she would be able to do it; she was confident that this would solve her problems. It was about time.

"Elizabeth," Margie, who was sitting in the back seat of the van with her band of nuns, yelled out to her, but Elizabeth didn't answer. *Thump, thump, thump.* Elizabeth could feel the van tremble and Margie was at her side in three large strides.

"Elizabeth," her voice boomed and Margie's face appeared, not the smiling, sweet Margie she knew and loved, but a face filled with fierce determination. "What's the matter? We're nearly there."

Elizabeth looked up from the safety of Jacob's chest and shook her head like a petulant child.

"No, don't do that! It's all set up. It won't be for long. We talked about it." Margie's clipped voice softened seeing Elizabeth's tear-streaked face. "You can do this, hun, you can and you must." She reached for Elizabeth's hand which flinched at her touch.

"But I don't think I can," said Elizabeth, looking up at her. Margie's round face bore a scowl that made Elizabeth shrink even lower into Jacob's chest.

"Don't give up now. Think about what you have lost and try to remember all you will gain from this. You can go back to your husband, your family."

At this, Elizabeth turned to Jacob, who was looking out the window trying not to interfere in this exchange. Margie had gotten to know Elizabeth well and knew of the situation at home, the physical abuse that Elizabeth had alluded to, rather than spoken of, the alcohol abuse on the part of both Mike and Elizabeth as well as the infidelity in their marriage. But she was a staunch Catholic and believed that the vows of marriage should be upheld, especially that of 'until death do us part'. There was no negotiation here. Divorce was not something Margie believed in and if Elizabeth even suggested such in conversation, Margie would shut the conversation down, bringing out her Bible and quoting her verses until Elizabeth could hear no more.

Besides, she had tried to leave him, numerous times, sneaking out of the house in the middle of the night, running from him while he showered her with words and lashes, but leaving him meant leaving the children too and even though she sometimes stayed away for a day or two, she always went back.

Knowing she had hit the right spot when she saw Elizabeth's eyes well again, Margie continued. "You can get your kids out of that school. You know what you need to do."

"I really don't think I can, Margie." Elizabeth sat up now, feeling bold, and faced Margie.

"You are a strong woman." Margie knelt down and put her face close to Elizabeth's. "It's a private hospital," she said in almost a whisper. "You will have the best care, good food. We will visit. Your family can come to see you too, if you want."

"I would never want my children to see me in that place," said Elizabeth, screwing up her face, knowing she was acting like a brat.

"Do you want to see your kids again? *Ever?*" Margie's stood up and her voice was hard again. "Because if you don't get yourself in there, you will die!" She was leaning over Elizabeth and shouting now and Elizabeth shrank back. Yes, Margie may have been soft and caring and for the last few years had tried to help by being Elizabeth's confidante, trying to find ways in which to keep the children out of that boarding school, and she genuinely wanted what was best for Elizabeth and the children, but being a teacher, she could certainly show her tough side when needed.

She looked at Jacob. "Take me home."

"Elizabeth ..." Jacob wavered.

"Please, Jacob, please take me home." Elizabeth was already shaken. She hadn't had a drink today and her nerves were shot.

"Jacob!" Margie moved closer to him.

"Margie." Jacob's eyes were pleading. Elizabeth could see he was torn between rescuing the woman he loved or sending her to rid herself of this disease. And the latter meant he would surely lose her, and forever.

"No, Jacob. We have to be strong. For her."

Jacob lowered his head, moving it from side to side and seeing him falter, the big sister act working on him, Elizabeth turned to him and grabbed his hand in both of hers. "I want to go home, Jacob. I can't go there. Not now. Just one more day. I will go tomorrow, I promise. Jacob, please."

"Elizabeth ..."

"No, Jacob, no. Take me home now." She felt her voice break.

"There is no home!" Margie was yelling. "You have no husband, you have no children. You have lost everything! This is your only chance to get them back."

"I have Jacob ..." Elizabeth said feebly.

"Jacob is not your husband." Margie didn't look at Jacob, who kept his eyes firmly on the van's dirty window. "You should be with your family, your *husband*. Mike, *that's* your husband, remember that. It is a sin what you've done. This is the only way you can get them back."

Elizabeth felt herself begin to shake, weeping now, and Jacob pulled her back to him.

The driver, having heard the whole conversation, crushed the stub of his smoke and stepped back onto the van. He looked at Jacob questioningly.

"Turn around," Jacob said.

"Still same cost," the driver replied, his eyebrows raised.

"Fine, just go back."

The driver shrugged and settled his puppy back into the towel.

Margie's footsteps were even more solid as she headed back to her seat without saying another word.

* * * *

It would be another year before Elizabeth made the same trip back.

This time was different; she was alone.

This time the place she was going to was also going to be different. This was not the Ritz as she had been promised the first time. The first time, she had money and she still had a few friends. Now she was penniless and friendless and would be admitted to the public section of the Yeruna Psychiatric Hospital, not the private, where she had been previously promised an easy stay.

But this time, she was at rock bottom, lower than she'd ever been. If her mother could see her now. Or her father! For the first time, she thanked God that her mother was far, far away and although she knew Doris would have heard stories of what was going on in Elizabeth's life, was not able to witness what her daughter had become.

The last year had certainly been the worst. More of everything, drinking, beating, infidelity; yes, Elizabeth too. She had had enough and was not going to sit by and be the good wife while Mike went away and got up to whatever he got up to. He barely tried to deny it anymore, when Elizabeth smelled the scent of a woman on him, when he went to work at the office and came home late in the night, when they went out and he disappeared with Barbara or Blanche, wives of his colleagues, friends that they sometimes entertained. She was sick of feeling like the abandoned wife, the one everyone looked at with sneers and pity. Bugger their pity, she didn't need it. She went out when he was away, to the bar, to the Derrum club, chatted with random men, strangers who made her feel more worthy than her husband did. She didn't care who saw her and raised her glass in defiance at any acquaintance who looked her way with a raised eyebrow.

She made love to Jacob once but they both knew it had been a mistake and did not speak of it again. His was a friendship she trusted in, and she knew it was foolish to risk it for the sake of feeling a loving body beside her at night.

And her children. Well, they never got out of that boarding school. Mike's job had taken them back to Bangalore, Madras, the moves too quick to bring the children home, to settle them. But they did come home for the holidays and for that period of time, Elizabeth tried not to drink as much, but once in a while she succumbed, throwing welcoming parties in celebration of their return, throwing goodbye parties the night before they were to return to school. In Bangalore and Madras, people didn't know her and she made new friends, ones with the same tastes for alcohol as herself. Mike didn't need to know about them. They visited when he was away and disappeared when he returned from his trip. Yes, she had her own life, most of which Mike didn't know about.

And yet she still couldn't stop loving him. She still wanted him more than anything or anyone and in some distant part of her mind, knew that he would come good, that he would give it all up for her, that if he did, she could give up the alcohol for him. That's what she told herself; that's what she believed. She closed her eyes in hope.

As the rickshaw neared the big white gate, she felt her heart beating its way out of her chest and willed it to stop. She looked at the driver who was tunelessly whistling a Hindi song. It was one she knew well. She wanted to sing along to try to calm her tattered nerves, but her throat was raw.

The large steel gates were opened by two men in uniform, brown cotton smocks and black shiny leather boots. As the rickshaw moved past them, Elizabeth noticed that one of each of their hands remained on the handles of their batons that were clipped to their hips. She wondered if the batons were just for show or if they used them often. She wasn't afraid of violence, she was used to that, but those batons looked menacing.

A man in a white suit, a stethoscope dangling around his neck, stood at the entrance. Elizabeth knew they would be expecting her and as the rickshaw stopped, the doctor walked towards her. She grabbed her handbag and still trembling slightly, got out. The doctor paid the driver and approached her.

"Elizabeth." Dr Patel was a little man, thin and angular, with glasses that covered most of his face. He led Elizabeth down a narrow pathway to his office. Even though it was the middle of the day, it was dim. Elizabeth expected to see patients strewn in the hallways, but there were none and she absently wondered where they were. A lone nurse walked by but didn't even glance their way. Elizabeth felt ashamed but tilted her chin upward—no one needed to know how she felt.

In his office, Dr Patel motioned for her to sit on a little stool while he took a seat in his big leather armchair. He leaned back and surveyed her.

Elizabeth, conscious that she was being assessed, looked around the room, a little square box painted the colour of vomit, without even a window. A large desk on which stood a lamp and two neatly stacked folders and the seats in which they were sitting were the only items in the room. She looked back at the doctor.

"I need a drink."

"Why are you here?" Patel asked, ignoring her words.

She hesitated. If she told him the truth right now, he wouldn't give her a drink. She could lie, just a little white lie, then after she had quenched her thirst, she would spill the beans. She just needed to take the edge off. "Well ..." She paused again.

"Admiral Dinay told me everything." So, he already knew.

"Anti-booze treatment?" she ventured.

"What is the problem?" he asked.

*Was the man mad?*

Realising what he had said, the doctor cleared his throat. He brushed his hand in the air dismissively and leaned forward. "You are admitting yourself. You need to know what is required."

*I'm admitting myself because I have nowhere else to go,* she thought, but she couldn't tell this man that. "I know," she said. She didn't know.

"You will be here for a three-month stay. You cannot leave the hospital by yourself so someone will have to check you out after the three months."

She lowered her head at that. Right now, there was no one.

"You will be put on a treatment program. You will stay in the

148

dormitory with the other women. They are here for many reasons. You are here for too much alcohol consumption, but your mental state will be evaluated. It is part of the admission process."

Elizabeth nodded.

"Did you bring clothes?"

Elizabeth shook her head.

"Give me the bag."

Elizabeth shook her head again and clutched her handbag tightly.

"Miss Elizabeth, you have to give me the bag," said Patel and moved forward, grabbing it.

Elizabeth gripped it tighter. She could beat this little man if she had to. *It's not too late,* she thought, but looking around again, she realised she was trapped. She thought about the guards at the gate with their batons. She wouldn't get past them. She released her hold on the bag and the doctor, still pulling at it, fell back. Even in her heightened state, she resisted an urge to laugh. The doctor did not think it was funny.

Patel opened the purse and immediately withdrew a flask of gin that was nearly empty. She had been taking sly swigs all the way here to keep her nerves at bay. Goshum had given it to her before she left the hotel. Patel placed the bottle on the table and upended the bag, its contents scattering on the wooden tabletop. A bottle of perfume was confiscated and anything that looked like it could be a weapon or could be a danger to her, a nail file and a lighter. She was allowed to keep her bright red lipstick after some convincing hysterics.

A nurse led her to a dormitory where she was assigned to a bed the size of a stretcher, two feet apart from another on each side. A folded grey smock was put on the bed and a pair of slippers were placed on the floor. The nurse walked away without saying anything. Elizabeth sat on the bed and leaned her head in her hands. She was hungry. But that was nothing new lately. Only yesterday, she and Goshum were pocketing leftovers from the hotel restaurant. But then they were caught. And now she was here.

She lay back on the bed and looked at the ceiling. Grey patches spread over a whitewash. Not unlike her home in Bangalore, where they now resided, her and Mike's rented three-bedroom house, where she was only a week ago.

That's where she should be, not a million miles away from home, away from her children who were still in their boarding schools. At least they were safe. She could feel her throat tighten at the thought of them. She wondered how it might have been if she had gone through with it the last time. If she had had the treatment, where would she be now? But she wasn't in any state to do it the last time. She wasn't in any state right now, but right now she had no choice.

The thought of seeing her children again strengthened Elizabeth's resolve; she could beat this devil, this drink. She had believed she could quit drinking by herself, she just needed a good reason to, and her children were everything to her, they alone were reason enough.

David, the eldest, was thirteen now. He was the responsible one, who made sure the others were looked after when she was unable to look after them herself. She could picture him now, his tongue sticking out of the corner of his mouth while he concentrated on getting the guitar chords right, while she gently encouraged him.

Robert, the rebel, always jumping into her fights with Mike. Stubborn and fiercely protective, unaccepting of strangers who came to their house when Mike wasn't home.

Faith, her loyal daughter, who stayed up with her late at night while she drank, listening to her stories, her eyes intermittently closing and her head dropping, to keep her mother company.

Genny, just eight, already in a boarding school for more than three years. Genny tried to stay awake with Faith, but her willpower was weaker.

And there was Mike. As much as he was a terrible husband, he loved her—and she knew she would never stop loving him.

Yes, she had to get her children back. They needed their mother. She may not have been a great mother so far, but she loved them, and they knew that. After all, it was about self-control. Yes, she had tried before, but not hard enough. Margie was right, she had made terrible choices, but she could get her family back; it was never too late.

She shivered. She felt so lost, so alone and so unloved.

There wasn't even Jacob anymore. He had abandoned her. Not then, like Margie had, but eventually. She thought about Jacob; he had been a loyal friend. Of course, Mike still didn't know about him, Jacob would be dead by now if he did, but whenever Mike had driven her out of her home, which in the last couple of years had been a regular occurrence, she had turned to Jacob, and he never let her down. She hopped onto a train and came back to Derrum where, under the safety of Jacob's watch, she had a drink, but he always made sure she slept it off, and then, after a few days, he sent her back to Mike, back to Bangalore. He was a kind man and Elizabeth knew she took advantage of his kindness and his love for her.

After her first failed attempt at admitting herself to the hospital, Jacob had taken her home, to his home, much to the chagrin of Margie, who washed her hands of the whole situation. Margie had stomped off the van without a word, clapping her hands together as she walked past Elizabeth. Her nuns had followed, their heads bowed. She had spent a week at Jacob's house, where she drank until she passed out. Then as usual, Jacob convinced her to go back to her family. She knew he was guilt-ridden and feeling weak for caving in to her weakness. She knew he wanted the best for her, even if that meant sending her back to her husband and her volatile marriage. He also knew she couldn't live without her children.

After helping Elizabeth to sober up, Jacob, with a hug and a promise to always be there for her, put her on a train to Bangalore and had asked Margie to send a telegram to Mike, who was to meet her at the station. Elizabeth hadn't spoken to Mike in weeks and was afraid of his reaction. Her fears evaporated when she saw the look on Mike's face as she stepped off the train.

"My baby girl," he whispered as he hugged her tightly. She knew this was home, in his arms, that this was where she should and always would be.

The children were still in boarding school and Elizabeth felt dejected when she came home to an empty house, even though Mary hovered, bowing to her and asking what she could get for her. She would go to see the children soon, Mike promised, and if things worked out, maybe they could become day scholars in the nearby Catholic school. How Elizabeth prayed that they would. She was already wondering if she could do this by herself, but with her children there, she may just have the strength.

Mike had missed her, she could see that. He showed it when he took every opportunity to hug her all evening, he showed it when he brought out the guitar and they sang their song, 'Unchained Melody', together, Mike staring into her eyes as he sang. And he showed it when he carried her to bed and made love to her.

Elizabeth loved him, she always had, and when she felt herself drift off to sleep just before dawn, she knew she had made the right decision. She had watched Mike sleep for the last few hours, resisting the urge to creep into the kitchen to find something to drink. Her shaking had stopped, she willed it to, even holding on to her clenched jaw with her hands to stop her teeth from chattering. And when sleep finally came, she welcomed it.

When Elizabeth awoke at noon, Mike was not in the house. She asked Mary, who told her that he had gone to the officers' mess, the place where pilots went to socialise with other pilots, and also do things that loving husbands shouldn't even think about. She felt a pang; she knew what that meant, but remembering last night, she forced herself not to suspect him of crimes he may not have committed. For the rest of the day, she walked around the house idly, plumping already plump pillows and fixing ornaments that seemed out of place. Eventually, she headed to the kitchen and helped Mary make dinner, trying to ignore the bottle of whisky that sat in the cabinet, smirking at her.

She shook her head at the unfairness of it. Mike was allowed to drink whenever he liked, often in front of her, but she wasn't allowed to and she resented him for it. Again, she shook her head, this time to clear away nasty thoughts. Things were looking up; she had to make an effort, a good shot of it this time.

Mike came home that evening and she knew. She couldn't explain it exactly, but she just knew. It was written all over him: the way he acted, the way he talked to her, his dismissive manner, his averted eyes. Elizabeth didn't ask him anything, he would just deny it as he always did.

"Off to bed," he announced, pushing his chair away from the table when he had finished his meal. "Early flight tomorrow."

"Oh, you didn't tell me about it. I thought ..." She thought she would spend some time with him, make plans to get their children home.

"Didn't get the chance to tell you." He leaned over and kissed her forehead. "Goodnight."

"But you haven't even packed."

"All done, Mary did it yesterday." He almost ran out of the room.

Elizabeth glowered at Mary, who was about to take away Mike's dishes. She had been with her all day and had not said a word! Mary tucked her head into her shoulders and scurried out of the room. Elizabeth sighed. How could she blame her after she could see how happy Elizabeth had been all day, carrying on about Mike and how things would be different and how they could be happy again. Mary had smiled, nodded and encouraged her.

Even through her annoyance, Elizabeth felt a little spark light up her heart. She could have a little sip while Mike was gone.

# Chapter 21 - The Year That Was

For the next year, life went on as it always had. Mike went on flights and while he was gone, Elizabeth drank. She tried to stick to her intention of having not more than a couple of drinks for the duration of Mike's absence, but a couple wouldn't even last the first hour he was gone. Soon, the neighbours would show up and the evening she began would turn into days of music, parties and drinking.

"But I miss them, Mary," she would moan when at night, the maid would try to pry the glass out of her hand.

"You will see them soon, Miss," Mary would say while she dragged Elizabeth to bed.

"Thank you, Mary," she said as Mary tucked the blanket under her chin. She grabbed her hand. "You are always there for me."

It was during Mike's second trip, when Elizabeth was drunk, she decided she was entitled to see her children. When Mike returned from his first, she had asked if he would take her to see them.

"Please, Mike," she pleaded. "It's been months."

"Maybe next time," he said. "I'm home for just a couple of days. There will be no time."

"But you see them all the time," she said. "I barely do."

"That's not my fault," he said. "I drop in when I can, when I'm stationed in Bombay."

"Can I come with you on your trip?"

He looked at her as if she was insane. "I work, Elizabeth! I'm not just gallivanting about everywhere. Someone has to bring in an income. I'm working as hard as I can."

"But the children. They are all alone ..."

"The children are fine. They're getting a good education, they have friends, they have me. Besides, Teresa goes to see them as well." He saw the expression on her face change at the mention of his sister and hastily continued. "She's there when I need her. She's helped out a lot."

"And who else?" Elizabeth snapped. She wasn't even sure what she meant by that but she felt a bolt of jealousy that other people were being allowed to visit her children while she needed to ask for permission.

"What do you mean?" His brow furrowed, his face grimacing.

"I mean, why can't they come home?" She lowered her voice.

"With you running off all the time? And you wonder why I don't bring the children back?" His voice was getting harsh now, bitter. "At least in that school, they have security, safety."

Before she could retort, he had turned on his heel and walked out. It was probably best she didn't anyway. She heard the front door slam and found her fists clenched, her heart thumping. Oh, he could make her blood boil! She should be happy that at least the children saw something of family regularly. As much as she resented Teresa for seeing her children more than she did, Elizabeth was grudgingly pleased that she looked out for them. Saint Martha's was a good school and although the boys and girls were in separate buildings, at least they were all together in the one large compound.

"Yes, I'm not a good mother," she said softly.

"You are, Miss," said Mary from the doorway and Elizabeth jumped. "But you must stop the drink."

Elizabeth was sick of everyone telling her to get off the drink. No one cared about what she wanted. Alcohol was sometimes her only friend. "Get me tickets, Mary," she said. "He leaves tomorrow. So for the day after."

"Will I be coming with you?"

"Yes, please, Mary. I can't do this by myself."

"But Miss," said Mary, a quiver in her voice.

Elizabeth understood. If Mike were to find out ... Mary loved Elizabeth, but she feared Mike more. But no, Mike couldn't stop her. Not when he wasn't around.

The twenty-hour journey was painful if uneventful, but Elizabeth was nervous. She hadn't seen her children for over two months and as the train brought her closer to them, her nervous excitement began to get the better of her. She was prepared. A flask, small enough to fit in her handbag, was intermittently sipped at. She ignored the looks of other passengers when she raised the flask to her mouth. She knew she needed it and it had to last. She also knew that

155

she couldn't appear to be drunk or Greta wouldn't allow her to see her children.

The train brought Elizabeth to the school at four-thirty in the afternoon, which meant the children would be at playtime. Without stopping at the headmaster's home, which was located beside the entrance of the school, Elizabeth almost ran into the yard and stopped uncertainly. A barrage of sounds rushed at her and she tried to peer through the masses of children of all sizes and shapes, to find her own. She needed to go to the headmaster's after all. But then through the crowd, she saw two figures bound towards her. She could already feel her knees going weak and she lowered herself onto her haunches. Her girls threw themselves at her with such force that she almost fell backward.

"Mummy, you came!"

"Mummy, you're here, have you come to take us home?"

Elizabeth just buried her head into them and tried to wipe her tears with their uniforms before they could see them.

"Where are the boys?"

"I'll go get them, they are going to be so happy," said Genny, bounding away.

"Can we come home now?" asked Faith.

"I promise, baby, very soon," she said. She looked towards the open gates and considered how easy it would be to walk out of there with all of them. Her hands shook with the anticipation of it. Jacob. She could go to Jacob, she could hide out there.

*Hide.* From what? Mike? How long would it be until he found her? And what would be the consequence? A beating? She could cope with that. But the children. He would take them away, maybe for longer this time. Maybe forever ...

"Don't cry, Mummy," said Faith, putting her head on Elizabeth's shoulder, and Elizabeth realised a tear had rolled down her cheek.

"I'm just so happy to see you," she said, nuzzling her head in her daughter's neck.

"And me too?" asked Genny who had returned.

"Yes, you too!" She tickled Genny over her ribs and pulled the laughing child onto her knee. "Look, here come the boys," she said as she saw her sons ambling towards her. She swallowed as she watched them approach, David, so tall, almost as tall as her, Robert, a twisted smile on his face, that expression he had when he was trying to play it cool but could barely contain his excitement. She opened her arms and they both fell into them.

The train ride back was sombre. There was no excitement, no anticipation—just a sense of utter desperation. Elizabeth felt like her heart was shattered, and this time there was no liquor to help her through it. Mary gently eased Elizabeth's head onto her lap and stroked it all the way home.

Home was not home without the children and Elizabeth and Mike continued their dance. He went on his flights and when he arrived home, Elizabeth reluctantly stopped drinking and the fights would ensue. They began the moment he stepped into the house and saw her with one of the neighbours or a friend. The guest would almost leap out the door, and Elizabeth would stare at Mike and then berate him for driving her friends away.

"These *gundas*! What sort of friends are these, letting you behave this way?"

"They are the only friends I have," she pled. "I'm so lonely and you are always gone."

He'd look at her incredulously. "Someone has to pay the rent. It's certainly not you."

Elizabeth barely batted an eyelid at this. It was often he blamed her for his trips away. "But Mike, you can work more from the office."

"No, I have to fly. I need to be away. It's how we can live in some comfort. It's how you can afford to have a maid, have this house."

"But ..."

He wasn't finished. "It's also how I pay the *bunya* every time you rack up the credit. It's how I pay the pawn shop to get your jewellery back. The things I get you, that you have no value for."

Elizabeth could feel her face flush, not just with embarrassment. It was true what he said. She had pawned her jewellery a number of times when she'd run out of house money and Mike had gone straight to the shop to have them returned, berating the owner for letting her put them in. But she was angry. If Mike was home more, if he paid her more attention, she wouldn't be lonely and wouldn't want to drink as much. In the back of her mind, she knew that was probably not the case but it was easier to blame Mike as much as he blamed her for everything that had happened. "I do," she replied, between clenched teeth. "I do value what you get me, but don't pretend that you can't wait to get away from here, from me."

"I have to work, Elizabeth," he said a little more gently but somehow that irritated her more.

"But you love it! You live for your work." Elizabeth knew she was trying to get a rise from him, anything for him to show some of the passion that he used to have for her. "You go everywhere, with all those sluts throwing themselves at you." She stopped, waiting for a response, waiting for him to pounce.

It never failed. With her taunting, he was usually on her in a matter of moments and she was fighting him back, biting and scratching wherever she could find a gap, while he punched, slapped and pulled at her hair. Vicious words were screamed amid a flurry of movement, arms and legs entangled, until Elizabeth lay either on the floor or on the sofa, unable to raise her head, or Mary came in and intervened, usually with a shriek or a broom.

Elizabeth sat at her mirror and brushed her hair, noticing long strands clumped together that stayed on the bristles of the brush. She stroked at her hairline, slowly receding, her hair not having the will to grow back anymore. She tried to pull at his too, but he had shorter hair, harder to grasp and his hair was thick, not a bald patch in sight. Mike loved his hair, massaged oil into it every morning, keeping it sleek and black, and thick. She smiled at the thought of his hair and scolded herself for her desire for him even after they had just been rolling around on the floor and not in the way she would have liked them to be.

She always fought back now. She had to; she wasn't going to lie down and take it anymore. She was not the only one who was in the wrong. She knew Mike was unfaithful. She heard about his dalliances and even saw things happen in front of her eyes. His affairs did not preclude her friends, or so-called friends, and his looks as well as his status was tempting to any woman. By the end of the fight, they would sometimes both have a drink and end up in bed together. Then Elizabeth would spend the next few days in misery, waiting until Mike left on his next trip to calm her nerves to feel like her life was somewhat normal.

By the end of the year, Elizabeth had gone to see her children at school a number of times and they had come home for the holidays twice and even though she knew Mike must have heard about her visits to them, either from Greta or the children themselves, he never mentioned it and she didn't either. She always vowed not to drink when the children were home, but her delight at having them around and actually having them home made her nervous as well—she wanted to be the best mother but knew she fell short; after all, they were in boarding school because of her and her inability to look after them. She tried to talk to Mike about bringing them home permanently, but he insisted they stay in boarding school for at least the next year or so, just until things were more stable at home. In other words, he didn't trust her—and if she were honest with herself, she couldn't really blame him.

But even with the children at home, Elizabeth's routine didn't alter very much. Mike would leave, drinking and parties would begin and even though they were at first reluctant, the children would join in their mother's fun, singing and chatting with her friends.

Her friends—what friends?

Elizabeth thought of the incident that had brought her here, to this place, to this prison.

A party for her thirty-second birthday had been impending and the week before, a few of her friends had visited her. They had been asking her what she would like as gifts and she refused to help them out. She didn't want anything from them, she was just excited about the party and having people around. Her children were back at school and she was lonelier than ever without them.

Blanche, who she'd suspected was in the middle of another fling with Mike, commented on her belly, which was a little bloated that day. "Are you pregnant?" Blanche blurted.

Elizabeth was taken by surprise and breathed in, holding her stomach tight. *How does one respond to a comment like that?* She wasn't sure if she should be angry or pleased that Blanche considered that she still had relations with her husband. "Yes," Elizabeth said laughingly and leaned forward conspiratorially. "That's what the party really is for, it's not for my birthday. To make an announcement." She watched their faces, especially that of Blanche who raised her eyebrows in distaste.

There were oohs and aahs from the little group and Elizabeth heaved a sigh of satisfaction. *Serves them right*, she thought, feeling quite clever for throwing them off track. They could have their little gossip, but she would have the last laugh. Only when it was too late she found out what a mistake she had made.

The party went well, with Mike even allowing Elizabeth to have a little drink, although he seemed to be watching her in a strange manner all evening, his eyebrows furrowed, his cheek dimpled from the twist of his mouth. Towards the end of the night, when the first of the guests was about to leave, Mike clinked his glass loudly and gestured for Elizabeth to come to him. The room quieted and all eyes turned to them. Elizabeth felt her heart race and grabbed the hand that was held out to her by him. She didn't know what Mike was up to, but it was her birthday and on occasion, he could come up with some really nice surprises. Two years before, he had bought her a hand-made shawl from the Middle East, her name embroidered in a pattern above the hem.

"Just an announcement," Mike began. "I wanted to thank you all for coming to celebrate tonight." There was a burst of applause and he waited for it to die down. "Tonight we celebrate Elizabeth's birthday ..." He looked at her and his face was not smiling anymore. "But this is also a farewell party." He raised his glass, turning to Elizabeth as he did. She looked at him in confusion. Was he going away again? "Surprise," he whispered in her ear. He turned back to his guests and continued. "A sad goodbye to Elizabeth, who will be going away for a while, back to Derrum."

Elizabeth just stared, her mouth agape.

"Her family needs her there and she promised to go," Mike continued and even though she tried to pluck her fingers from his grasp, he clutched them more forcefully. "So this is your chance to say goodbye tonight, because you will miss her ... as I will too."

He planted a kiss on Elizabeth's forehead while her friends rushed around to question her. Elizabeth just stood there, surrounded by people, her eyes staring blankly ahead, her body numb. "Just for a while," she croaked out to the waiting guests. "I don't know why Mike is spoiling me!" She tried to smile and lifted her glass as Mike dumped her hand and strode away from her and she watched as he disappeared into the garden, a knot forming in the pit of her belly.

She couldn't get Mike by himself all evening and when all the guests had gone home, having filled up on laughter and booze, Elizabeth found him in the study, packing his attaché case. She put her glass on the table with a thwack, ready for a confrontation, but he was clearly ready.

"The train is at eleven in the morning. You will be on it. Go to Derrum, go stay with your relatives there for a while. They can take care of you. Your mother can send for you. You can go to Canada, or else, do what you want; I'm done, I'm washing my hands. Either way, Dimple is expecting you, I sent her a telegram." He pulled out a one-hundred rupee note and shoved it in her hand. "I'm off. I won't be back for a couple of days. You won't be here when I get back." With that, he clicked down the lid of the case, turned on his heel and walked out of the house, leaving Elizabeth staring at his disappearing figure, her mouth agape.

Mary took Elizabeth to the station the next morning and touching her feet as she stepped on the bus, she turned around and left. She wasn't coming with her. As much as Mary cared for Elizabeth, she knew where her bread was thickly buttered. She knew Elizabeth couldn't give her what Mike could, and Elizabeth understood. One needed to live and Mary had a village of people to send her pay home to.

# Chapter 22 - Goshum and Other Things

*When she got the telegram from Mike, Dimple was not pleased one bit. She was not happy about taking Elizabeth in. It would ruin her name. Elizabeth was not someone who one would want to socialise with, not anymore. Those days were gone. If Sadie, that silly niece of hers, wanted to say kind things about Elizabeth, that was her problem, but she didn't have to put up with it. And being ordered by Mike to take her in! Who did he think he was? Why did she agree? In her heart of hearts she knew why. She didn't want any problems. She didn't know Mike well enough but she knew he could be stubborn, had a temper, everyone knew that. What if he decided to enquire about Elizabeth's parents' house? What if he decided to fight for it so Elizabeth would have somewhere to stay? Dimple was in a quandary. She did not want to be saddled with that drunkard. She would have to let her stay. And she was family. What would it look like if she didn't take her in? But she was certainly not going to put up with any of her crap, that was for sure.*

Elizabeth was still in a daze when she reached Derrum; she hadn't really had time to process what had happened and had such a hangover, she had not remembered to take a bit of the hair of the dog with her for her trip. Which was fine because she slept through most of it anyway.

Her aunt met her at the station and took her to her house, the same house in which Elizabeth had been born, had spent her childhood. She had been brought up in that house, it should have been hers. But as the rest of her family had gone to Canada and she had been living around the country with her husband, moving from place to place, her aunt had taken it over. She looked around and saw paintings that her father had created lovingly and patiently; on the mantel was a sculpture carved in wood, a miniature panther. She moved towards it and let her fingers slide over it. She felt a pang of nostalgia and missed her father terribly, the only man who had ever stood up to her husband.

Her aunt was irritated, Elizabeth could see that, her pursed mouth making that quite plain. Dimple didn't want to be laden with this woman, whom everyone in town knew about. Elizabeth had created quite a reputation for herself. From a rebellious teen to the success story, by marrying a most eligible bachelor, to the drunk, the alcoholic, to losing her children. She had done it all and was gossip fodder for everyone in town, even those she used to consider her closest friends and family.

"Why are you here?" It was the first thing Dimple said the moment Elizabeth had put her suitcase down.

"I don't know, Mike told me to come. He said you were expecting me." Elizabeth shrugged.

"Yes, because he told me to take you." Dimple didn't mince her words. Her next sentence shocked Elizabeth. "Are you pregnant?"

"What? No!" Even in her haze, Elizabeth found that shocking.

Dimple put her hands on her hips and narrowed her eyes. "Don't lie to me."

"I'm not!" Elizabeth was indignant, unsure whether it was what Dimple said or how she said it that made her blood boil.

"Well, your husband thinks you are. And he knows it's not his."

"I need a drink." Elizabeth sat down, barely comprehending what her aunt was saying. She was tired. Not just physically but of everything.

"You can't drink when you're here." Dimple remained standing.

"Aunty, please," Elizabeth pleaded.

"No, that's the end of that." Dimple was tough. Elizabeth never really warmed to her, even as a child, when Dimple would spend time at their house sucking up to her mother, and when her family had left, Dimple had little time for her. Except when, of course, she had come over to take what she could from Elizabeth when parcels were sent from Canada.

"Then I can't stay here." Elizabeth stood up.

"Good, then don't," Dimple said and picking up Elizabeth's suitcase, placed it on the doorstep. She then shoved Elizabeth out the door, closing it behind her.

Elizabeth lifted her suitcase and with her head held high, walked to the nearest park bench where she sat down, trying to work out what was going on and why Mike would think she was pregnant. Then it clicked. Blanche! She must have told Mike about their conversation. Elizabeth slapped her forehead. How stupid of her. But Mike, why would he think that it ...?

It dawned on her then—they hadn't been intimate with each other for a little while, which meant he suspected an affair and between the drinking and the fights ... and affairs ...

"Well, bugger him," she said aloud, anger and frustration shaking her body.

She picked up her suitcase and walked to her cousin Sadie's home, but after waiting for an hour at her doorstep, she realised that she wouldn't be returning home anytime soon. Sadie's mother lived in Goa and she was probably visiting with her as she often did. Sadie had her own life now, two children to contend with. Elizabeth couldn't just stand here at her door.

She thought she would try her old drinking buddy, Sandra, but after knocking at her door a few times, she saw the movement of the curtain in the window and realised that nobody in this house would be welcoming her in.

She got the same treatment from a couple of other friends and cousins and some even boldly told her they had no room or time for her. These were people Elizabeth had grown up with, people who had clambered to be her friend not so long ago, the same people who came flooding to see her and pluck at the booty she had been sent from her family in Canada. She had always let them take whatever they eyed, knowing that these people rarely got to have what she did. Even Margie, who she would have trusted with her life, wasn't around anymore; she had finally taken up residence at a convent in Delhi.

As it began to darken, Elizabeth sat on the side of the road to consider her next move. She was tired and hungry, but most of all, she needed a drink.

Jacob! Elizabeth picked herself up and hailed a rickshaw.

She arrived at Jacob's home at close to one in the morning. A sleepy Jacob opened the door, but Elizabeth could tell he was not happy to see her, even through his smile, wan and tired. The last time she saw him was when he put her on a train back to Bangalore a year ago and she hadn't been in touch with him since. But he was a kind man and she knew he wouldn't let her down. He let her walk into his arms.

After spending the night in Jacob's bed, while he slept on the sofa, Elizabeth awoke to find him sitting in an armchair in the corner of the room, gazing at her. He motioned to a cup of coffee that sat on the bedside table and even though she would have preferred it were vodka or gin or even wine, Elizabeth gratefully drank from it. She had had two drinks the night before and Jacob had told her that enough was enough. Elizabeth hadn't protested too much; she was exhausted from an evening traipsing her old neighbourhood.

"I've booked you into a hotel on Main Street for a week."

Elizabeth looked at him in surprise.

"It's all I can do. It's paid for, so you don't have to worry about the money. I can give you ..."

"I don't want your money!"

"From what you told me last night, you don't have much to survive the week."

"The week?"

"You need to go back to him, explain that it was a misunderstanding. He will understand."

"You don't know him," said Elizabeth, almost to herself.

"What do you want to do?" Jacob was not smiling. He leaned forward.

"I don't know ... stay here for a while, until ..."

"Until what, Elizabeth?" Jacob's gentle voice made Elizabeth feel guilty, and she didn't answer. "I can't be your halfway house anymore. My heart can't take it anymore."

Elizabeth looked at Jacob, her eyes wide, and he laughed a small gurgling laugh.

"You're not a stupid woman. You know I've loved you from the moment I met you. I am your friend, but I can't take you coming into and going out of my life whenever you and Mike have problems, which is more often than not."

Elizabeth stared down at her coffee at this. She knew how Jacob felt, but thought he had settled on friendship. She began to understand.

"I'm sorry, Jacob. I never meant to be a burden."

Jacob came to her and sat next to her on the bed. He took

her hand. "You've not been a burden. I just don't have the capacity to do this anymore."

"Do what?" Elizabeth could already feel this friendship slipping away.

"Watch you do this to yourself. Again and again." Jacob stroked her hand. "Go back to Mike. Leave Mike, go back. It just goes around in circles. You know you will go back. I know you will too. And I cannot be the one to watch you drink yourself to death. Because that's exactly what you're doing."

"What will I do after the week?"

Jacob laughed, a hearty laugh that held no humour.

"You go back to him. Spend the week on your own. Mike would have cooled off by then and you can go back. As much as I hate to say it, I know you still love him."

After Elizabeth had bathed and dressed, a rickshaw was called and Jacob, with a hug that said this would be his last, put her in it. He gave the driver the address and paid for it. He knew Elizabeth wouldn't take his money, so that's all he could do for her. As the rickshaw bumped away from Jacob, Elizabeth looked back to see him turn slowly and walk back into his house, running his hand through his hair. She shut her eyes tight and turned back around. She would find a way to make it right with him. Margie too. They had been so good to her.

But go back to Mike? After a week? Elizabeth realised that Jacob didn't know Mike very well at all, even after all she had told him, which by now was almost everything. She needed to get her head together before she made her next move and what that would be, she didn't know. She had a week to figure it out.

At the Hotel Raj, Elizabeth felt lost. After putting her suitcase on a chair, she sat on the bed in her room and looked around at what was to be her abode for the next week. It was a pretty nice place, the bed was soft and clean, the curtains on the window plush, shutting out the harsh afternoon sun. There was even a silver bowl in the middle of the round dining table, with little gold chocolates. She knew Jacob was no scrooge. But now what? Stay holed up here for a whole week? Elizabeth still had the money that Mike had given her and knew it would need to last for a while, but one-hundred rupees was not much. As always, with a soft, "God will provide", she headed to the liquor store.

She sat in the foyer of the hotel, sipping at her gin, and rested her head on the lounge. It had only been a couple of days since she left her home, but it felt like a long time ago. She began to relax, feeling the familiar liquid flow down her throat. Before it could take effect, she was already feeling better; she felt hope, things were not so bad. She would get through this part too. She watched people come in and out of the large sliding doors, businessmen, families. Her heart caught in her throat when she saw a young girl around the same age as Genny, hanging on to her mother's hand. She could feel the tears start to well and quickly turned away. She had to get them back. She took a swig of gin.

Her eyes fell on a well-dressed Anglo-Indian man who seemed to be hovering about without much purpose. At first, Elizabeth was amused as she watched him move quickly between pillars, his eyes darting about; he was clearly avoiding the staff, particularly the concierge, who was alert, his head turning with oddly sudden movements. Elizabeth realised that this man was more than just a beggar—apart from his apparel, which she admitted looked slightly grubby, his posture was perfect, and he had something cheeky in his eyes.

"Sir," called Elizabeth to the concierge, who looked annoyed at his detective work being interrupted, but when he set eyes on Elizabeth, he put on a smile and came over to her.

"Yes, madam?" he said with a small bow of his head.

"I think those people at the elevator are having some trouble," she said, pointing to a man and woman who looked a bit lost. The concierge looked over to where Elizabeth was pointing and nodded.

"Thank you, Madam," he said, his vacant expression unchanging, and walked swiftly towards the couple.

Elizabeth smiled at the man who was now observing the exchange and he grinned sheepishly back and looked towards the elevator, which the concierge was stepping into with the couple. He grinned again and moved to where Elizabeth sat.

"Goshum," he said holding out his hand.

"Elizabeth."

Elizabeth liked Goshum immediately. He was funny, smart and his swarthy looks could more than rival that of Amitabh Buchchan, one of the greatest and most handsome Indian actors. She learned that he was down on his luck and was living on the street, having been thrown out of his house by his wife three weeks earlier. He spent his days sneaking into the hotel foyer and staying there at night, avoiding the staff, until he was eventually discovered and thrown out again. Then he would swap to another hotel that was more than five kilometres down the road, a little less swanky, until the same happened and then he would return.

"It keeps life interesting," he said with a laugh.

Elizabeth formed a friendship with Goshum and shared some of her food with him. An alcoholic like herself, he also shared her gin and she was soon out of money. Eventually she didn't even have money to buy food which would usually be fine as she barely ate when she was having a drink but being sober, particularly after coming off a binge, made her hungry and she wandered about during the day wondering how she was going to eat. It was only day two.

"I got this," said Goshum. He was crafty, had his own way of filling his stomach. Watching patrons in the large dining hall leave after their meal, he would rush in and grab their leftovers, buns, chapattis and sometimes even a piece of steak. Then he would dash outside the hotel where Elizabeth would be waiting and the two of them would feast on their meal. Even though Elizabeth ate the food feeling like it was the best thing she'd ever tasted, once her belly was sated, she felt disgusted with herself. She knew she had sunk low before, but this was a completely new level. She even began to help Goshum retrieve food after diners had left their tables, and the both of them became somewhat a tag team of food theft. It was on the fourth morning of her stay that she was caught and together with her suitcase, tossed on the street again—she was back to square one.

"Where will you go?" Goshum asked.

"I have no money left. I have no place to stay." Elizabeth was not feeling sorry for herself anymore, she had left that feeling behind a long time ago.

"You could go back to your husband," said Goshum.

Elizabeth shook her head. It was too soon, she knew that much. Besides, she had never seen Mike so cold. Ranting and raving, maybe, hitting her, sure, walking out in a fury, sometimes, but the icy way in which he left her was something she hadn't seen before. She didn't even know how to react to it at the time, it was so out of character for him. "I can't," she said.

"You need help," said Goshum. "I want to help you but I

don't know how to do that."

"I don't either," she said, her eyes creased, trying to think. She could telegram her mother, perhaps she could send her some money. No she couldn't do that. She never wanted her mother to know her situation. Besides, how could she ask her mother for money when she knew her mother was working hard to live in a country that was so expensive? And how long would that money last with her? It would buy a few days of alcohol and then what? But even a few days of ...

A realisation began to sink in. It was the alcohol. Here she was, destitute, hungry and yet dying for a drink. She had lost her family and friends and everything in the world she cared about. But she had her faith and she was not going to give up now. She understood the problem more clearly now and was determined not to let it beat her. How she wished she had gone through with it the last time. Where would she be today? Maybe with Mike still, but also with her children. Maybe she could have gotten a job even; she had helped Margie teach in the kindergarten, perhaps she could be doing that again?

She could be something. If she could beat this thing, she could be someone again, someone her children, and even Mike, could be proud of.

She had no choice but to be cured of this disease. She wracked her brain to think of whom she could go to for help and suddenly remembered Admiral Dinay. He now worked at the military hospital in the psychiatric department. Perhaps she could ask him to be admitted there until she could work out what to do. She remembered the man, a burly, but caring man. Mike had sent her there a couple of years ago to get her help for her drinking. Dinay had spoken to Elizabeth and then asked to speak to Mike. Mike was having none of it.

"Why does he want to talk to me? I'm not the mad one!" he declared and had flatly refused to see him.

Elizabeth laughed cynically as she related the incident to Goshum.

"You must go to him," said Goshum. "He seems like a good man, a kind man."

"Yes, I think so too," said Elizabeth, still wrestling with her decision to banish alcohol from her life. She felt like she would be killing her fifth child, her love of the bottle, but rather that than lose the rest.

"Then you must go. He will help you."

Elizabeth nodded.

"Wait here," said Goshum and Elizabeth waited, sitting on her packed suitcase outside the hotel.

In half an hour he was back with a brown paper bag.

"This will be your farewell to alcohol," he said and shoved the paper bag and a two-rupee note in her handbag. "For bus fare," he said. "And don't ask where that came from." He chortled. "And this is goodbye from me too," he said and hugged her.

# Chapter 23 - Hotel Yeruna

Elizabeth was dropped off at a bus stop, some several kilometres from the hospital as that's all her fare would allow. After getting directions from the driver, she made her way to the hospital on foot. It was a long walk and she had abandoned her suitcase on the side of the road along the way. At the gate, she smoothed back her hair and wiped away smudges around her eyes. She was glad she had put on fresh jeans and a flowered top this morning. She lifted her chin and pressed on the buzzer.

Admiral Dinay was in and his face registered surprise at the sight of her but he covered it with a welcoming smile. He ushered her to his office, where he indicated for her to tell him what brought her here. She sat on an armchair and could barely face him but she took a deep breath. There could be no shame now. She needed his help.

"There's something wrong with me," she said after she related her situation.

"Nothing is wrong with you, not mentally, and I'm not sure what I can do to help," he said, sitting back in his chair. Elizabeth felt her heart drop. He suddenly leaned forward. "Wait here." He left the room and Elizabeth fidgeted with her fingers, waiting for him to come back. Now what? What would she do if he couldn't help? Not a few minutes later, Dinay returned and sat back down in his chair. He smiled, a hopeful smile. "So, at Yeruna, they are trying an anti-booze treatment that may be helpful. You would have done well to stay the first time. But you can still go there. The public section is free, so they will admit you. If you agree, I can call them now and they will look after you." He picked up the telephone and dialled, speaking in Hindi. Elizabeth understood a little of what he was saying and twisted the sleeve of her blouse while she waited, hoping that they would take her and somewhat hoping they wouldn't. Dinay hung up the phone and smiled.

Putting her into yet another rickshaw and wishing her luck, he bade her goodbye.

Now as she stared at the ceiling, her thirst growing with each passing moment, she was wishing she had been sneakier. She could have stuck the bottle of gin under her coat. They had let her keep her coat. Sure, there was only a swig or two left, but it would have been enough to calm her nerves for a little while longer.

"God! Help me!" she cried and threw herself back on the cot. Her life in prison had begun.

That it was hard to get used to was an understatement. Elizabeth never got accustomed to the place in the four months she remained there. The treatment, which consisted of medication taken with large amounts of alcohol, was designed to make the recipient sick. This treatment was given to Elizabeth each week and she was violently ill each time, but the moment she felt better, the first thing she thought about was how much she needed a drink. She harboured thoughts of escaping and looked around for any weak links, a window ajar, a nurse's head turned the other way, and then she always thought about the guards with their batons at the gate.

She thought about her children often too, her children languishing in boarding school because of her and the guilt she felt about that nearly consumed her. Every time she considered any possibility of escape, the thought of her children steeled her resolve and she put her mind to making her stay here as pleasant as possible.

Elizabeth became popular with the patients. Always having time for them—really, she had nothing but time in there—she would read them stories from the Bible, which was given to her by a visiting missionary, embellishing and creating worlds to which they could escape, at least for a while. Most evenings, during down time, she could be found on her bunk, with a variety of patients, from schizophrenics to alcoholics like herself, gathered around her while she explained stories patiently to them.

One young woman in particular, just eighteen years of age, had become very close to her and very rarely left her side. Nanda, shapely figured with a round face and big green eyes, seemed as normal a person as Elizabeth had ever met.

"Why are you here?" Elizabeth eventually asked her one day.

"I'm a nympho," Nanda replied, quite matter-of-fact.

"Oh." Elizabeth was a little confused. She had watched for some sort of odd behaviour and so far had not noticed anything. She wondered what a nympho actually did to be admitted here.

It was the day after that when the doctor, an older man of around fifty, Elizabeth guessed, had come into the dormitory, that Elizabeth understood. Elizabeth had been sitting with Nanda, helping her with reading from a children's book and Nanda was spelling out the letters one by one. It was an arduous task and time consuming but in here, Elizabeth had nothing but time and as she was on a reprieve from the treatment, she needed something to fill it.

Nanda, upon seeing the doctor enter, rose from her bed slowly and spread her arms out in the manner of an eagle's wings. Then she strutted towards the doctor like she was on a catwalk, winking at him as she walked past. Once past, she turned around and did the same again; this time, she didn't wink, she very deliberately lowered her gown to expose her breasts. The doctor didn't flinch. He called to one of the patients and turned to walk out. Nanda flounced behind him and beating him to the door, stood with her back against the wall and put her hand out, blocking his exit. All the while, her eyes fluttered while with her spare hand she caressed her breasts. The doctor gently removed her hand from the doorway and walked out. It was like a switch had been turned off. Elizabeth watched, mesmerised, as Nanda pulled up her gown to cover her breasts again and walked back to where Elizabeth, whose jaw had dropped, was sitting and picked up the book. "More reading?" she asked and Elizabeth dumbly nodded.

Elizabeth thought about the episode that night as she lay in bed, listening to the moans of other patients, something she was now used to. She understood Nanda's obsession and in the same way she could see that was what she was doing with alcohol. She was a different person when drinking, craving things—company, love and attention. When sober, though, all she craved was the liquor, which would again turn her into that person. It was a vicious cycle, but the freedom she felt when drinking was unlike anything else. She closed her eyes and willed sleep to come to her. This nightmare would end more quickly if she was unconscious more often. Hopefully it would all be worth it.

"You are losing too much weight," Dr Patel said when she went to see him for her weekly check-up. She realised that other patients were not afforded the luxury of a check-in but she gathered that by now, Patel knew her connections and was therefore taking an interest in her wellbeing.

Elizabeth nodded. She didn't like the man, had still not forgiven him for taking away her last drop of gin. She plucked at the skin on her arm. "Yes, I guess I have lost some weight."

"That will not do any good," he said.

"I throw up," she said, staring at him in defiance.

"Yes, that's the treatment," he replied.

*How do you expect me to put on weight?* She looked at him, incredulous. The man talked in riddles. Either that or he was just a nut himself! "Isn't that what the treatment is supposed to do?" Elizabeth raised an eyebrow.

Patel cleared his throat, again realising what he had said. "Well, you have to keep food down. Too much weight loss is not good either."

Elizabeth shrugged and left his office, wondering why he even bothered to see her. But he was right. The food was awful and as hungry as she felt, she couldn't bring herself to eat any of it. Even the scraps she and Goshum collected were better than the food they served here. She would sit back and watch the other women gobble their food down and when they had finished, they would look at her untouched meal. She would nod and one or more of them would reach out to grab at it. They wanted it more than her and she was more than happy to share what she received. There were times when Elizabeth was called to the doctor's office and she would receive a parcel that had been opened. The parcels would usually be snacks, sent from Admiral Dinay, but she also received Chinese takeaways from her cousin Sadie, who clearly knew where she was. By now, most of Derrum would know where she was.

Right now, she didn't care.

It was two months into her stay when Elizabeth became violently ill. The vomiting wouldn't cease and she felt like her insides were being ripped out of her through her throat. She lay in bed, heat coursing through her veins one moment and icy jabs all over her skin the next. There were minutes, hours, days, she couldn't remember, could never recollect about that time. What she did remember was being in an hallucinatory state, muttering incoherent words. She could hear what she was saying, but they weren't the same words that were in her head.

*Maybe I'm going mad, maybe I belong here.* Elizabeth became worried that she was becoming like the people around her.

Perhaps she had been spending too much time with her fellow patients, they had rubbed off on her. *Maybe I've been mad all along?*

Delirium, that was the word given to her much later in her life, but that didn't help her then. After a few nights in which nurses came in constantly to stop her from screaming, she was put into a private room to be observed.

"Mrs D'Souza." She felt a prod at her arm. The voice was familiar and with as much effort as she could muster, she tried to turn her head. "No, Elizabeth, rest," said the voice and she let herself relax in exhaustion.

Elizabeth sat on her bed in a lone room. Her body was weak, her stomach cramping, but she was feeling better, her head clearer. She tried to remember her life, her children, Mike and almost cried with relief when she realised she did. She had not lost her mind after all! It made her miss them all so much but at least she wasn't crazy. She had eaten a full meal, some brown rice with dhal, but it was one of the tastiest she'd ever had. She heard a knock on the door and looked up to see Admiral Dinay poke his head through the door. She knew that voice sounded familiar.

"You're awake," he said.

"Hello," she said, her throat sore with the words.

"How are you feeling?" he asked and sat himself down on the chair beside her bed.

"I really don't know," she said, coughing.

"No, no. Don't speak. It's good to see you up."

"What are you ..."

"No, I said don't speak. You need to rest everything, even your voice."

Elizabeth's eyebrows creased in confusion.

"Dr Patel called me a few days ago. He ... um ..." Dinay paused and Elizabeth nodded her head for him to continue. What was going on? She was beginning to feel a rush of worry now.

"Nothing to worry about now," he said quickly. "But ..." He paused again and seeing her eyes narrow, hurried on. "You were inadvertently given the wrong medication. Which made you sick. It also explains the hallucinations, the shivers, the fevers. It took a couple of days for them to work out what happened." He put his hand over hers and Elizabeth realised that her eyes had widened and that her fingers were clutching tightly at her bedsheet. "But they realised in time," he said. "You will be fine. Back to normal in no time."

When Admiral Dinay left the room after consoling her and telling her he could check on her more often, Elizabeth rested her head on her pillow in wonderment. She didn't know what to think anymore. Where was she? How did she get here? This place was supposed to cure her, not kill her!

Elizabeth was nursed back to health, at least to as healthy as she had been previous to that episode, and she was force-fed to make her gain weight. But at night, she would convulse and awaken to find herself being held down by nurses. This became a regular occurrence and the nurses, toughened by experience, did not have the time or energy to sympathise with her. They would throw her back on the bed once they were sure she wasn't going to die.

The day Elizabeth was informed of her fate, in the small office of Dr Patel, she became hysterical.

"What do you mean?" she cried.

"Electroconvulsive therapy. It's fairly standard these days," said Dr Patel, clearly nervous at having to break the news. No one wanted to hear they would be getting an electric shock through their brain. "It's shock treatment," he reiterated, looking at her horrified face.

"I know what it is!" she cried. "No!" She was terrified. She had heard horror stories, the pain, the damage to the brain. She'd also heard some of the noises that emanated from the treatment room and didn't want to think about what happened in there.

"Elizabeth," said Dr Patel in what he thought was a calming tone.

"No!" she shouted and stood up. She saw him signal to a nurse who was standing at the door for situations such as these. She looked around her and seeing a pen on his desk, grabbed it and brandished it in front of her. "Stay away from me!"

A guard who had suddenly materialised grabbed her from behind. The screams were piercing and she knew they came from her, but she couldn't see anything anymore. She had kicked and punched everyone as they tried to take hold of her. Then she saw the batons, two of them that were held in the air and the view was suddenly clear. With one swift blow, her weapon had fallen to the floor and she felt a searing pain on her forearm. They were upon her then and the last thing she remembered was a fog that clouded over her eyes.

Elizabeth woke up alone in a dimly lit room. She knew she was in isolation from the state of the walls, fingernails still stuck on the bricks from previous patients who had tried to escape or had gone mad. As she tried to haul herself off the cot she was on, she found she was unable to move her arms. Looking down she saw that she wore a straightjacket and tried to move about but she couldn't. She could feel panic rise again and she struggled with all her might, screaming as she did, but also knowing that no one would come. She lay back on the bunk and prayed.

Two days later she was released from her jail. With a nurse holding her up, she followed the guard to Dr Patel's office, where she was told that the procedure would be taking place the next day. She nodded, resigned to her fate and was given a parcel that was delivered. She sat on her bunk and shared the *biryani* that Sadie had brought for her with her friends.

*This may be my last supper.* Elizabeth took in a deep breath. She was damned well going to enjoy it.

By morning, Elizabeth had worked herself up again and when the nurses came to collect her, they had to drag her kicking and screaming to the therapy room. She could feel herself losing control again and screamed at the top of her lungs.

"Help me, Jesus!"

In that moment, she felt a tranquillity take over her body and her mind was suddenly peaceful. All the panic, the thoughts that crowded her brain, the terror, the confusion suddenly drained out of her. She stopped walking and struggling and when the nurses tried to take her arms again, she held still. She looked at them calmly. "Please take your hands off me. I will go with you."

The faces of the nurses registered shock. Elizabeth could see that they had never seen anyone go willingly to the treatment room before. They always expected a fight and they always got it. They released Elizabeth tentatively and she walked into the room, lifting herself up on the table and lying down. Just before she closed her eyes, she saw the expression on Dr Patel's face. His jaw had dropped.

Not many words Elizabeth could think of could describe what it was like. But the word *horror* came pretty close. There was no anaesthesia, as she thought there may be, and although it lasted less than fifteen minutes, Elizabeth was awake for only a few moments before she passed out when it felt like her brain had been squeezed out of her skull. She knew that no feeling could be as exquisitely barbaric as this.

It would be another two months that Elizabeth would remain in Yeruna hospital. The anti-booze treatment was supposed to be administered for three months, but she was there for four. Feeling well and still craving a drink, her time was done at three, but there was no one to release her to. She was not allowed to leave on her own, a caregiver was required to sign her out, and who that may be, she didn't know.

No one came. Not even Margie. Not even Jacob.

One rainy afternoon, while playing a board game with Nanda and a couple of other patients, she was called to Dr Patel's office. She thought it was odd because she hadn't been summoned there since before her treatment. In fact, she had seen the man no more than a handful of times when he came into the games area to summon a patient. He always kept his eyes off her.

Upon entering the little room, her eyes fell on Mike sitting on the same stool that she had sat on when she was admitted. He looked at her and she saw his face crumple. He stood up and his eyes filled with tears.

Elizabeth stood still at the door, staring at him, her heart beating fast but not knowing what she should do. She knew what she looked like. She could feel her fragility and by the look on his face, she knew he could see it too. Her cheekbones jutted out of her cheeks and her collarbones seemed to have a life of their own, independent to her body. Mike moved slowly towards Elizabeth and gathering her in his arms, he wept on her shoulder. Elizabeth stood unmoving for a moment, but against her will, she encircled her arms around him and wept too.

The doctor stepped out of the room, closing the door behind him.

It was some months later, Faith told her one day, when they had come home for the holidays, their father had gathered them together and had asked them if they wanted their mother back. His question was met with a mix of pleading and screams of excitement and it had made his decision.

She had been home for three months. Her children were pulled out of boarding school to attend school as day scholars and Elizabeth was finally happy. She had her children with her and her husband back, Mike as affectionate as he was when they were first married. She had put on weight and was feeling healthy. She read her Bible often and attended AA meetings regularly. But the devil was never far from her thoughts and she pushed temptation back with all her heart and mind. Her life right now was worth it. She was going to make this work. It was a small concession for everything she'd gained.

It was a sunny afternoon when she waited at the gate for her children to return home from school. Mrs Slattery, the neighbourhood gossip, an older woman whose hair seemed to be perennially in rollers, strolled over to her to tell her something important. She knew better than to listen to gossip, but Elizabeth didn't know how to get rid of her.

"But I'm just letting you know," Mrs Slattery finished, after relating a tale about Mike being seen at the officers' mess with another woman the week before. "It's taken a while to tell you because I didn't know if it was the right thing to do." She put her hand over her heart, a look of distaste on her face. "But I think you have a right to know," she said before walking away.

Elizabeth held her head high and nodded slightly, but her throat was tight. When Mrs Slattery was out of sight, she walked into the house.

"Mary," she called. "The children will be home soon but I'm going out for a little while."

Mary shook in fear, knowing what that meant, and knowing that she would have to deal with Mike when he found Elizabeth gone. But all her begging, pleading and hand kissing were ignored.

Elizabeth picked up her purse and going back out into the street, she hailed a rickshaw.

"Where to, madam?" said the chipper driver.

"Ryder's Tavern, please."

# Chapter 24 - Daddy's Home

*The sputtering woke her. A car idling.*

*Genny looked over at Faith, who was making a soft gurgling sound in the bed next to hers. She hadn't heard it, but Faith could sleep through almost anything. She was going through puberty, which she thought gave her licence to do whatever she wanted, including sleeping until all hours. It probably didn't help that she had been up until the early hours of the morning. Genny couldn't stay up that long no matter how hard she tried.*

*She lifted her head, listening for sounds around the house.*

*All was quiet. She put her head back on the warm pillow and sleep called to her. As she began to close her eyes again, a thought struck her. Cars didn't often drive by their house. Motorbikes, sure, scooters, all the time, but very few cars ...*

*Her eyes were wide open now.*

*She leapt out of bed and ran to the window—luckily it was one that faced the street.*

*Her fears were realised.*

*"Faith!" she yelled to her sister as she watched her father helping his chauffeur remove his luggage from the boot of the car.*

*Recollections of the previous night flooded her mind and for a moment she was frozen.*

*This was it. It was bound to happen.*

*All hell was going to break loose.*

There was a party the night before.

In fact, there were parties quite often when Mike was out of town. And Elizabeth, being lonely and having a love affair with the bottle, sought solace in the company of strangers, men and women alike. A social being, she felt the need for more than just the company of her children. Most of her friendships were platonic, as all she craved was adult company. But there were times when it was more, and more than once the children discovered her in compromising positions with strange men. The booze and the loneliness made her do things that she knew she never should. It didn't help that she had heard about Mike's many dalliances and exacted revenge by drinking, partying and taking lovers.

This was when they lived in the hills in Hyderabad, where a sprawling land lay behind the house. From the backyard, all one could see were large boulders over larger boulders that spanned beyond the horizon. A tall fence blocked immediate access but Elizabeth, along with the children, would climb over the wooden fence to explore, and lying on a large rock with the sun beaming upon their already tanned faces was as close to being in Heaven as there ever could be. There they would stay, unaware of the prickly rocks beneath them, tugging at stray blades of grass that poked through the stones, reading a book or just staring into the skies. Lizards would scurry past and some would even settle on the rocks beside them, undaunted by their presence. Elizabeth sometimes headed back in or watched as the children wandered around. She knew they were safe there. They had been in this town for over a year and had already made many friends. They were doing well and when she wasn't with them, they had each other.

It was particularly special when at times, while lying on those boulders, they heard the drone of their father's plane. The large grey Dakota, a black square on its underside, would fly low over the house, its thunderous sound vibrating through the rocks on which they sat. They would jump up and down trying to cover their ears and waving at the same time. As it moved above them, its wing would dip. Mike was announcing his arrival home.

"Daddy's home," someone would yell above the din and all the children would dash into the house to await him, with joy, but sometimes with worry. It was bittersweet. Usually there would be evidence of their mother's habits—empty bottles and, on occasion, random men.

As much as the children loved their father being home, it also meant arguments, sometimes violent ones, and Elizabeth felt for them, felt torn between keeping them away from it all and keeping herself away from the bottle. The ritual rarely varied. When Mike left, with a prayer by the altar and hugs and kisses for Elizabeth and the children, it would begin. Elizabeth would send the children to see a movie, while she set off to the bar, sometimes by herself, but mostly accompanied by Mary.

She didn't even try anymore to resist. What was the point?

She saw the faces of the children when they got home, resentment but resignation. They knew what to expect, the sound of her music always wafting through the street, calling in the neighbours, announcing the departure of her husband. She saw David's hand tighten around Genny's, a reassurance that it would all be okay and even though her heart fell at what she was doing to them, it also puffed with pride. She could rely on her children, particularly David, to take charge. Just a teenager himself, he was now the man of the house and his back would straighten and his chin would rise, a smile plastered on his face. He was not going to upset his mother; he was used to it.

On entering the house, the children were usually confronted by the usual scene—Elizabeth and one or two people, mostly strangers, listening to music and sipping on gin or some other version of alcohol.

Seeing their faces, Elizabeth's eyes would shine with pride and she would call out to them and introduce them all one by one to her guests. She knew they would, perhaps reluctantly at first, eventually get into the spirit of the party. The guitar would appear, and David would be coaxed into strumming it while Elizabeth's voice, clear as a bell, would echo through the house, mesmerising her guests. The rest of them croaked in harmony, just happy to be in the presence of their mother.

By the end of the evening, more neighbours had flocked to the house, the music and noise pulling them in. Most of the neighbours were scared of Mike and the invitation to visit when he was out of town was hard to resist. Many of them worked hard, ate little and drank even less—their lifestyle couldn't afford that to which Elizabeth's family were accustomed. When Mike was out of town, they knew they were in for a treat, a party, food and drink, and they enjoyed visiting with Elizabeth and her family—without Mike there. It wasn't that he was nasty to them, it was just that his general demeanour was intimidating and his booming voice, residual effects from his Air Force training, caused them to shiver in fear.

Most of the guests retreated to their own homes, usually towards the early hours of the morning, but some stayed longer, depending on how well they knew the family. The festivities would continue for days and when her company eventually left, Elizabeth would either coax one or more of the children to stay up with her or go out to find other companions. This would continue until she ran out of the money Mike left for them, and when that happened, she would purchase food on credit from the corner store. Mike always came home knowing the first thing he had to do was to pay a visit to the *bunya* to settle the bill.

When Mike returned from one of his trips, he never knew what to expect, but most often his fears were not realised. The dip of the wing of his plane, they all suspected, was a warning sign to Elizabeth. *I'm nearly home, get yourself together.* There were, of course, times when he arrived without warning, having taken another route home. He would discover that, as usual, the money had run out and Elizabeth was nursing a hangover and sometimes, he would walk right into the house while she was still drinking. For the most part, she was lucky, and he never found strangers in the house, but just the fact that she was drinking was enough to throw him into a rage.

"But Mike, I've missed you," she would plead. "I'm so lonely when you're gone."

"Enough!" He would move towards her and banish the children to their rooms.

Then the pushing and pulling and yelling would begin. All the while, Elizabeth would excuse herself to go to the bathroom, where she would guzzle gin from her hidden stashes, and then she would return to Mike to continue the row. The children would huddle together in one of their bedrooms, listening to the commotion, waiting for it to end.

At times, depending on the foulness of Mike's temper, they would try to intervene and would usually get rewarded by an accidental knock on the head or an elbow in the ribs. Robert once nearly got his thumb bitten off. It had lodged itself in Elizabeth's mouth and thinking it was Mike's, she had bitten—hard. It was lucky it hadn't been bitten right off!

The stoushes would eventually end and Elizabeth and Mike would happily go off to bed at the end of the evening, leaving their children to sit with each other, wondering if this pattern would ever end and praying that it would ... and soon.

The days that followed Mike's return were wonderful: Elizabeth and Mike, singing together, talking with each other and walking on the terrace holding hands, while the children giggled at their amorous behaviour but knowing that it was only a matter of time before Mike left again.

And he always did. And the drinking would begin, and the strangers would appear again.

There were three men, boys really, in their mid-twenties. Michael, Mario and Trevor. Elizabeth had befriended them at a bar and brought them home to continue their drinking and conversation. These boys were different. They just loved music and most of the evenings were spent singing and playing the guitar. Mario had a glorious bass voice and along with Elizabeth's own stunning soprano, theirs was a duet made in heaven. Trevor and the children usually joined in providing back-up. There was nothing romantic between any of them and Elizabeth and as such, the children became quite fond of the trio. On occasion they spent more than a few days with the family before going back to their own homes, wherever that may be.

The three of them had come over one evening knowing that Mike was out of town and the usual shenanigans began and went on late into the night. Neighbours had emerged from their own homes to join the party and this one turned out to be a smashing one where everyone donned some of their finest outfits, happy to forget their troubles for a night. There was singing and dancing and teasing. Mario had bought himself a wig as even at the tender age of twenty-four, his hair was thinning. The wig became a party favourite, with everyone trying it on and throwing it to each other. Mario, unimpressed, ran back and forth trying to retrieve his hairpiece and there were cackles of delight from observers, all of whom wanted to be part of the fun.

"Not funny," he growled as he tucked the hairpiece into the pocket of his pants, trying to shove it all the way in.

"Here, give it to me, that looks ridiculous," said Elizabeth and put it on the bookshelf. She looked at the others who were still giggling. "Nobody is to touch this," she said in warning. "Come on, let's sit outside."

After the neighbours had gone home, Elizabeth was tired and saying goodnight to everyone, retreated to her bedroom. David and Robert stayed up the latest; they always did. They were the *bouncers*, the men of the house. They were the ones who made sure that nothing got out of hand and would not go to bed until all was well. At fourteen and fifteen, it was a huge ask, but they never thought to consider their age or question their responsibility.

The three young men, taking off their shoes and socks and shirts, placed themselves on mats on the living room floor and settled in for the night. David and Robert retired to bed.

Elizabeth could feel herself being shaken. She moaned. "A little longer," she cried. She hadn't drunk all that much the previous evening but felt she could use a little more sleep, there was nothing so important to wake up to today.

"Daddy's home," she heard Faith's voice, a whisper.

"That's nice," she said sleepily and rolling over, tucked her hand under her pillow.

"Mum!" Shaking again. The realisation set it. She ignored the banging in her head as she bolted upright.

"The boys!"

"Robert's getting them up," whispered Faith, and Elizabeth dashed into the living room where the three young men lay asleep in various positions on their mats, Robert pushing his foot into Trevor who was rolled into a ball, resisting the kicks. Michael seemed to be spooning him. Mario was laying prostrate, loud snores lifting and dropping his bushy moustache. On any other occasion, Elizabeth would have laughed at the sight but at this moment, there was no time for hilarity.

"Get up," Elizabeth said, bending down to push at them too but there were sounds of groaning. "Mike is home!"

Just the mention of Mike was enough to make them jump to their feet.

A flurry of activity followed.

Faith was now out of the bedroom, understanding without needing to be told what was going on.

There was a bang on the door.

It was as if time froze and froze everyone with it. Then in unison, they all turned to the front door which opened straight into the living area. They all looked at each other. The thud of Elizabeth's heartbeat seemed audible, and she pressed on her chest, hoping to soften it.

Another two knocks, more like loud raps. Everything Mike did was loud.

David moved first.

"Who is it?" he called, almost sung out, while the three young men began to gather their shoes and socks and bolted out of the back door, Mary, already now a part of the scene, at their heels holding their guitar.

"Daddy's home. Open the door." Mike's voice, exasperated.

David ran to the door and put his hand on the knob. He turned to Elizabeth and the look of fear that was on his face was almost palpable.

"It's already open," he mouthed.

"Open the door," Mike called out again. He was getting impatient. It didn't take very much.

Everyone quickly looked around for any traces of the boys, but also for traces of alcohol. Mary and Genny scurried about picking up empty and not-so-empty glasses, ashtrays, a pair of glasses that didn't belong to any member of the family.

"I'm trying," David called through the door, using all his might to push the door in the other direction. "It's stuck."

"What's going on in there?" Mike was not a stupid man.

Elizabeth looked around the room. The place looked decent enough and she turned to David and nodded.

"Let him in," Faith whispered, just as she snatched up a wallet that lay under the centre table.

David stepped back and Mike pushed the door open.

"What's going on?" He looked around in suspicion.

"Dad!" the children called out together, running over to hug him. They always missed him and even though their hearts were pounding in fear, they were happy to see him.

He bent down and enveloped them all in his large arms.

"Where's your mother?"

"Darling, you're home," Elizabeth's voice sang to him. She had taken the chance to pat down her hair while the clean-up was underway, so Mike wouldn't suspect anything.

Mike stood up, went to her and hugged her quickly. Then he stepped back and appraised her. "You've been drinking?" Suspicious always, albeit with reason.

"No, of course not. I just woke up." She pulled him to her again. "I do need to use the bathroom. I'll be back in a minute. Sit down, Mary will make you some coffee." She signalled to Mary, who seemed to be happy to get away from the scene.

Elizabeth went to the bathroom and pulled out her bottle of gin from behind the commode. She sat on the edge of the bath and took a swig. "Elizabeth," she heard Mike call. She wiped her mouth and secured the bottle back in its hiding place.

"I'll get Mum," she heard Genny say loudly and heard the pattering of feet outside the bathroom door. She opened it.

"Mum! He's going to catch you," Genny whispered, looking over her shoulder.

"I'm coming," Elizabeth said, snatching the bottle back from behind the toilet and taking a quick swig with a shaky hand. She saw Genny waiting nervously, hopping from foot to foot. "Where are the boys? Did they make it over the fence?" she whispered after returning the bottle to its position.

"They're gone, it's okay. Just come out," Genny urged, tugging at her arm.

Elizabeth took a deep breath, and poised herself. Her hands were not shaking as much anymore and she lifted her chin in the air. It would be okay. They would be okay. She walked to where Mike now sat on the sofa and took a seat beside him, crossed one leg over the other and leaned a hand on his shoulder.

Mary was already bringing out two cups of coffee which she placed in front of them. Elizabeth tried to stifle a shudder of disgust. That was not what she wanted.

Mike took a long gulp and he rose, turning to head to the hallway that led to the bathroom. "I have to use the bathroom," he said.

Elizabeth's glance roamed to Robert who had his eyes so wide, they looked like they were going to pop out of his head. Elizabeth followed his gaze and it was at this moment that she saw it.

The wig!

It sat on a shelf that was right beside the hallway. It was so large and curly, it couldn't be missed. Elizabeth froze.

"Dad!" Genny called out and Mike turned around. Faith had also spotted it at the same moment and jumped up. Genny ran over to Mike and jumped into his arms.

"What is it?" Mike said as he pulled Genny up. She wrapped herself around him, hugging his neck tightly.

"I just missed you so much, that's all." She squeezed him tight, while over his shoulder, she watched as Faith swiped the wig and shoved it into her pyjama bottoms.

Mike smiled and squeezed Genny before putting her down and he pinched her cheek, as he always did. Then he continued on his way to the bathroom.

The moment he was out of sight, the children as well as Mary raced to the back door. There was no sign of Michael, Mario and Trevor. Then, Faith pointed to one of the many boulders in the distance. The top of a head glistening in the now hot sun could be seen from behind a rock. There was an audible sigh of relief, a chorus from all of them, including Mary. The three of them had made it past the fence and in record time. Mario turned around and on seeing the little group, nudged his friends, whose heads popped up, one by one from behind the boulders. They waved to signal that they were okay. Michael fluttered his shoe at them to let them know they were getting dressed.

What a strange sight it was. Three grown men, sitting on rocks, tying their shoelaces. This time, they did laugh, even if it was just from pure relief.

Faith waved Mario's wig and his wallet at him. Then she quickly ran to the fence and tossed them over. He knew better than to come back to retrieve them right now.

"Where is everyone?" boomed Mike's voice from behind them and they all scuttled back into the house to enjoy his homecoming.

# Part Three: New Beginnings

## 1985-1988

# Chapter 25 - Australia—Here We Come!

"Say goodbye, everyone," Mike called out, a sing in his voice.

"Goodbye, India," said Faith.

"See ya," said David.

"Good riddance," said Robert.

"Bye, India," said Genny.

Elizabeth herded them onto the plane and looked back across the tarmac. Her heart was heavy. She was leaving her home, everything she knew and loved. But really, what was there to love anymore?

"Why do we have to go?" she asked Mike when the okay had come through. It was a dream for everyone to live overseas but now that it was becoming a reality, Elizabeth was scared.

"It's for their future," he had said, throwing a glance in the direction of the children who were sitting at the dining table, some doing and some pretending to do their homework. Robert had questioned why they had to do any at all if they were leaving before the end of term anyway. "Because you have to do what you have to do." When Robert tried to protest, Elizabeth had shaken her head at him. It was best to just do what Mike said.

And now here she was, arguing, almost for the sake of it. She knew their fate was sealed, no discussion was going to change anything and in reality, she knew they stood more of a chance of being happy in a place far away from here, where she didn't have to be reminded of the girl she was and the woman she'd become.

"But Mike, they are in the best schools, they are all smart, they will be okay. I mean, you are okay. You have a good job. They can do all the things they want to do right here."

"Do you know how hard I had to work to get where I am?" He was indignant.

"And they can't?" Elizabeth felt a little offended that Mike didn't have enough faith in his children to become as successful as he was.

"Elizabeth, I work hard, I get paid well but we barely manage."

"I could work too. To help out."

"But that's not the point. I want the children to live well, to have careers that they will love, to work hard, yes, but to be able to do it without as many sacrifices as I had to make. My parents had to help me, and God knows, they struggled too."

"And how are your parents doing in Australia?"

"Well, they're too old to work now, but Teresa looks after them well. She has a great job, so does her husband. They live a good life."

"So it's about having money?"

He shook his head and knitted his brow. "Elizabeth, this was our dream, a better future for us, for the children. And after all we have been through ..."

"A change," she had said in acknowledgment. She had to admit it was what they needed. Something to jolt them out of the life they'd been living. Maybe it was best.

She felt a shove from behind her and jolted forward towards the door of the airplane. She hoped things would work out. This was a new beginning, a new hope for them all. She had made promises and hoped she could keep them. No alcohol. She swallowed.

"Remember," said Mike, as they sat together on the balcony of Joshua's apartment in Bombay, from where they were to board their flight. "This is for us all." He held out his hand and she took it.

"This is going to be so wonderful, Mike," she said. She was excited for him. He would be reunited with his parents, and his sister had permanently moved there two years before. Only Joshua had stayed behind, not wanting to give up his own life and even though Mike tried to convince him to go with them, he was happy where he was. "Will you ever come to Australia, Josh?" Elizabeth turned to him now and immediately felt Mike's fingers tighten over her hand. She tried not to react, not even bothering to wiggle her fingers out of his grip. Even with his own brother, he was jealous. She had given him reason enough to be now. She was, in effect, a female version of him.

Joshua swirled his whisky in his glass, unaware of the interaction between Mike and Elizabeth. "Why would I?"

Why would he indeed? Joshua, now a businessman in uptown Bombay, could want for nothing. He had invested well and had a glorious bachelor pad overlooking the Arabian Sea, four full-time house people including a chef and a driver, he could come and go when he pleased, did not marry, even though he had come close twice. But he seemed lonely, had a faraway look in his eyes as he took in the view.

Elizabeth immediately thought about her own family, her mother, her sisters, her brother and would have killed for the opportunity to go to Canada instead. "Well, I guess now that all your family is there anyway?"

Joshua snorted. "I didn't see them when they were here." He glanced at Mike.

"I suppose everyone is busy with their lives," said Elizabeth. She changed the subject. It was no secret that Joshua was not who his parents wanted him to be, a family man who gave them grandchildren, who behaved in the right way, who didn't screw around with every woman, married or not, who was not a blight on their good name in their hometown. "So, how is the new girlfriend?"

"Girlfriends, you mean," Joshua said with a laugh.

"You're not getting any younger," said Mike, looking pointedly at his brother's torso.

Joshua laughed again and rubbed at his head which was still thick with hair. "Still got this though," he said. "So do you, little brother."

"Good genes," said Elizabeth. It was almost a sin the way they were so vain. Mike still got up every morning and dressed like he was going to a party even when he stayed at home. He didn't leave the bathroom without applying grease to his hair, having a fresh shave and applying buckets of cologne. Joshua seemed a little less vain but in his mid-forties, he still had his good looks, albeit a subtly developing belly.

"I'm off to bed," said Joshua. "You two can make your plans and enjoy your last night in this country." He gave them a little salute and a quick wink before closing the sliding door behind him.

Elizabeth got off her chair and went to Mike, placing herself on his lap and taking his arms, wrapped them around her. "Mike," she said. "It will be wonderful, won't it?"

He squeezed her. "Yes, it will, of course it will."

"A new start?"

"A new everything," he said.

"What will I do?" She said it for no particular reason. This conversation had been had a few times already. She just needed reassurance that they were doing the right thing.

"Anything you want ..."

"Will it be hard?"

"I'm sure it will take some adjusting, but once I get my licence and begin flying, it will be wonderful."

"Will it be hard, you know, to get back to flying?"

Mike laughed. "Elizabeth, I am the best. Any company would be lucky to have me. Any country, for that matter."

Elizabeth smiled. Yes, he had many offers he had to turn down. Good ones lately that would have taken them to Kashmir and to Bombay, but none that could be taken. The end game was Australia. It had been a continual topic for the past year. She had expected the okay to come much later—her own parents had to wait for years. Perhaps Mike had applied much earlier than she'd presumed. Perhaps even before ... "Mike," she said, turning to face him, a little fearful now. "Why are we doing this?"

She saw a flicker of doubt rush over his face. "Because there is no future for our children here. Australia is the land of opportunity, that's what they say."

"Who says that?"

"Everyone." There was a silence except for the rush of the waves over the sand on the beach. It should have been romantic but it came off as foreboding. "Brian, you remember Brian?" Elizabeth barely remembered Brian, Mike's cousin, who had taken his teenage children to Australia a decade before. "His children are doing really well. One is a lawyer and one is a nurse. And he got a job as a teacher. They send money home to their parents every month." He kissed the back of her neck. "If it gets tough, remember that's what we will be doing it for."

"And us, Mike?"

"What about us?" His kisses paused on the nape of her neck.

"Will we be okay?"

"As long as we don't start the old habits ..."

Elizabeth knew what he meant. If *she* didn't start the old habits. He could never understand how it felt, how when she was not busying herself with him, with the children, the thought of alcohol pervaded her mind. All the time. But she had to look at the bigger picture. It wasn't just about her; she couldn't lose the children again. She was determined it was going to work and she was going to do her damnedest to keep away from it. Maybe if Mike didn't start *his* old tricks ... maybe ... She hated herself for already looking for a reason.

She sighed. They had broken up and made up so many times, more than she could count on all her fingers, even her toes. She knew it was futile, even the thought of being without him was frightening, not just of being by herself, but actually being without Mike by her side. When they had gotten the okay to come to Australia, Elizabeth thought it would change things. In fact, the last year in Derrum was wonderful. Yes, there had been fights, yes, there were affairs, on both sides, but the excitement of beginning a new life made all the other things pale and Elizabeth tried not to drink so much, and instead, sitting together with the children, made plans for their new life. Genny wanted new shoes, David, a guitar, Robert wanted a bike and Faith, a new hairstyle. She worried about her children sometimes; would they have the same thirst for booze as she did? She hoped not and spent time talking to them about the dangers of the drink. She knew she didn't need to, they saw the damage it could do, Elizabeth walking in pain, a bend in her back, even though she still kept her chin high and insisted that heels were not hurting her.

Their life back in Derrum became more than just tolerable. Even though she didn't see Dimple, refused her friendly advances once Dimple knew Elizabeth and Mike were together again and back to being the most sought-after couple in town, she forgave her other more near-sighted friends. Even Margie had come over once or twice even though their friendship had never quite fully recovered. But overall, the last year had been one of the best they'd shared, all of them.

"I'm going to miss Mary," said Elizabeth. "She was with us so long. She became a wonderful friend and housekeeper."

"Yes, she was a good housekeeper," Mike agreed without too much emotion but Elizabeth knew he had put some money in her hand thinking that Elizabeth hadn't noticed. He still wanted to be seen as a tough employer, but it was that soft side that Elizabeth adored and wished he'd show more often.

"Thank you for setting her up," said Elizabeth. In addition to his secret gift, Mike had given her three months' worth of pay and had found her another place of employ with one of his colleagues, an officer who Elizabeth knew would not give her the benefits that Elizabeth had given her. Mary had cried loudly, tears and snot dripping all over Elizabeth's sleeve, had hugged the children so hard. It was an awful sight and the children all sobbed in the taxi that took them away from her.

Mike's hands closed around Elizabeth's waist. "What do you say?" he said. "Once more in this country?"

Elizabeth loved that he still wanted her as she did him. She giggled. "The children are probably still awake," she said.

"Then we will need to be extra quiet," he said, prodding her off his lap.

She skipped behind him to the guest bedroom, excited to feel his arms around her. *Yes*, she thought. *This is going to be exactly what we need.*

A new start.

# Chapter 26 - Adjustments

## 1986

"How can I leave him?" She couldn't even look at Vince, the purple on her skin growing darker every passing hour. She didn't need to explain to Vince what happened. He had been around for nearly a year, had found the family when he knew they'd migrated, six months after they'd arrived in Sunshine, Melbourne. The son of one of her mother's youngest cousins, Vince was closer to her children's ages, and had therefore found a place in the family, even though he only came by on the weekends and the evenings that Mike was working.

"Elizabeth, it's about time!" Vince's voice was harsh. He usually had a gruff voice but it always lacked an edge. This time he was not going to mince words and Elizabeth was afraid of what she may hear, the truth which she'd ignored. Things were different here; there was help, not like in India, when she was on her own, with no support from the government or her friends, most of whom had turned their backs on her. Here in this country, it was possible for her to leave him and survive financially on her own.

"Vince, you don't understand ..." Elizabeth shrugged her shoulders. "It's not like, I don't know ... it's not like he's seeing anybody. He made a mistake."

Vince looked at her through his eyebrows that folded over his usually twinkling green eyes. "You will always make excuses for him, won't you?"

"No," she said with a deep exhale. "I just don't know how to do any of it anymore. I just don't have any fight left, you know?"

"I'm here," said Vince and rose from the table. It was late at night and even though they were second cousins, Mike didn't like the idea of Vince hanging around too often. His suspicious mind knew no bounds and Elizabeth gave up trying to convince him that Vince was a good friend—to the whole family. "But it's late, so I guess I'm not." He gave a chuckle of resignation. "Bye, Elizabeth," he said, bending down to kiss her on the cheek. "Say goodbye to the children for me."

Elizabeth watched him walk out the door and smiled. Vince had been a godsend, had been good to the children, had been an ear for her whenever she needed one, which in the last year and a half, had been a lot. He had been the reminder of home she needed, something familiar in this alien country, a crutch for when she felt alone. More than Mike these days, and if she really thought about it, more than Mike at any time.

Mike had been in such an awful mood. And who could blame him? Elizabeth felt sorry for him; he had tried but was unable to secure his pilot's licence. In India, he was almost godlike, admired and respected, with a job he loved almost as much as he loved his children. She couldn't begin to imagine what he must feel like.

Elizabeth could see what he had given up for his children, for all of them. She knew he missed flying and going away on trips, where he got to play the bachelor. Women fell at his feet, a man in uniform, as handsome as anyone with a smile that lit up the room. Men wanted to be near him, to have some of the magic he emanated rub off on them. He missed the parties, the gatherings with his friends at the mess, and he didn't look at her now the way he used to, the sparkling trophy wife, who he displayed on his arm, looked up at adoration when she was on the stage. She even missed him beating up on some man who said something complimentary to Elizabeth or even smiled her way.

That was before. Before they came to this new world. Before they came to this new life.

Being stuck in the same house day after day was something Mike found hard getting used to. Now, he trudged to work in his green puffy jacket with *The Met* emblazoned on his lapel, catching the train to the city station, and there he would stay for the day, and sometimes the night when he was on a nightshift, standing at the barriers, checking the tickets of often disgruntled passengers.

He was embarrassed. He would come home from the station and Elizabeth would pour him a drink. Then he would tell her how people would push past him and how some people even yelled racist slurs at him if he demanded that they show their tickets. He had never been disrespected before and to have it done to him, sometimes by children, he found utterly unspeakable. He found it hard to comprehend that young people could speak in the manner they did.

"In India they would be walloped!" he complained. "What sort of country have we moved to?"

Elizabeth sympathised with him but didn't know how to help. She just watched as he sipped on his whisky, wishing that it was her lips on the rim of that glass.

"My God, if my friends should see me like this!" He would shake his head. "What have we done, coming here?"

At times, Mike was asked to sweep the platform. He related to Elizabeth, amused and also indignant, how a Japanese tourist asked if she could take his picture. He leaned the broom against a pole and puffed his chest out ready for the shot when the woman gestured for him to pick up the broom and sweep. Then she began snapping away.

Elizabeth could almost feel his humiliation and just stayed silent, nodding and patting his arm, which just seemed to annoy him. She tried to help financially, had secured a job working in a kitchen in the city, washing dishes and preparing food for factory workers, but the wages were menial. Not having had much work experience in her life, she was unable to find much else and was taking temporary work offered to her by the Employment Service.

She wanted to have more hope for Mike. Perhaps if he got his licence, became a pilot here, maybe things would get better, be a little easier. Maybe their dreams for this country weren't as sour as they seemed. Mike still dreamed of flying. He talked about it incessantly and had not considered that in moving to Australia, he would be giving up what he loved. The cost of applying for an Australian pilot's licence was much more than he expected, and his Indian licence didn't count for all that much, regardless of the experience he had in the Air Force and as a commercial pilot. There were numerous stages involved in the process and each one required a hefty fee, the first of which was a physical. When Elizabeth got her income tax return, she insisted Mike use the money to take the first step in his endeavour, the medical. He knew it was a long shot by this time. He was at an age where his experience didn't matter. He also knew he was in a country that preferred to take their own and especially with his accent and the colour of his skin, it was going to be tough. He didn't pass his vision test and Elizabeth could see he was spiralling into a depression, something she hadn't seen in him before.

Sure he had a temper, got into fits of rages, but he was sometimes so quiet, so morose and nothing she could ever say or do helped.

He came home from work, drank, complained and wished he were back home. He was curt and rude to Elizabeth, and she tried to understand what he was going through, but he knew, as she did, that it was a little different for her. Even though she was new to the country too, Elizabeth was accepted more readily by Australians. For one, her skin was lighter, and most people thought she was of Spanish descent, which made her exotic and interesting. Her demeanour was also more inviting to others and she didn't experience as many racially demeaning comments as Mike did. She did wonder at his rigidity with other people. He had always been strict and unmoving, and she wondered if maybe he just gave a little, people would treat him differently. But she dared not tell him that. That would be insolence and would probably be answered with a slap even though she had to admit that he had really tried to control his hands since they had made their vows to turn over new leaves.

At one stage, Mike even discussed the possibility of moving back to India and although Elizabeth was not enthusiastic about the idea, knowing it was just a matter of time before they became acclimatised, she didn't argue. She knew he needed more time.

"It will work out, it always does," she tried to tell him.

"What do you know? You're not out there every day, working in this place. We were better off where we were."

"Remember why we came here." She tried to turn his attention to their ultimate purpose for migrating, his very idea. "For the kids, their future."

"I know, I know." He was soothed, but only for a moment. "I just didn't think I would be giving up mine. I was a respected officer ..."

Elizabeth nodded, trying to be as supportive as she could, also knowing how his position as 'respected officer' had contributed to his philandering and had compromised their marriage. She didn't say this, of course, but then he turned it on her anyway.

"We should have stayed there, we were better off. If you weren't such a drunk, we could have been happy," he spat.

Elizabeth was beginning to get worked up now, and she knew better than to exacerbate his mood, so she just got up and left the room. Lately she had been leaving the room often. She was just glad for the most part, he didn't follow her to continue the argument.

The verbal abuse continued, but soon and inevitably, it turned physical again. A hard pinch or a slap as she walked by him. Elizabeth could see the signs that things were about to get worse. She tried to stay as far from him as possible, going to work, now as a door-to-door salesperson, lugging large paintings to the homes of families, people who she knew would never buy them. She would come home sometimes very late in the evening, have dinner with the children and wait until they went to bed. She would then sit at the kitchen table and stare at Mike's bottle of whisky, laughing at her from the top shelf. How she ached to lift it off its perch and take a sip, just one sip. She would light a cigarette and pray that Mike was asleep before she went to bed.

One evening, she came into the living room after having an afternoon nap and heard Mike's voice: not a snarl, no irritation, the gentle voice he used to have. She stopped at the door of the living room and leaned her back against the wall beside it.

"It will be okay," he was saying. "We'll get you a new one."

"But the old one was nice," Genny said.

"But it's gone. If you didn't see who took it ..."

"I know," said Genny, a tremble in her voice.

"Then how about we go to the Salvation Army and buy a new bike?"

"But mine was new. Mum and you spent so much on it."

"Then how about we get you a used one and when it's your birthday, in just a few months, we will try to get you a brand-new one?"

"I don't mind a used one," Genny said and Elizabeth could hear the smile in her voice.

There was a momentary pause. "What is this weird show we're watching?" Mike said and she heard the vinyl on the sofa creak.

"It's *Skippy*," said Genny with the sputter of a laugh and Elizabeth put her hand over her mouth to stifle a laugh at the sight of Mike watching a show about the adventures of a kangaroo. "No, Dad, stay here for a bit," Genny said.

"All right, all right," he said in a grudging voice.

Elizabeth lowered her head and as the smile on her face broadened, her eyes became wet. She loved so much that he still could be so gentle, so kind. The old Mike still living somewhere in him. He was never violent with the children. Yelled about the house sometimes, made them scamper to their rooms but he never laid a finger on them. When he said, repeatedly, that he had done everything in his life for the children, including the move to Australia, he meant it. She saw that he put up with what he did because of them, to give them a future. How easy it would be to return to India, to his glory days. She knew he never would. He loved those children.

But where was the love for her anymore? She winced with the pang of pain she felt in her heart. She never saw any of that love, any of that care. She resented him for the fact that for some reason he couldn't give that love to her. She tiptoed to the backyard, wanting a cigarette and as she passed by the kitchen, she paused. Should she? Could she get away with it? She hurried past, knowing she had to defeat her own demons if her marriage were to survive.

## Chapter 27 - One Christmas ...

Although Christmas was usually a time of celebration for the family and Mike never scrounged on money for gifts and decorations, in the Christmas of '86, he didn't offer anything. Elizabeth understood that money was sparse—between rent, bills and other house expenses, there was not a lot left. Elizabeth put a little aside from the grocery money he gave her but inevitably it would be spent on something that came up, shoes for the children, books that they needed and other incidentals.

Vince, who had been in the family's life for a few months, offered to help Elizabeth buy gifts, at least for the children, and wouldn't take no for an answer. He was working as a taxi driver but insisted he didn't have many expenses.

"I can't take your money," Elizabeth said, feeling humiliated that he had seen her predicament.

"Elizabeth, it's just me. I have very few expenses. I live in a flat and pay very little rent."

"That's not the point," Elizabeth said. "I've never had to take money from anyone." She tried not to think about Jacob and how much he'd helped her. She tried not to remember the humiliations of asking for credit at the corner store when she lived in India. But that was before. When she was inebriated and didn't feel it as acutely as she did now.

"Okay," Vince said and she could see him thinking about how he could convince her to take his money. "Well, whenever I'm over, you feed me ..."

"Don't you dare," she said and stood up, feeling even more demeaned. "You are part of the family ..."

"What about a loan then?" Vince said quickly. "Pay me back when you can."

Elizabeth sat back down and considered it. "I don't know."

"Okay, so I don't give you the money. How about I take you to the shopping centre? Get the presents with you?"

For some reason that sounded more reasonable. Taking money from him seemed filthy, untoward, like she was a beggar. But if he bought them himself ... *Oh, Mother! Why did you make me believe all this bullshit? All these stupid proper ways?*

But Elizabeth was grateful. A basketball shirt for Robert, a car wash pack for David, makeup for Faith and a set of books for Genny. She even bought Mike a new pair of dress shoes, a tradition she'd started since they'd first married. It was not extravagant, but it was something for them all to open under the Christmas tree when they came home after Midnight Mass.

Mike's own family, his parents and his sister and her family, all of whom lived very close to them, didn't sympathise with her. She knew she had no support from them, even though she tried. They, in fact, took to babying Mike and would take every chance they got to make Elizabeth believe the situation they were in was her fault, going as far as to directly blame her alcoholism on their financial situation. Elizabeth wanted to remind them that she had not had a drink since they had arrived in Australia but knew there was no point. To them, Mike was a saint, albeit a very scary saint, and she was responsible for making him unhappy.

"Hush, Elizabeth," Alma said one day when Mike had walked out of the room in a huff, using all manner of profanities, and Elizabeth had put her head in her hands. "He's finding it hard. You just have to be a good wife."

"I am," Elizabeth replied without conviction. They didn't seem to care so there was no point in trying to get them to see her side.

"Yes, you can be," Alma said and Elizabeth looked up in surprise to see Alma's usually hard-set eyes soft. "We have to be patient with him."

Elizabeth smiled unsteadily. There was something that resembled understanding in that face. "Yes, I'm trying."

After Mike's parents had left, Elizabeth pondered the woman. There were moments of warmth from her, moments of understanding in those usually hard eyes, the unbending stance. Had Mike's father been the same? Had he used his fists on his wife as well? Joshua had alluded to it when they had sat on the terrace all those years ago. Did he manipulate her and have other women as well? Did she know if he did? Was it in his blood? Was it an excuse?

She had no answers for any of those questions, had never come close to understanding his family. She figured they just wanted their son to be happy and he wasn't happy at all, hadn't been for the last eighteen months.

They never considered how unhappy she herself was without something to look forward to—the relief of a drink. The urge was always there, it had never left. It wasn't just when Mike talked down to her or hit her; it wasn't just when she worried about their finances; it wasn't just when she felt joy at one of the children's academic achievements or even when they went to a family gathering. An occasion wasn't necessary for Elizabeth to think of the bottle. It just became unbearable when these things came up. With Christmas on the horizon, Elizabeth knew she would have to keep busy.

It was also the Christmas when two of Elizabeth's second cousins, Donna and Valerie, the daughters of Sadie, just a little older than David, had arrived from Adelaide to spend a few days with Elizabeth and the family. Elizabeth was glad for the company and also for the feeling that she too had someone on her side for a change. Vince was invited as he was a second cousin to them too and Mike was not happy about the arrival of these invaders, but Elizabeth put her foot down this time and insisted they were welcome. Mike acquiesced, but never missed a chance to let them know they were not welcome—a snide comment about the house being too full, a remark about running out of groceries. It had never been like him to make a guest in his house feel unwelcome, but who he was now, she didn't even know.

It was a somewhat sombre lead-up to Christmas, the second in this new country, but Elizabeth and the children tried to make it as fun as all their previous ones had been. The house was decorated with tinsel, the tree, picked up at the Salvation Army, courtesy of Vince, glittering with baubles and other ornaments sent by Elizabeth's mother from Canada. Elizabeth began to feel as though things would improve as Christmas was always a special time and Mike had always enjoyed the occasion, revelling in the festivities. The whole family walked to Midnight Mass together and as usual, when they got home, gifts miraculously appeared under the tree. Mike had reluctantly stayed with the party and Elizabeth was grateful to him. When he saw the shape of the brightly wrapped box with his name on it, he even laughed in pleasure. Elizabeth was hopeful, feeling that life may be returning to normal, whatever that may mean.

It was a few days after Christmas when Donna approached Elizabeth, who had been laughing with Robert over his assembly of a jigsaw puzzle that had to be started from scratch. Even at sixteen, Robert's concentration was short and his temper even shorter. He was about to upend the five-hundred-piece puzzle and Elizabeth was trying to fix some of it to encourage him to keep going. She was trying to instil in him a sense of accomplishment and stickability, but Robert, at that age, clearly needed more than just a puzzle to achieve that.

Elizabeth looked up at Donna, who had nudged her with her knee and the look on her face made her blood drain.

"What's the matter?" she croaked at her, a familiar pang nudging her heart.

"Can you just come with me. I need to talk to you," said Donna, her voice quivering. Her eyes looked red and splotches of mascara dotted her cheeks.

Robert looked at both of them, also knowing this was not a good sign. He quickly turned back to the task at hand, shifting around the jigsaw pieces which seemed to be worse than they were before.

Donna pulled Elizabeth out in the backyard, away from the children's ears.

"Mike ..."

"Mike what?" Elizabeth already knew what was coming, but she wanted to hear it anyway. A sensation went through her, a nervous tension, and she almost enjoyed the feeling. It was familiar. She was comfortable with it. It meant things hadn't strayed so far off course that she couldn't get her life back to what it used to be.

"He tried to ..." Donna stopped again.

"Just spit it out, Donna." Elizabeth was beginning to get frustrated, her heart already thumping wildly. She just wanted to hear it said out loud.

"Nothing, it's nothing." Donna turned her back to Elizabeth and burst into little sobs.

Donna was a beauty, but at twenty, she was young and inexperienced, and Elizabeth could see she just didn't know what else to do.

Elizabeth sighed. "It's okay, you don't have to say anything."

"I didn't do anything," Donna pleaded with Elizabeth.

"I know you didn't. It's not your fault." Elizabeth was torn between hugging the girl and confronting Mike. She decided to do both.

"I want him to admit it," she said to Donna. "Where did this happen? Where is he?"

Donna burst into fresh sobs. "I was going into the lounge room and he came out of the bedroom and pushed his ... his, you know ... against me. I didn't know what to do, so I moved, and he grabbed my arm and he ... he kissed me."

"And then?"

"And then, Faith walked in and saw us, so he let go of me and I ran to you."

Elizabeth felt the bristles stand up on her arms. Faith had been there! She knew Donna was telling the truth and she had felt this feeling so many times before. When someone told her about Mike, when she just knew, suspected somehow ... She took a deep breath and looked at the trembling girl.

"I want to confront him." Elizabeth knew how much she was asking of this young girl, but now she was livid and didn't think about how Donna may be feeling. In the back of her mind, she felt a pang, an excuse ...

Donna, clearly so relieved that she was believed, nodded emphatically. "Yep, I'll come with you."

Hand in hand, they headed to the lounge room, where they found Faith standing at the window, staring outside, resembling a prisoner planning an escape. Faith turned when she heard them enter and just looked back outside again.

"Where's your father?" Elizabeth asked her.

"I don't know," Faith replied as if in a trance.

Elizabeth, torn between confronting Mike and talking to her daughter, chose the latter. Leaving Donna standing at the door, she approached Faith and encircled her arms around her shoulders. She felt Faith heave.

"I'm sorry, baby," she whispered.

"I'm fine, Mum," Faith sniffed, still staring out the window. Elizabeth could read in her forlorn face that she was sick of everything; she looked like she was thinking about how quickly she could get out of this house. Faith patted her mother's arm and gave her a lopsided smile. "Really, I'm okay."

Elizabeth kissed Faith's hair. She couldn't do this to them

anymore. These kids had seen and heard much more than they should have in their youth. What would become of them? What would they turn into, with everything they'd seen and been through? This had to be affecting them mentally. Worse, what if they turned into her? Abused, alcoholic women?

By the time Elizabeth had gotten back to Donna, who was hopping from one foot to the other now in the doorway, she was seething again. She pulled Donna to the bedroom, where she found Mike sitting in an armchair reading the paper, or at least pretending to read it. He didn't look up when Elizabeth barged in, Donna in tow.

"Did you?" she demanded.

Mike looked up and shrugged.

"How could you?" Elizabeth wanted him to deny it, wanted at least an argument.

"You women are all the same, getting upset over stupid things," he said flippantly.

"Stupid things?" Elizabeth screeched. "You just tried to come on to my cousin! Stupid things?"

"Sorry, Donna," he said, looking at the trembling girl, and went back to looking at his paper.

After helping Donna and Valerie pack their things, Elizabeth asked Vince, who was playing cricket in the backyard with the boys, to drive them to the station. She went with them and said her goodbyes, apologising profusely for the conduct of her husband. She wasn't just humiliated, she felt disgusted and angry with herself for putting up with his behaviour for so long. On the way home, she just stared out of the window, wondering what was going to happen when she got home.

"What's the matter?" asked Vince.

Elizabeth trusted Vince and related the incident to him, barely feeling the betrayal anymore.

"When are you going to stop taking all this bullshit?" Vince said after driving for ten minutes in silence, while he let Elizabeth contemplate her position.

"What can I do?"

"You can leave him!" Vince banged his hand on the steering wheel.

"What for?" said Elizabeth with a shrug of her shoulders. "To go back again, like I always do?"

"You're in another country, Elizabeth. He has no rights here."

"I have no one here, Vince."

"You have me! We are family. I can help you." Vince was indignant.

"Help me to do what?"

"Get away from him, Elizabeth."

Elizabeth was silent for a few moments. "But I love him, Vince."

After Vince dropped her home, she went to Faith's room, where she found her lying on her bed, reading. She sat beside her and looked at her daughter, who looked back at her with what she could just assume was resentment.

She made up her mind.

Elizabeth had put up with Mike's moods, mollified him, taken his verbal and physical abuse, and now this. She believed that coming to this country meant a new start to their life together, and that meant leaving all their bad habits behind. She had certainly kept her part of the bargain; she had not touched a drink since the plane touched down at Melbourne Airport. She had made excuses for his behaviour towards her, blaming his moods on his position, but he had not a care for her feelings or even that of his kids anymore. She had had enough; she knew she had to leave, love made no difference anymore.

She spent the night on the couch praying she was making the right decision and when Mike left for work the next morning, she called Vince.

# Chapter 28 - Freedom—For Now

On her first night of freedom, Elizabeth had her first real drink in over two years and she barely paused for the next seven months. It was like welcoming back her closest friend in the world. She stayed at Vince's house for three days while he helped her find a flat not very far away from her and Mike's home in the western suburbs of Melbourne. That way she could still be close to the children. Faith and Genny wanted to go with her and Mike had no choice but to let them. David and Robert were left with the brunt of Mike's temper when he found they had gone, but Elizabeth trusted that his love for his children would keep them safe. David told her that Mike had taken the news better than they expected; he had gone to his parents' home, had come back and stayed up all night drinking. The next morning, as usual, he woke up and went to work.

Elizabeth went back to drinking and partying as she did in India and soon her little flat was filled with music and laughter. Her new neighbours were friendly and many stopped by to welcome her to the neighbourhood. Many took advantage of her hospitality and her state of mind and it wasn't often when the flat didn't contain one of her new friends, singing and talking late into the night, and sharing her liquor.

Elizabeth could see that the girls missed their father and she encouraged them to see him as much as possible, but when they were there, not a word was mentioned of their mother. She tried not to grill them but they said that Mike didn't ask about Elizabeth; it stung a little but she knew his pride wouldn't let him, and they didn't volunteer any information about her either, they were too afraid of his temper.

Elizabeth was happy for a while. She missed her boys, who came to see her on weekends and although she took a lover or two, she missed Mike. She knew she still loved him but at least she wasn't looking over her shoulder at every moment, wondering when the next punch or kick would come her way.

But mostly it was the freedom. She could do as she pleased and have a drink when she liked. As the girls saw their father often, she knew he was coping, so she felt less guilty for leaving him. His family had rallied and, as usual, they were mollycoddling him, but this time she felt grateful for them.

Elizabeth's drinking was beginning to take a toll on her health, and she lost a lot of weight. Even though she cooked for the girls, she barely ate anything herself. Her life was a routine of drinking and hangovers and she had never felt so free.

*Genny arrived home from school to find her mother passed out on the sofa in her underwear, an empty gin bottle and two glasses sitting on the table beside her. Genny sighed and dropped her schoolbag on the floor next to the door. She knew Elizabeth had been on a bender and hadn't stopped now for more than a week. She picked up the glasses and the bottle and put them on the counter in the kitchen. She looked around and found, as she feared, that there was no food cooked. She looked into the fridge and saw that it was empty, a pack of butter and a nearly empty bottle of milk the only items in there. It was shopping day and Elizabeth had promised she would do it during the day. Genny felt a surge of anger even though this was nothing new.*

*"Spent it all again!" Genny slammed the fridge door closed.*

*She walked to where Elizabeth was lying and picked up her purse, which sat beside her. There was no money in it and she wondered if she had even been out. She looked at her mother, who looked so peaceful, she didn't want to wake her. She considered going to her father's house to see if there was anything there, but the look on Elizabeth's face bore a strange expression. It was ... too calm. She knelt beside her and gently shook her arm, which flopped to one side.*

*"Mum," she said softly, not wanting to give her a fright.*

*Still no movement. She shook her again, this time a little more forcefully, feeling a small panic begin to hurry her heart. Genny looked around her, for what she didn't know; no one else was home. Faith had lingered behind after school to chat to her new love interest and Genny was not interested in waiting for her. Now she wished she had hurried her home. She put her hand on her mother's chest and waited for the rise and fall, which didn't come.*

*Now dread had well set in. She put her ear to her mother's nose and couldn't feel anything. She wasn't breathing! Putting her hands on Elizabeth's chest, she began to pump, trying to emulate what she had seen in movies.*

*"Get up!" she called out to Elizabeth, tears streaming down her face. "Get up, get up, get up," she repeated with each pump of Elizabeth's chest. After a few minutes, with no response from Elizabeth, Genny slumped to the floor and sobbed, her head in her hands.*

*She heard a sound at the door and looked up to see her sister looking at the scene before her, her eyes wide.*

*"She's dead," Genny cried out to Faith through hiccups.*

*"She's not dead!" said Faith and pushing Genny out of the way, began to shake Elizabeth violently. "Get up, Mum!" she kept saying while she shook her.*

*There was still no response, the body of Elizabeth flopping from side to side, and after a few minutes, Faith found herself on the floor next to Genny.*

*"Ambulance!" she said and ran to the phone.*

*"What can they do now?" Genny replied. "Call Dad instead."*

*"We can't give up," said Faith and dashed to the telephone.*

*The ambulance on its way, Faith and Genny sat huddled together, staring at the body of their mother. They had called their father's house, but he wasn't home. David and Robert were on their way over instead. They were coming on their bikes, so they wouldn't be too long.*

*Soon, the wail of the ambulance could be heard and Faith went to the bedroom to retrieve a blanket, which she placed over her mother's body. Even in this state, she was trying to save her modesty.*

*The boys came in at the same time as the paramedics and they tried to run to their mother. David's usually tanned face looked a pasty grey and Robert's was just plain white. The paramedics, a man and a woman, pushed the children out of the way and the kids moved to a corner of the room while they let these people do their job. David held his sisters' hands, while they whimpered, and Robert paced up and down the length of the room, swearing under his breath.*

*"She's dead," said Faith to David and hid her head under his arm, while David watched the medics put a blood pressure glove on his mother's arm.*

*"She's moving," David said suddenly, and Faith's head*

*popped out from under the protective arm.*

*Genny kept her head down, not wanting to get her hopes up. She was hating herself for what she sometimes thought, the thoughts that she pushed out of her head often. "What if ..." She often wondered how things would be if her mother were not around. Not just somewhere else, because she knew there was the possibility of her returning. No, she often wondered how things would be if her mother were never able to come back. Like if she ... she could never get the words out, not even when she hated her at times. Now all she felt was guilt and dread. She made this happen, by thinking it, even if it wasn't just now. Now she just wanted David to be right. She wanted her mother to move.*

*She felt David push at her shoulder, and she looked up.*

*The lady medic came to the group and Robert rushed over to join them. "She's going to be fine. We need to keep an eye on her for a while."*

*"What's wrong with her?" Robert blurted.*

*The medic looked at him, sympathy oozing from her eyes, and Genny looked away. It wasn't the first time strangers had looked at them that way.*

*"She's just had too much. She was in a very deep sleep."*

*"But she wasn't breathing," said Genny.*

*"She was, very slowly," said the medic and smiled. "But she will be just fine."*

*"Children," they heard their mother's voice from the sofa, and they all rushed over.*

*Elizabeth's eyes were still half closed. "Why all this?" she muttered slowly.*

*Robert blurted again. "Genny thought you were dead!"*

Elizabeth tried to open her eyes fully but couldn't. "But I'm fine, I'm just very tired." Looking at each of the faces of her children, Elizabeth realised what they had thought but she didn't have the energy to say anything else, so she raised her arms slightly and they all clambered into them.

The incident shook Elizabeth up. Knowing what her children must have thought broke her heart. "Please give me the willpower!" she cried to the heavens. "Or at least some control. I can't bear this burden anymore."

When she made it through the horrible hangover, Elizabeth decided she had to try much harder to slow her drinking and for the next few months, she did, drinking for a couple of days at a time and trying to stay sober until the time came when she couldn't take the thirst for it anymore. Then she would walk to the corner store, return with a bottle of gin and soda and settle down on her favourite armchair. She knew the looks she would get when her daughters came home from school and she dreaded it, but she told herself she was getting better. At least there were no parties anymore, just the odd neighbour at times and Vince who checked in on them, but mostly, she was happy to sit in the evenings with her girls and talk with them about their lives and school and boys, relating her own tales of her youth. She knew they treasured this time as much as she did. It was enough. It was more than enough. She didn't need Mike; she didn't need a man to take care of her.

And then came Joe. Joe, a divorced father of two. Joe who lived in her building, just a floor above her. Joe, who always checked in on her, who put out her bins, who sat with her until it was time for him to go to his own flat. After all, Joe had a job; he woke up very early to go into the city, on a train, to put pavers down on the streets of Melbourne. And stopped to poke his head in at the door of Elizabeth's flat when he got home.

Elizabeth found herself looking forward to the man, somewhat weathered, but with blue sloppy eyes that were so kind and caring, coming to see her. She invited him in on one of her drinking bouts but he declined and she thought no more of it.

One evening, Elizabeth was pruning the little garden beside her porch steps when Joe's car drove into the compound. She straightened her shirt and put her hand over her eyes to shield them from the sun. She watched as he opened the back door of his car and pulled out his work bag.

"Hi, Joe," she called.

"Hey, Elizabeth," he replied, a smile gracing his face when he saw who had called to him. "Nice day for gardening, eh?"

"Yes, it is. Do you have any place for a garden up there?"

"No," he said with a laugh. "Just concrete everywhere."

"Well, when I get an itty bitty table and two chairs, you're welcome to come down and enjoy mine."

"Oh, I already do," he said. "But wait. I have a couple of

dining chairs. Will they do for now?"

"Only if you can spare them."

"I'll bring them right down," he said.

"Would you like a cup of coffee? Tea?" Elizabeth hoped he wouldn't say tea. She didn't have any in the house.

"I'm Spanish," he said. "I drink coffee, like water."

"Good, I'll get it ready."

Elizabeth was surprised how quickly she fell for Joe. He was a big, hearty man but softly spoken and kind, so kind he reminded her of Jacob. His teenage son lived with their mother who had left him because he couldn't give her the life she wanted. He had to travel an hour away, into the Eastern suburbs, every second weekend to see his son, for just a few hours.

"I want to have enough money to get a place that's closer," he said. "So I can see my Pablito more often."

Elizabeth felt for him. So many things she took for granted now. She had lost her children so many times and yet here she was, still allowing the devil to get the better of her. And here was this man, working so hard, his skin tanned and peeling from the sun, so that he could have the opportunity to spend more time with his child.

She looked forward to the days he came over, now even when she did have a drink and one evening, when Faith and Genny were at their father's house and Joe was having dinner with her, she leaned over the dining table and kissed him. He let himself be kissed but then stood up and excused himself, letting himself out the front door and going up to his flat.

"Why?" Elizabeth admonished herself. She cleared the table and washed the dishes, feeling like she needed something to calm her from the embarrassment she felt at his rebuff. But it was more than just embarrassment. It was disappointment. She had seen the way he looked at her, mostly sly glances, and was sure he felt the same way about her. Perhaps she had lost touch. Maybe she just didn't know what anything meant anymore.

"Can I come in?" Joe was outside the screen door.

"Yes, of course," Elizabeth said, putting down the tea towel and opening the door.

"I'm sorry," he said.

"No, I am." Elizabeth went back to the dining table and sat down. "I misconstrued everything."

"Elizabeth ..."

"Joe, don't let that be something that comes in our way, okay? I value your friendship so much, so can we forget that even happened?"

Joe grinned. "I don't want to forget that," he said. "I want to do that again."

Elizabeth felt a buzz about her body. She hadn't been separated from Mike before, not really. Everything she did with other men was something to be despised. She hadn't felt a genuine connection with anyone. Now here was this man, who was as free as she was. What did they call it? Consenting adults? She relished the feeling. "Then do it, Joe." She let herself be taken into his arms.

It was a wonderful two months, Joe being everything she ever thought Mike could be. He was warm, caring and made her feel like a woman again, a worthy woman. For a short amount of time, she felt she could find happiness with this man. Even her drinking slowed, the thought of not seeing him frightening her.

She was careful not to allow Faith or Genny see how she felt about Joe. She had no idea where the whole thing was going but for the first time in a long time, she felt loved again. And she was in love too, looked forward to his visits, rushing up to his flat sometimes if he got home from work early to see him, to feel his loving arms around her, to savour his kiss. For the first time in a long, long time, she had hope. She could be happy again.

# Chapter 29 - Back to Life

On a Sunday morning, one of the rare moments when Elizabeth was completely sober, not having had a drink for a few days, Mike came to pick up the girls for church and Elizabeth followed them to the door. The boys were in the car as well and they waved at her. Even though this was a routine, she had only recently found the nerve to wait at the door. She'd seen him, but he never did acknowledge her and she always walked back into the house with a feeling of dejection. Why couldn't he just be a little normal? Why couldn't he be more like Joe?

She waved at the children now and her eyes widened when she saw that Mike waved back. Emboldened, she went to the car and stood at his door, shifting from foot to foot. The girls scrambled in the back, their eyes wide, wondering. Their parents had not seen each other, not really, in over six months.

"Hi, Mike," Elizabeth said with a smile.

Mike looked different, calmer. He put his hand on hers. 'We'll talk when I get back," he said.

Elizabeth nodded and stepped away as the car reversed, the kids waving at her from within. Elizabeth shook her head and took a deep breath, her heart beating fast. She was already beginning to feel the urge, but she knew she needed to focus on what was important. But what was important? She took an upward glance. Joe would be waiting for her. They always had breakfast together on Sunday mornings when the girls had gone to church with their father. She suddenly felt dizzy and let herself down on the sofa. What was going on? She was in love with Joe. She had told him as much not so very long ago. She had imagined they may one day have a future together, as a family. Although the children didn't know what was happening between her and Joe, they liked him very much, always had nice words to say about him, always greeted him with friendliness and respect. Why did she now know that was all over?

She had missed Mike so much at the beginning, her heart hurt and she tried not to think of him. But at night, alone in her bed, or in the lounge room with a drink in her hand, uncalled thoughts of him would rise to the surface and she would wonder if she had made a mistake leaving him. The beatings had already dimmed in her memory and she began to remember the Mike that was good and kind. And sexy. They had always been a passionate pair and her admiration of his looks had never waned, even when age put wrinkles in the corners of his eyes.

"Do I want to go back to him?" she said to herself and a fresh bout of dizziness hit her. She wasn't going to beg to go back, making him promises she didn't intend to keep. Things couldn't be the way they were when she left. He would have to give a little too, but she knew how stubborn he was. Still, she had the upper hand this time. She had left him, made a new life for herself.

She walked around the flat and looked around her. It was clean, it was always clean when she wasn't drinking, but she tidied up and paced nervously, waiting for the hour to go past, when Mike would return, hoping Joe wouldn't come down looking for her. Almost on the dot, she heard his car drive up and went to the window. She saw the children scramble out and checking herself in the mirror, she went to the door. The kids came in, her sons kissing her, but Mike remained in the car. Elizabeth furrowed her brows. She thought he was going to come inside.

"Will you come in?" she asked when she got to him.

"I'm not going in there. Come for a drive," he said gruffly.

Elizabeth looked towards the flat where her children stood on the doorstep, their eyes wide with excitement and their mouths smiling. They waved at her and she laughed as she got into the car. As the car moved away she glanced to the flat above hers and saw the curtain in the window move.

She moved back into their home that very day and between tears of love, Elizabeth had promised Mike that she would never drink again, and he promised never to lay an angry hand on her again. They both meant it this time.

# Chapter 30 - Back to Square One

Elizabeth went back to her flat the next day to pack her things and waited for Joe to come home, allowing him time to get into his flat before she made her way up there. She was not going to say goodbye to him in the middle of the compound. "I'm sorry, Joe." She wanted him to take her into his arms again, to tell her to come be with him. Yet, after last night, after making love to her husband and feeling like that was where she belonged, she wasn't sure what she wanted.

"You have your family, Elizabeth," he said. "It's where you should be. If I had the chance for my family to be whole again, I would take it."

"You still love your wife?"

"My ex-wife. And how could I not? She gave me my son. But no, not in the way you think."

She threw her arms around his neck, knowing she loved him, knowing he loved her. They had felt love, never made love, but felt it. "Go be happy with your family," he said and squeezed her tightly for a moment. Then he let her go. "Yes," he said looking into her questioning eyes. "I will be all right."

She fled then, took as much with her as she could manage when David came by with Mike's car to help her with her things, and she never went back. But for the rest of her life, Elizabeth could not wipe the image of Joe, his eyes shiny and wet, his tender face, out of her brain.

Elizabeth knew that she had to make it last this time, and to make a real try of it; she had to ignore the itches. She hated what she'd done to Joe, hated herself for giving in to her husband, but he was just that—her husband—they had made promises, till death do them part, and now, promises to work things out.

The promises lasted less than a month.

Although she and Mike never discussed the incident with Donna, the thought of it made Elizabeth ill. It was one thing to make advances on strangers and even her friends, which had happened on occasion, but her family? A twenty-year-old? It was a whole new level. Elizabeth tried to understand, knowing what Mike was going through. His confidence was shot and although he still held his head high to the world and even to his family, she could see it was a hollow shell he possessed; she knew him too well. His ego was damaged and his advances on Donna could very well be some sort of validation. For his manhood.

She had tried to understand him, had really tried after they had left India. Before then she knew she had been a brat herself. Who was this man she married? Really, who was he? Was he the man who could make her feel like the only woman in the world? Or was he a bully who used his fists to get his way? These were two extremes, she knew that, but how could someone so loving be so tyrannical?

And she? Who was she? Was she someone who took revenge on him by having other men? Could she once again be the devoted wife she began as? Or was everything in a puddle? A dirty mucky puddle and both of them were drowning it, trying to see through the scum, to save each other—or themselves?

How could it work now when nothing had changed? He still didn't want her to drink. She could never trust him. Was their being together because of the children? She remembered something he'd said to her, the night she returned home when she'd asked if the only reason he wanted her back was because of the children. "It's you, always was you. The children are a product of what I feel for you."

She held on to that. She needed to keep that with her, memorised the words, how he said them, his eyes boring into hers. It was the closest she had felt to the intensity of their first few months together, when she felt like she was the only thing he saw.

She kept herself busy, tending to the household chores and taking care of the children, who, although happy that their parents were back together, lived in fear of their bubble shattering again. They all knew that it was only a matter of time.

One evening, when Mike sat down after work with a glass of whisky, Elizabeth sat beside him.

"We can have a drink together," she ventured.

"We both know where that will go," he said back.

Elizabeth knew this would be his response, so she was

prepared. "It's only fair that if you drink in front of me, that I can too." She was pleading with him. "What can happen? I'm in the safety of my home ... with you. We'll have a quiet drink and go to bed together and it will be fine."

"You won't stop tomorrow," he said flatly.

"Mike, please, if I didn't have to hide, I would be able to stop because I know that it wouldn't be a problem and I can have one again the next time you do. We can have a drink together, in each other's company, safe, with no one else to wreck things."

Elizabeth could see him thinking and her hands began to shake in excitement. Mike nodded. Elizabeth smiled; it was a win.

Music wafted outside while they reminisced about their youth and laughed at their antics. They talked about how much they missed their old ways as well as their struggles in this country and dreamt of when they would be able to afford a trip to India to visit their friends.

"Dance with me," Mike said then and held out his hand to her. Elizabeth took it and they danced slowly to the music, an old song, one she knew well. She hummed to it as she ran her fingers through his hair, feeling his hand pressed against the small of her back and for a moment she was transported back to the time they were in love, so in love that they couldn't see anything else. When they were young, when the only troubles they had were how they were going to see each other. A flash of Andy came to her brain and she smiled. What if she had stayed with Andy? Where would she be now? She never would have loved Andy like she loved Mike. She never would have had these four beautiful children. She chose not to think about all the horrible things that she may not have had to endure if she had chosen Andy. Besides, she would have been bored to death. At least with Mike ...

The clouds parted, the moon shining upon them and Elizabeth looked at the night sky. It felt like a sign. This was it. This was the new beginning, not what they had been through already. This was the life she'd envisioned. Sitting together, dancing forever with the man she loved, sipping their drinks together. She felt his hand take hers, closing it to his chest and she closed her eyes, her face still tilted to the stars. She wanted to hold the moment, the peace she felt, the love she felt for this man, mirrored in the way he clutched at her hand, not forceful, not threatening, soft, gentle, hers only. She was here with Mike, the man who she loved absolutely.

She leaned her head back and looked deeply into his eyes. "I'll always love you, Mike."

He didn't smile, just let his eyes bore back into hers. "You will always be mine, baby."

She awoke to the alarm the next morning, Mike's arms still around her, and she sank her back deeper into the recess of his body. She could hear the children move about the house getting ready for school and groaned. She hadn't drunk all that much but her body ached and in a good way.

"They're old enough to get themselves ready," Mike said sleepily.

"I know," she said and closed her eyes but not a few minutes later, Mike was scrambling out of bed himself. She stifled a laugh. Mike never could sleep in on the best of days. He was always up with the birds and even after the night they had had, drinking, laughing and making love late into the night, this was no exception.

But the hair of the dog called to Elizabeth, even though she hadn't drunk enough to have a hangover. The children had gone to school and Mike, on afternoon shift, left at twelve. She spent the morning getting his lunch ready and tidying up, looking at the clock and cursing its hands for moving so slowly. She berated herself and then decided she would do the right thing. She had promised Mike and she had promised herself. She thought of the possibility that she could still get to have a drink with Mike on the odd occasion and not go overboard. It could work.

Yet the moment she waved Mike's car out of sight, she found herself hurrying to the cupboard where Mike kept his alcohol. She wrinkled her nose at the bottle of whisky, she still didn't like how it tasted, but she found herself pouring a finger of it into a glass and skolled it. She put the bottle back and went about her day, trying to focus on the tasks at hand. She hated herself for wanting more. She drummed her fingers on the sink as she looked out the window. Was it boredom, perhaps? Maybe she needed to find a job again? But Mike had made it clear that he wanted her home now that his salary was covering costs, now that he had accepted that he would never fly again.

Distraction, that's what she needed, something familiar, something to keep her mind off the alcohol.

She called her mother. She only ever spoke to her mother or sisters on special occasions and it was usually them that called her. Overseas phone calls were expensive and she knew Mike would be furious but she needed something to keep her away from temptation, something safe.

"It's me, Mother." Elizabeth's heart constricted at the familiar gentle tone that answered the phone.

"Hello, Elizabeth," said Doris, tentative. "Is everything okay?"

Elizabeth heard the note of alarm in her mother's voice and swallowed. She had always been the trouble child and now, even in her forties, she still was. She hated that she worried her mother, she wished she could have been nearer to her. "Yes," she said, swallowing again. Her heart ached to see her mother's beautiful face. It had been so long, not since David was twelve, when Doris had brought Molly to Derrum. Tess, Audrey and Freddie had families of their own, people she saw in photographs but had never met. When Doris and Molly had left after a three-week stay, she had cried for a solid week, had drunk herself silly. "Everything's fine, Mother." She laughed shrilly, trying to sound chipper.

"Why are you calling?"

"I just wanted to talk to you; I miss you, that's all."

"How are the children?" Doris's voice still sounded rattled.

"Everyone is fine! Tell me about Molly's new baby." She knew she had to distract her mother and her grandchildren were the light of her life. She already had twelve, including the four Elizabeth had given her.

"Oh, he is the cutest," said Doris, her voice relaxing, becoming almost songlike. "He has big stretchy ears like his father but he is Molly all over. She's doing well ..." Doris paused. "My girl, can you afford to call like this?"

No, Elizabeth couldn't afford to call at all, but she needed to feel the safety in her mother's voice. "It's okay," said Elizabeth softly, then reconsidered. "Can you call me back then?"

"Elizabeth, I will call you on the weekend when the rates are cheaper, okay?"

Elizabeth didn't want to remind her about the time difference; it would be early morning when the rates were cheaper. And she needed her mother now. But she couldn't be selfish. Her mother had her own financial problems, saving her money to send gifts to

Elizabeth and the children, monetary gifts in the cards they received for Christmases and birthdays. "Okay, Mother. I love you."

"I love you too, my darling. Give my love and kisses to the children."

Elizabeth hung up, noticing her mother didn't mention Mike. Why would she? Everyone knew what he was. They had tried to convince her to leave him so many times but she couldn't. Sometimes she resented them for leaving her alone. In their defence they thought they had left her with a family around her in Derrum. How they had all let her down, save for poor cousin Sadie.

She missed her brother who had married soon after they had gone to Canada. He'd become a writer for a newspaper, was dabbling in novels now. Tess and Audrey also married soon after, Tess preferring to stay at home with her children while Audrey became a beauty consultant. She smiled at that. She always thought it would have been Tess who would have gone that way, she had been so obsessed with her looks. Molly was also successful, not married, preferring to focus on her career as a businesswoman, what business Elizabeth was not sure, but she always marvelled at the suits Molly wore in the photographs. Now she had a child, all on her own. Good for Molly.

Elizabeth sat with the receiver still in her hand and looked into the dressing table mirror. And what was she doing? Elizabeth with all her talent, her brains, her looks? Nothing. She was the one who took life by the throat, never waited to be asked. Now here she was, having everything and having done nothing.

She remembered the conversation her parents had all those years ago. Maybe her mother had been right all along. Maybe she should have learned to be more restrained. Maybe her father had it wrong all along. She missed her father, wished he were around to wipe the smears from her face, the tears she didn't realise had been streaming down her cheeks. She hung up the phone and lay on the bed, wrapping the blanket around her. She shut her eyes tight and tried to keep the face of her father before her. Before she knew it she was asleep.

When she awoke, just past two in the afternoon, she took a deep breath. No, she told herself. This would work. It was not too late to exercise restraint. She tried to remember last night, how good it had been, how that moment in time would come again, that moment she looked to the stars and felt like this was exactly where she was supposed to be. That moment that had felt like home.

She got out of bed, had a shower and walked into the kitchen. She opened the cupboards, trying to work out what to prepare for dinner. And her hand kept returning to the cabinet that held Mike's whisky. "Just this time," she said to herself.

Elizabeth found ways. Just a swig here and a sip there. She would only drink a small amount and replace it with water. As she usually poured Mike his drinks, he would never notice it. She began to buy her own alcohol with her weekly shopping and hid her bottles carefully, behind the toilet, under the towels in the laundry, even in her children's sock drawer. She knew she couldn't go overboard and even though there were times when Mike suspected, he gave her the benefit of the doubt, because things right now seemed good. They were both making an effort to make it work. Sometimes there were physical altercations, but Elizabeth could deal with them and now they were few and far between. As long as she let Mike think he was in control, things would be fine. She was at home with her husband and all her children, which was where she always wanted to be.

# Chapter 31 - The Visit

Elizabeth was propping a cushion when she heard a sound from the street. She smiled and leaned over the sofa to part the blinds.

Carolyn. She was here! It had been a while since she'd seen her and she always relished sharing memories with her best friend. Elizabeth had spent the morning and afternoon cooking and cleaning with the help of the children and was preparing for a cosy catch-up with Carolyn. She expected to stay up late into the evening chatting of old times and reminiscing about their youth, hearing about Carolyn's children and sharing stories about her own. Carolyn had been Elizabeth's best friend since as long as they both could remember and had kept in touch through mail. They had visited each other a few times during the last couple of years but as Carolyn lived a good hour's drive away, it was hard for them to see each other often.

Mike and Elizabeth had just celebrated their wedding anniversary and decided to make a night of it with her best friend. Mike had gone to pick Carolyn up from the train station and she would spend the night in the girls' room, with Mike to drop her back to the station the next day.

Elizabeth saw the car roll into the driveway and raced to the door. Carolyn threw herself at Elizabeth and hugged her tightly and Elizabeth felt a surge of warmth flow through her. She ushered her in and the children came in to greet her, quietly disappearing after the obligatory greetings, and they settled in for a chat.

Carolyn bought Elizabeth a grey silk scarf and Elizabeth had thrown it around her neck immediately to show her appreciation. Mike came out of the kitchen with a bottle of whisky and two glasses. He placed one in front of Carolyn and one in front of himself and proceeded to pour the whisky.

Elizabeth laughed in indignation. "Did you forget mine, Mike?"

"You're not having any," he said simply.

Carolyn looked about her and giggled nervously.

"What do you mean?" Elizabeth felt a pinch in her chest, an uneasy feeling. "It's my anniversary too."

"Elizabeth," Mike said with a snicker. "You won't be able to hold yourself."

Elizabeth didn't quite know how to respond. She was dumbstruck, humiliated that Mike could say something like that in front of her friend. Sure, everyone knew about Elizabeth's drinking but to demean her like that ... Her skin bristled and before she would allow her eyes to well, she got up and walked out of the room. She leaned against the kitchen sink, expecting one of them to walk in after her but no one did. Her eyes were stinging. She and Mike had spent many evenings drinking together in the last year. He knew she could hold her liquor; recently she hadn't drunk anywhere close to what she could but she held off, using her willpower to stop before things got out of hand. It had worked, was still working. Why would he now, of all times, not allow her to have a drink?

A thought struck her, but she pushed it from her mind. Mike perhaps ... but Carolyn was her best friend. They had been friends since they were children; she would never betray her.

Yet Carolyn didn't come to find her.

She took a deep breath and as embarrassed as she felt, walked back into the room and sat down next to Mike. The evening passed with a lump in Elizabeth's throat, but she smiled and took part in the conversation as normally as she could, looking for signs that something else was happening and when she saw Mike brush a little too close to Carolyn as he walked into the other room to refill their drinks, her heart shuddered.

Mike returned Carolyn to the station the next day and Elizabeth went into the laundry and took a long swig of gin from her stash under the sink. "Why didn't I go with them?" she asked herself. "To drop Carolyn off?" She knew why. She could already begin to see the writing on the wall. For one, she needed to let whatever was going to happen, happen. Besides, she knew all she wanted to do was have a sip of gin. She had watched the night before as they both drank, her lips pursed, her mouth watering. She had gone to bed, a rumble in her belly with the ache of the craving.

She let herself slide to the floor and put her head in her hands. Then she went to the bathroom and gargled.

Elizabeth could pinpoint the moment things took a turn for

the worse. It was that moment when Mike came home from the station.

"Did she go off okay?" asked Elizabeth when he came through the door.

"Yes," he replied and walked straight past her to the bedroom without looking at her.

She followed him and stood in the doorway, watching as he changed his clothes. Why he needed to change, she couldn't fathom, but he put on a sweater and walked out, pushing past her as he did.

"Where are you going?" she asked.

"My parents' house," he replied and Elizabeth followed as he walked out the front door without any further explanation. Elizabeth sat herself down on the sofa next to Faith, who was doing a jigsaw puzzle.

"Help me, Mum," Faith said and Elizabeth smiled, happy for the distraction. She looked at the pieces of the puzzle and couldn't figure what was what.

"Where are the others?" Elizabeth asked.

"David and Robert went out somewhere and Genny is in our room doing some art thing."

"And tell me, Faith, more about John."

"Mum!"

Elizabeth poked her daughter in the ribs. "Come on. Are you in love with him?"

Faith shrugged and she lowered her eyes.

"Make sure it's more than love," said Elizabeth. "Make sure he is a good man, can take care of you, can treat you well."

Faith stopped and looked at Elizabeth. "I'm sorry, Mum," she said.

"What for?" Elizabeth said in surprise.

"Just because," she said, and shrugged again, her eyes back on the puzzle.

Elizabeth squeezed her eyes tight, her heart torn. She still loved Mike, but she didn't know whether that love was enough anymore. Sometimes she could hate him as ferociously as she loved him.

Mike came home late that evening, claimed he ate dinner at his parents' house and went straight to bed. He was up early every day, out of the house sometimes before Elizabeth even roused herself out of bed and returned home late at night. When he was on nightshift, he still awoke early and on the rare occasion when he was at home, he avoided her and spoke to her in monosyllables. His moodiness permeated the air and the children avoided being in the same room as him which was not hard as he was not often around. But this time, Elizabeth couldn't fathom why. What had happened that had turned him around again, and so suddenly? There would be times where he slapped her for no other reason than she was in his way.

They didn't drink together anymore, as the relaxing evenings that used to be usually ended in an argument. Most evenings Mike spent at his parents' home, coming home late at night and in a foul mood, and she'd usually serve him his dinner and turn in for the evening. She had to wait up for him or she knew he would yell and wake up the rest of the house. She was at a loss as to how to make things better again and Mike was not a man for talking: "weak men talked, strong men did", that was his motto. And Mike did. It showed on Elizabeth's face and arms and even on her shins.

She tried to talk to his mother about it, but Alma would not hear a bad word about her son. She made excuses for his moods and asked Elizabeth to forgive his foul language and loud voice. She refused to acknowledge that Mike was violent and literally looked away when she saw it happen in front of her very eyes.

Once, when she confronted his mother after she had gotten a backhander from Mike in front of her, she saw the old woman's head jerk backwards in shock.

"Did you see that?" Elizabeth said triumphantly, hoping she would be believed now.

Mike's mother quickly corrected her face after Mike had looked at her for support. "I saw his hand slip," she said. "He was trying to pick up the cushion and his hand slipped."

Elizabeth knew it was useless. The old woman was sweet to her at times, but she would defend her son until the day she died.

Elizabeth couldn't bear it anymore. It had been weeks of this, weeks of spiralling, weeks of sneaking around trying to quell her fears with a sip of gin, and she spent her days tidying up and cooking and dreading the moment Mike came home. She even began to look for a job, hoping that she would find something else to keep her busy and perhaps if she was contributing to the household, Mike may respect her a little more.

One spring day, when the sun was shining so brightly that Elizabeth had to leave her gardening to get out of it, something hit her. This was no life. The children were at school and Mike was at work. Mike had kicked her out of bed the night before, quite literally, and she had landed with a thump on the floor. The humiliations she felt were becoming a normal part of life, she was being treated worse than a stray dog in her own home and she spent a sleepless night on the sofa, knowing she had to retaliate, or at least have something that made her happy.

When Mike left for work and she had done her daily chores, she took a deep breath, felt the fear and dismissed it, called for a taxi and directed the driver to the local bar.

Although terrified of what she was doing, the sensation of freedom ran through her body the moment she stepped into the doors of the bar. The familiar smell of liquor accosted her senses and although she was not a fan of beer, she welcomed the aroma just floating about in the air. No one here to hide from, no one to tell her not to do it and no one who would make her feel like she was nothing. Elizabeth had always been a person who drew people to her and soon, she was singing and dancing, chatting and laughing, feeling her old self again. No one judged her here.

A couple she had met at the bar dropped her home and Elizabeth spent the evening trying to sober up with hot coffee and laps around the backyard with the help of her children before Mike came home.

"What do you need, Mum?" David asked when Elizabeth asked him to go to the shop.

"I need more coffee," replied Elizabeth. "Dad can't function without coffee in the morning and I don't think there's enough."

"Sure," said David and called for Robert to come for a drive with him.

"Could you get my purse from my handbag?" asked Elizabeth. Her body was tired from dancing, even though her mood was bright. She hadn't had so much fun in such a long time.

"It's not here," said David, rummaging through the handbag.

"It should be," said Elizabeth and took the handbag from David, upending it. Lots of things fell out—a lipstick, keys, a nail file—

but no purse. "It has to be," she said, panic beginning to rise. "It's got to be there ..." There was a scramble, everyone, including the other children, participating in the hunt, from the letterbox outside the house to the backyard which Elizabeth had been pacing.

"Maybe you left it at the bar?" Robert suggested when Elizabeth let her hands flop onto her lap in desperation.

"That's what I was afraid of," she replied.

Before she could finish her sentence, Faith was already picking up the Yellow Pages. "What's the name of the bar?"

"Hotel West," she replied, glad she had remembered the big sign when the taxi had driven into its gates. She spoke to the bartender who looked around and told her that he couldn't find anything that resembled her purse. She left her number with him and hoped for the best. She replaced the receiver and she slapped her forehead with the back of her hand. "The bills," she groaned.

"What about bills, Mum?" asked David.

"The gas bill. It was in the purse. I kept it there to remind me to pay it because it's overdue."

"You can call the gas company," suggested Genny. "You've done that before. Make them send you a new one?"

"Yes," Elizabeth said, a little less panicked. "I can do that." Her head was still spinning but this was a calamity that could be avoided. She would call the next day.

When Mike got home from work, he barely noticed her shaking hands as she served him his dinner and after he had eaten, he left to go to his parents' house. Elizabeth was relieved. She sat in the living room, watching a movie with the children, glad for their presence, their quick thinking, their support.

It was two days later when Mike picked up the ringing phone. It was a day on a week when he worked nightshift and the children were all at school. Elizabeth thought nothing of it as his mother or sister called him often, but the tone of his voice made her slow her movements, while she tried to decipher what was being said. She slyly looked at him and saw his head turn to her as he spoke into the phone and she began to tremble when she saw his jaw tighten and his eyes narrow.

"Where's your purse?" he asked, after he hung up the phone.

Elizabeth just shook her head. Her brain was searching for something to say to him.

"Where is it?" he demanded as he walked towards her.

Understanding what the call was about, Elizabeth lowered her head. She felt herself fall to the floor from the weight of his hand.

It was one of the worst beatings she got from him, even though she fought back, scratching and biting and trying to protect her face and head. It only stopped when David walked into the house and screamed for his father to stop. Mike's crazed eyes looked at his son, and he got off Elizabeth and stormed out of the house.

David helped his mother into her armchair. "It's okay, Mum, it'll be okay," David offered while he wiped her forehead with a wet towel.

Elizabeth just lowered her head, feeling the soothing hands of her son on her face. It made her want to cry more than the beating and all the humiliation Mike put her through.

# Chapter 32 - Freedom

*It was the seventh night in her daughters' room. Theirs was quite a large room; in fact, one could call it a double room. It looked as though it had been made for a rich lady as it was a large-sized cube with an attached area that resembled a study; they believed it may have been a dressing room and Faith and Genny would lay their hairbrushes and costume jewellery out on their own dressing table as they thought a grand dame might. Elizabeth had created a makeshift bed in that space, even though her daughters insisted she could sleep on one of theirs. Elizabeth didn't want to put them out, saying she felt more comfortable on the floor; however, sometimes at night, she felt one or both of the girls snuggle up beside her.*

She knew it couldn't last forever.

Elizabeth could feel the need, the thirst for alcohol. At night, her body shook and her skin tingled and she had to put her hand over her mouth for fear of her teeth chattering. Gin was her devil, but the way she felt at this moment, she would kill for a cheap cask of wine. Wine made her ill, but she would take anything right now. The thought of it made her mouth water and her heart beat faster. She prayed for strength and for a moment, felt a calm behold her. She held on to the prayer, hoping she would be asleep by the time it ended.

She knew what desperation was, she had felt it more than she should have in her forty-one years of life. She remembered the hard times, when she was alone, she remembered being without her children for all those years, she remembered losing everything she cared about, her family, her first baby; and she remembered the mental hospital, which had almost broken her. She survived all that and she knew she would have to survive more that was still to come. This was no life.

She wasn't ready to let go of the booze yet; she couldn't, she knew she was still too weak.

Booze—what a wretched name for it, it gave her that label, *the alcoholic,* but the word, even in her prayers, was enough for her to feel her belly tingle. Sobbing quietly, her mind went through the available options—and none were good.

Mike had found her hiding spots that morning and had smashed bottle upon bottle into the kitchen sink. He held her wrist and even as she yelled and twisted in defiance, he held one of the shards of glass to her face.

"Do it!" she yelled, sticking her chin out, as he raised the bottle over her head.

"Daddy!" Genny screamed and Elizabeth and Mike both turned to see their youngest daughter standing in the doorway, her large brown eyes pleading with him. Mike lowered his hand and he smashed the glass in the sink, pushing Elizabeth away roughly as he did. He strode out of the room and Genny watched as her mother held on to the edge of the sink.

As though in a trance, Elizabeth watched as the gin, working its way through the shattered glass, slithered down the drain. She put her hand in, retrieved the bottom of a brown bottle and looked at it. She could see that it contained clear liquid with shimmers of glass twinkling and snickering at her. She swished it around slowly, considering ...

"Mum!"

Elizabeth dropped it back into the sink and walked slowly to her daughter.

"I'll clean it later," she said, patting Genny on her head as she went past.

"I'll do it," Genny said as she walked to the littered sink. Elizabeth walked to the door and turned around. Genny was already picking up bits of glass, tears rolling down her face. Elizabeth's heart shattered in as many pieces as the bottles in that sink but she didn't have the energy anymore.

"Need help?" David must have come through the back door. He was beside Genny and she shook her head silently. He put an arm around her shoulders and squeezed gently, while she leaned her head on her brother's chest and sobbed.

Elizabeth stood there for a moment watching them. At least they were there for each other. They had to be. But they just couldn't go through this anymore, day after day and night after night. She went back to her daughters' room and sat down on Faith's bed. Faith was at the dressing table, trying on the new earrings John had bought her. She looked at her mother through the reflection and got up to sit beside her.

"I'm okay, I'm fine," Elizabeth said, seeing the crease between her daughter's eyes.

"He will calm down, he eventually does." Faith said.

"I don't know this time. But it will be fine." She managed a smile, trying to reassure Faith, but she knew she wasn't fooling her. "Go back to your homework, don't you have an exam coming up?"

Elizabeth didn't wait for Faith's answer. She could feel the desperation begin to envelop her again and she walked to the door. Peeping out of the room, she didn't see Mike anywhere. She tiptoed to the bathroom slowly.

"Where are you going?" she heard his voice boom from the living room.

"Bathroom," she called back and kept moving. She closed the door of the bathroom and turned the lock. She hurried to the commode and looked behind it.

Gone.

Elizabeth had hoped he hadn't found this one. It was small enough to stash underneath the siphon but the spot was empty. She pushed her hand through, hoping it may have moved to the other side, but no, nothing.

She could almost hear him sniggering at her. She could feel her face flush and looked around again, her heart beginning to beat faster. Above the toilet, on the windowsill, she saw a bottle of Pine O Cleen disinfectant, a small amount of the green liquid left in it. She grabbed the bottle, opened it and put it to her lips. As she felt it burn her throat, she came to her senses and spat it out into the toilet bowl. She shoved her fingers down her mouth and felt as the warm vomit soothed her burning throat. Rushing to the sink, she poured handfuls of water into her mouth, bringing more out. Then she sat herself on the edge of the bathtub as tears ran down her face. She knew something had to give.

Mike was very angry, more so than usual, and this time she was scared.

This time she was also very tired, just tired of it all. Most days she just wanted to curl up in a ball and die. She called to God to let her die, but the thought of leaving her children terrified her. She had already missed out on much of their lives. They had spent so much of their childhood in boarding schools while Mike was working, and she was ... she could barely even remember where she was for most of that time. She just knew the booze came first then and it couldn't anymore.

She sighed heavily. What life was she giving them now? One of fear and worry for her. She knew she was better off without Mike and he was better off without her. He had most of his family here in Australia, while all of hers was in another country. His family would look after him, feed him, make sure he was okay. But she wondered what leaving again would accomplish. She had done it so many times already and either she had always returned, or Mike had always brought her back. The last time was promising. It was the furthest she had come to having her own life. And Joe ...

But she'd come back. What was the point?

It had to happen, she surmised. She was being careful but this time she had slipped and when he had gotten home from work and smelled whisky on her breath, Mike had gone in search of her hiding places and had found her bottles. And he had made her stand by and watch while he smashed them all. He was livid that she had outsmarted him, more so than because she had been drinking in the first place.

Finding the bottles had made Mike's moods even worse. He swore at Elizabeth when he saw her and never missed the opportunity to give her a pinch or a slap when she was within reaching distance. The days were a reprieve, and when Mike came home from work, she stayed quiet, taking his physical and verbal abuse, not wanting to aggravate him even more, hoping things would get better. She thought that at some stage, his attitude towards her would improve, but even as the days passed, there were no signs of improvement.

Life had now become hell for Elizabeth. The children took to staying in their rooms; the atmosphere was toxic. Although Mike never touched the children, his tempers scared them and they knew that this time it was worse for Elizabeth. It came to the point that every time she would cross paths with Mike, he would slap her, even in the middle of the night, coming into the girls' room, where she now took to sleeping, to throw vile words at her. He accused her of sneaking away and drinking and of despicable behaviour, saying things that shocked her, and by now not much Mike did or said could shock Elizabeth. Even the children's presence didn't deter him. She couldn't figure it out and she was sick of trying. She realised she would never understand him.

Mike was completely in control now, ridding the house of all the liquor, including his own. He didn't trust Elizabeth with money anymore, sending the children to buy cooking needs on a day-to-day basis.

When Elizabeth took to sleeping in her daughters' room at night she began to consider leaving him again. When she thought of it, she brightened, but realised that it would end the same way, back in his house, taking his abuse. She knew the children were better off if she and Mike were not together, even though she could still picture the joy on their faces when she had returned the last time. This was no life for them either but leaving and returning as they had been doing for most of their married life was not much better. She had even given up the chance of being happy with a man she had managed to fall in love with. But she knew she couldn't go backwards, not again. She resigned herself to living like this for the rest of her life and the thought repulsed her. She was a free spirit, loved by all who met her. Her mother would be horrified if she knew, but her mother was not here. Even though Elizabeth hated feeling sorry for herself, this time, she indulged it.

"I am not a worthless human," she said to herself. She didn't know where that came from but the words made her sit up. She thought back to her childhood, her adolescence, the bold girl she was who took no one's nonsense, her father's words—"you are spirited, don't lose that". She thought back to the days where she had the world in her hands, bright and sparkling. She had a voice which everyone wanted to hear which now was silenced. She remembered being the person who could outrun everyone in the neighbourhood, now she had a broken back, a broken heart, a broken spirit.

She had it all. Then she met Mike.

Mike was on nightshift and the children were doing their own thing around the house and she looked around her. She had a lovely home, decorated with whatever she could manage to afford, a trip to a garage sale or the op shop, some items sent to her from Canada. It was a cosy home, lamps giving the living room a warm glow. A façade.

This was not a cosy home. This was hell. "Enough," she said to no one.

"What, Mum?" Faith, who was with her boyfriend, John, stopped in the hallway.

"I'm going out," said Elizabeth.

"Can we come?" Faith's eyes lit up.

Elizabeth considered this. Yes, it would be nice to have them along. Sure, she would be taking them to a bar but John was of age and he was responsible. He would make sure Faith was all right. "Yes, let's call a taxi."

Mike usually didn't get home until 1:00 a.m., so Elizabeth, with Faith, and John in tow, went to a bar. Again she felt the freedom that was so elusive these days. A band played rock and roll, while she danced and drank to her heart's content. Every time she began to fear the repercussions, she shoved it into the recesses of her brain. Nothing she could get from Mike was worse than what she was going through right now.

That night was also the night she realised she was a woman who was worth more, deserved more.

Pete and Tina. Elizabeth noticed them eye her when she was on the dance floor and she was suddenly aware of how it felt to be looked at like that again. She smiled brightly at him, she couldn't help herself, and that was enough of an invitation for Pete to stroll over, take her hand and twirl her under his arm.

When they sat down at a table and chatted about nothing in particular, the weather, she recalled was part of that conversation, Elizabeth felt the ache and gratification of social interaction, which she hadn't even realised she was missing. Tina was a little younger than her, but she was bright and fun and there were no strings attached and no impressions to be made. Elizabeth was having the time of her life but before she knew it, it was time to leave. They knew they had to get home before Mike did and Faith called for a taxi. They bade goodbye to their new friends, but by the time they got outside, the cab had sped away. They called for another.

Waiting outside the pub, Faith and John looked at their watches. Time was running by too quickly and it was already 1:00 a.m. when the cab arrived.

"We can't go home," said Faith, fear in her eyes.

"No more fear," said Elizabeth, knowing what awaited them

if they went back home. They all trudged back into the bar and explained their predicament to Tina, who offered to let them stay at her place which wasn't very far away. After a few more beers, they all headed back to Tina's home.

They stayed up all night in worry and fear and in the morning, Elizabeth decided she was not returning home. She couldn't live in fear anymore. "Go home," she told Faith.

"Where will you be?"

"You can stay here for a few days," Tina piped in.

Elizabeth smiled. That's all she needed, one kind word. "Thank you," she said, touched at the gesture of a virtual stranger. "May I use your phone?"

"I'm staying too," said Faith, looking hopefully at Tina, who nodded, and Elizabeth lifted her daughter's chin.

"It will be hard," she said.

"I know," said Faith. "What about the others?"

Elizabeth considered this for a moment. "That's up to them."

"You're not going back?" Faith asked, a little twinkle in her eye, and Elizabeth knew the answer.

Elizabeth could never have predicted the impact of that decision. She never could have foreseen how her unrestrained drinking would affect her physical and mental health. She could never have anticipated how this decision would impact her children. And test her faith.

She couldn't see and she didn't want to see.

She was free.

# Epilogue

## 2023

Freedom, she pondered one day, was a state of mind.

"How philosophical of you, Mum." Faith laughed.

"But you know what I mean," said Elizabeth. She snickered. When did it happen that the children thought they knew more than her? Maybe when Faith turned fifty? No, she gathered. For the most part she had been the child herself, even when she herself was fifty.

"What is freedom anyway?" asked Robert. "It's what you think it is."

Elizabeth tried not to roll her eyes. She used to worry about Robert, how he constantly tried to work out the past, how he tried to figure out his mother and father, like putting the pieces together like that jigsaw he had worked so hard on would somehow make sense of his own life. She nodded, hoping one day he would find his way, knowing he was stronger than both she and Mike had been. "How is your father?" she asked.

"Same ol'," said Genny averting her eyes. "Um ..."

It was sometimes hard for the children to talk about Mike with Elizabeth. She wanted the best for him but she also resented him. She resented that he had gotten on with his life when she had left him, remarried, bought a house, settled into the life she had once despised. She had not seen him in over thirty years. Once on a street, when he acknowledged her with a wave but he made it clear there was no room for her in his life. And for her part, Elizabeth felt the same. He had taken too much already. She was happy. Alone, but sober for more than ten years.

It had been hard, she had drunk herself into a stupor. Her freedom wasn't freedom as she had thought then—from Mike maybe, but not from the booze. There were a couple of close calls, she had been close to death on a number of occasions. Freedom had not been the saviour she had hoped for.

No, her saviour had been her faith. One day, after Faith's fortieth birthday party, she had put down her glass and had never touched alcohol after that. She didn't know how it happened, could not have in her wildest fantasies believed she could do that. She called it a miracle. It was a miracle, there was no other word for it.

That was freedom. Real freedom. She became the mother she knew she had been all along. But now she was able to show it. She regretted the years she'd wasted but what was the point of regret? It was forgiveness she needed. From her children, but mainly from herself. That was the hardest thing to do. But when she looked around at her children, so close to her, she knew she must have done something right. She said a silent prayer of thanks.

A knock on the door saved Genny from delivering an answer.

"David," they all called out in unison.

"We're talking about Mum's story again," warned Faith. Sometimes these discussions didn't have a nice ending. When Elizabeth recalled some of the things that happened, albeit funny, she felt her heart melt at the thought of what her children went through to protect her.

David laughed. He loved to rock the boat, get everyone started. "Oh, are we remembering the day she fell out of the taxi?"

"No, not that one," said Genny.

"When Dad flung her wig off her head at the dance?"

"It was when she hauled Faith off to live with her and Tina," Genny replied.

Elizabeth glanced at Robert. He was clenching his teeth. He had never warmed to Pete, who Elizabeth began to see seriously after leaving Mike. Rightly so. Pete took another twenty years of Elizabeth's life, and not in a good way.

"And what about Pete? What about that story?" David nudged at Genny.

"That's a whole other story," said Elizabeth. "Let's have dinner."

The End

# Acknowledgements

A lot of thanks due here – this book was four years in the making.

My parents – for teaching me in good ways and bad, the way to navigate life, to be accepting of no matter who or what came our way.

My siblings – we always had each other's back, and we still do.

My children – for reminding me that it's so easy to fall back on what you know rather than learn from it – they do this without even knowing they do.

John – because no one will love me like you do – and because you have so much faith in me, it's uncanny.

My editor, Anita – this is the tenth book you've edited for me: you really are the easiest person to work with.

Julia Kalman – wow, what a find. Our collaborations have just expanded and made me a better writer – thank you for your foreword (I'm especially chuffed at the comparison to Virginia Woolf).

Dawn – for helping me come up with the title – perfect!

My beta-readers – you gave me such wonderful feedback, most of which I took to heart and used.

All the people who have encouraged me without even realising you did. Thank you.

And of course, thank you dear reader, for taking the time to go on this journey with me.

# ABOUT THE AUTHOR

Rita H Rowe is a teacher and author with a Bachelor of Arts, a Diploma of Education, and a Masters in Writing. Her journey into writing began as a lifelong dream that she was finally able to pursue at the age of forty-seven, resulting in her first novel, Never the Moon. Rita pours her heart and soul into her writing, incorporating her personal experiences with love, romance, hurt, and abuse. To Rita, writing is both a form of therapy and a way to connect with like-minded readers on a deeper level. As an author, Rita hopes to be remembered as someone who created worlds that readers could lose themselves in, even just for a little while. When she isn't writing, Rita enjoys playing pool, painting, going on motorbike rides, and spending time with her children and mother.

# Other Novels by Rita H Rowe

## NEVER THE MOON

Two men who could not be more different.

One woman caught between them.

When Jennifer loses David, the love of her life, her world falls apart. Fleeing to New York for a fresh start, she meets Jack, rugged and handsome, everything she could hope for.

But her world is unexpectedly plunged into chaos and violence. An abusive husband, a loveless marriage - and no way out.

When David comes back into her life; Jennifer is torn between the man she has always loved and a life she has now chosen...

Never The Moon interweaves the lives of Jennifer, David and Jack, revealing the power of love - and the destruction it can leave in its wake...

*'Inspired and emotive, a great romance and heart-string tugger of a story...well done to a new voice of romance...' Debra, Indiebook reviewer.*

## SHE REMEMBERED

Her beauty is a curse. Her memories a void. Elena cannot remember. All she has are fragments of a past life that feel foreign to her, only glimpsed in fleeting moments through violent nightmares. Struggling to put her life together and find acceptance, she takes comfort in Luke, a charming boy who seems to like her as much as she likes him. But nothing has ever come easily to Elena—and when she wakes up between blood- soaked sheets next to the body of a man recently stabbed, what little stability she had comes crashing down around her. With no one to help her and nowhere to go, Elena has to salvage the broken pieces of her life all on her own. If only she could remember

...

*'I didn't predict the outcome and I thoroughly enjoyed the journey to get there. Definitely 5 stars from me.' Umm Ibrahim, Amazon reviewer.*

## DANCING WITH GHOSTS

Alex will never dance again. Her parents and her dreams, all lost in one fateful night. Unable to put her faith in love and happiness, not even for Nicholas, the man she loves, she escapes to Chernut, a country town far from the reminders of her past. Here at the beautiful Lovelet Manor, inhabited by a family who are as lost as she is, Alex finds solace in the picturesque gardens of which she is caretaker, accepting that her life can never be full again. But when she meets Edward in the grand gazebo, she discovers that her heart may not be done with her yet. And for the first time in a long time, she allows herself to be loved.

But is she losing her mind? Will the ghosts of her past keep her running forever?

Or will Alex find herself before she runs out of time?

*'Binge worthy. This is a ghost story with romance and characters so very real they are believable. I loved it.' Amazon reviewer.*

## THE BAD SEED

Love, betrayal and murder. He's the new kid in town, complete with a sordid past and a tarnished family name, doomed to fail even before he begins. Jenna is the only person who sees beyond Joey's past and they fall deeply in love. But there are already forces determined to separate the pair by any means necessary. Tommy, the thug, who is hell-bent on breaking Joey by brute force, Jenna's mother, whose connection with Joey cannot be ignored, and Joey's own past, the strongest weapon against them. Only Tim, the local police officer, shows any compassion to the plight of Joey and Jenna, but is Tim all he seems? And what role will he play in their fate? Can young love survive in a town filled with discrimination?

Can Joey and Jenna get out before they fall apart, or is it already too late?

*'A thrilling, heartbreaking read. I finished this book four days ago and I still can't get it out of my mind.' Tina MK, Amazon reviewer.*

## BECOMING RUTHLESS

When all the men she knows are liars, maybe it's time to become one too. Ruth is young, excited about life and not looking for love. Yet love finds her, and Ruth is thrilled. But she is left devastated when she finds out that the man she loves has deceived her. Still hopeful, she embarks on another relationship only to find herself in the same predicament. Ruth becomes disenchanted with love and decides that if she can't beat them, she may as well join them and begins a journey that will change her very being and endanger her life.

Can Ruth find herself before it's too late? Or will she become what she has always despised—a loathsome liar?

*'When I tell you I was excited for this book, I'm not kidding! I read it in one sitting, and absolutely could not put it down.' Rebecca, Amazon reviewer.*

## THE IMPOSSIBLE CHOICE

Mary, still reeling from the loss of her husband, is living a quiet life, running a boarding house in the seaside town of Righteous Creek, her only priorities her two teenage daughters.

But the tranquillity in which she lives is about to be rocked with the appearance of Lawrence, ten years younger and with demons of his own.

And there is more at stake than just a love that cannot be fulfilled. Just when Mary defies her heart, her world is turned upside down again and she is left to make an unthinkable decision, an impossible choice.

*'The rollercoaster of emotions that Ms Rowe manages to evoke in each one of her books is astounding and this novel is no exception. A little gem of a book with a conclusion that you will never see coming.' Amazon Reviewer.*

## DOUBLE DECEPTION

Tess has the perfect life, a beautiful family and a successful career. But when she meets Brian, she realises what has been missing in her life.

Love. The type that makes your toes curl, that makes you do crazy things.

But Brian has a family that he cannot leave, even if his own marriage, like hers, is a loveless one, and as their romance deepens, Tess cannot imagine     a       life       without      him       in       it. What will it take for Tess to make Brian hers, and hers alone? How far will she take what has now become an obsession?

*'Double Deception is a thrilling, twisted tale that hooked me from the first page. From the moment Tess meets her handsome former classmate Brian, it's obvious her attraction to him will be her undoing. It isn't long before friendship turns to lust and then to an unbearable love she cannot deny. Each step she takes toward obsession feels real and full of emotion, and though I knew she was on a path to self-destruction, I could not look away. If you enjoy a well-written story with some non-explicit spice, you will not be disappointed. Highly recommend.' Amazon Reviewer.*

## ALMOST HAPPY

Meet Beverley: she's timid, shy, struggles in social settings and has health problems that prevent her from living life to the full. She is, however, appreciative of the things she does have, a bond with her sister, Dina, who is so different from her, and the love of Troy, her childhood sweetheart who may be caring, but can also be controlling.

When Troy leaves her, Beverley feels free. She meets Jay, thoughtful and unlike any love she has ever felt before, and a lifetime of happiness beckons. But when Jay abandons her unexpectedly, she feels like her world has fallen apart.

Troy is never far away, and when he returns to Beverley's life and asks for her hand in marriage, she accepts, realising that it's better to be almost happy than not at all. But these slivers of happiness are threatened when Jay returns, bringing with him secrets that could destroy her world. A world that is so carefully held together with hope.

How can Beverley ignore the betrayal that has torn apart every fabric of her life? How can she leave everything she loves, so she can finally be free?

*'Oh wow what can I say? For the first couple of chapters I wondered if I was going to get into this one but then it hit me and I was completely absorbed. This novel is strikingly sad if you look deeply into it but comes across as only tinged with sadness. The theme of emotional abuse and threatening behaviour may be hard for some to read but I felt it was handled well and made for an enjoyable read. For me it had vibes of "never the moon" by the same author so if you enjoyed that, I feel you would love this too.' Amazon Reviewer.*

## IT'S JUST CHEMISTRY

Is it love, or is it just chemistry? Fiona and Danny are about to find out.

They say opposites attract, and that is true with Danny and Fiona. He is athletic and the star of the soccer team. She is a dreamer and the star of the stage. Sparks fly when they meet and fall in love.

But can you stay together when you have differences as significant as they do? Their love for each other is immense, but so is the jealousy that comes with such great love. After three tumultuous years, Fiona is faced with the ultimate betrayal that will see her wipe Danny out of her life forever.

Fate, however, has other ideas and keeps drawing them back together. But how can two people who are so different, so unwavering in their life choices, be together when their lives are so far apart?

What is it that pulls them together time and time again? Is it something deeper, or is it just chemistry?

*'I'm quite a fan of Rita H Rowe and this book is no exception. It's spread over a long time period but it moves along easily and keeps you guessing what the final outcome will eventually be. The novel tells the story of the relationship between Danny and Fiona which is so on-off and volatile that there's simply no way to guess what will happen in the end ....and I'm not going to spoil it by saying!! Read it and find out and I hope you enjoy it as much as I did.' Amazon UK Reviewer.*

## EVERYBODY's GOT A BILLY

Everyone has a first love, someone who touched their lives in some inexplicable way, someone who they remember, either with fondness or with regret. Maybe a shiver when they hear their name mentioned, maybe a yearning when they see their face in person or in a photograph ...

This book is a collection of their stories.

A meeting at a nightclub that turned into a perfect match. A man who still remembers fondly the girl he loved when he was eleven. A woman, happily married for twenty years, who can't explain why she is still in love with her high school sweetheart. A young woman who had no choice but to break her boyfriend's heart because he didn't have ambition. A tale of betrayal and a tale of manipulation. And so much more love ...

From the heartwarming to the heartbreaking, these stories are taken from real experiences - some filled with pain, some beautiful forever love stories, but each of them unique and personal to its owner, an experience that will remain in that heart forever.

*'From the tingling highs of love, to the titanic lows, this collection of stories had me reading a few every night. Short and sweet and sometimes sour, each one was more heartfelt than the last. Highly recommend for any short story lover and collector of poetic works in the journey of love, heartbreak and fate.' Amazon reviewer.*

*Follow Rita H Rowe on Facebook or Instagram or visit her website www.ritahrowe.com. Leave a review or drop her a line. She loves to hear from her readers.*